"YOU CAN DO THIS, PHIL. BE KAT, BECOME KAT."

As if she stripped every night, Philamina Zorn sauntered into the dimly lit dance room, a sultry smile hovering on her lips. The music swelled, and so did her pride. She wasn't a drug addict, and she wasn't a whore. Phil was a good girl gone bad for the night, and all for a cause.

Ty stepped forward but something inside her snapped. She waved him off. She wasn't a fool who needed rescuing. Maybe a long time ago she needed rescuing, but not now. She was a cop, hell, a woman who could do anything she set her mind to. Her pride shoved her good girl aside and let the bad girl loose.

GOOD GIRL GONE BAD

KARIN
TABKE

GOOD GIRL GONE BAD

POCKET BOOKS
NEW YORK   LONDON   TORONTO   SYDNEY

POCKET BOOKS, a division of Simon & Schuster, Inc.
1230 Avenue of the Americas, New York, NY 10020

ISBN-13: 978-1-4165-2485-4
ISBN-10:   1-4165-2485-1

This Pocket Books trade paperback edition September 2006

10   9   8   7   6   5   4   3

POCKET and colophon are registered trademarks of
Simon & Schuster, Inc.

Designed by Jan Pisciotta

Manufactured in the United States of America

For information regarding special discounts for bulk purchases, please contact
Simon & Schuster Special Sales at 1-800-456-6798 or
business@simonandschuster.com

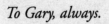

To Gary, always.

ACKNOWLEDGMENTS

Wow, I finally made it! My first published novel-length book. It took a village to get me here, too! So without further adieu, let's get to it.

To Kimberly Whalen, my agent, without your confidence in my writing and in this story, this novel would not have landed on Lauren's desk. Thank you for your leap of faith.

To Lauren McKenna, a real-live working editor, thank you for giving me the opportunity to write for you, and big hugs for making the revision process so easy. Ty and Phil are forever grateful to you for making them a stronger couple.

Megan McKeever, thank you for always returning my emails with a "?" in the subject line.

To my CPs, Liz Krueger and Michelle Diener, much thanks for your red pens and patience with the first draft.

To my über CP, Edie Ramer, you went beyond the call of

duty on more then one occasion. I love you, and you have my undying gratitude and respect.

To my little sister, Rae Monet. Hey, chica! Thank you for gluing all of my hair back on my head after my many meltdowns. Ready to do it again?

To Amy Knupp, Jan Kenny, and Sharon Long, thanks for being sounding boards and always lending your support when I needed it.

I want to thank my girls of the small but mighty RWA chapter the Black Diamonds for your wonderful support, and for being normal.

To my mom, Iyone Stanton, who also seconds as my pimp, thank you for stalking those book sellers. And thanks, Mom and Dad, for taking such joy in my success. I love you both.

To my mother-in-law, Marlene Tabke, my biggest fan. Thank you for always wanting more, even if it was at 1 a.m. in the morning. Thank you for threatening me with violence if I ever stopped writing. I love you.

Thank you to Larry, my father-in-law, for not bitching all those nights when Mom read into the wee hours of the morning and was too tired the next day to fix breakfast.

To my kids, Jenn, Rhianna, Jeff, and Will, thank you for always understanding writing is my bliss.

To Gary, my husband. You are my true inspiration, my rock, my best friend and my mentor. Thank you for hanging in there with me when we hit those rough spots. Thank you for your humor. Thank you for putting your plans on hold to indulge mine. Thank you for being the consummate gentleman that you are. And thank you for never allowing me to give up on my dream. I love you.

GOOD GIRL GONE BAD

Internal Affairs HQ, interrogation room number 2

"Are you trying to tell me, Sergeant Jamerson, you didn't lay one finger on Jesse Rivera?"

Ty looked hard at the investigator across the table from him. He didn't see a woman. He saw a career killer. His gaze narrowed to the sleek tailored suit that accentuated more curves than it camouflaged, the firm set of her jaw, and the sensible bun curled tightly against her neck. Yeah, a career killer, and the worst kind. The kind that crucified her own by stripping them of their badge and honor. He curbed a sneer.

If she didn't have Internal Affairs stamped on her forehead, he would have smelled her out for the rat she was just by her arrogance. He gritted his teeth.

"On the contrary, I laid all ten and then some. You've seen the booking photo, I presume?"

Her dark blue eyes widened and her lips pursed at his confession. "Booking photo? I shot a whole roll of film documenting his injuries. Under color of authority, you've violated his rights."

Ty swiped his hand across the stubble on his chin and shot his union rep at his side a glare. Ponch shrugged lazily. "You know the drill, man. She can accuse all she wants." Without moving a muscle, Ponch speared her with a glare. "Now prove it."

Ty smiled. Ponch was a reticent man. It's what Ty liked most about him, that and he knew how to maneuver IA without them even realizing they'd been had.

He looked back at the salivating IA officer. He didn't have time to dick around with a trumped-up brutality charge, but he'd make her think he had all day and night.

Her nostrils flared like a she-wolf scenting the kill. He silently cursed. This one smelled blood, all right—his.

He leaned back into the straight-back chair, caught her gaze, crossed his right foot onto his left knee, and pulled a piece of hard candy from his pocket. Not breaking eye contact, he casually unwrapped it and popped the root beer-flavored candy in his mouth. He set his hands on his thighs, tapping his fingers in a slow rhythm, and sucked.

He'd done this routine in this same ten-foot-by-ten-foot drab-colored room too many times to count, but never had he had the misfortune of getting jacked up by a newbie IA, and a female one to boot. How damn low could a department sink?

She leaned forward. "Do you really expect me to believe, Sergeant, Rivera's wounds happened *before* you cuffed him and not after?"

Ty leaned toward her. When she didn't retreat, he leaned closer, so close he could see the wild pulse of silver-colored flecks in her irises. For a brief second the unique color caught him off guard. If she weren't on the other side, he wouldn't mind a quick roll in the sack. Her skin was smooth and flushed pink and her lips were full, like he'd just kissed them stupid. He grinned when she licked them. His cock twinged. Oh yeah, he could get into that. He slowed his breathing to long deliberate breaths. Yeah, he could get into her, after he taught her a few things about eating her own words.

"I'm not *trying* to tell you anything, young lady. I've *been* telling you for the last half hour, I chased down that punk after he ripped off my snitch. Bonedick wanted to see who was faster. I won, and when he resisted I used a necessary force to overcome his resistance."

"You didn't call for backup," she challenged.

"Backup?" He bit back a harsh laugh. "There is no backup in undercover work. If you ever become a real cop, you'll learn that in deep cover you're on your own."

"Watch your insinuations, Sergeant Jamerson. Remember who you're speaking to," she snapped.

"The last time I checked, a sergeant still outranked an investigator, *Officer* Zorn." Ty sat back in his chair and glanced at his overfed rep. "Do I have to continue this song and dance or what?"

"Officer Zorn, are you going to formally charge Sergeant Jamerson?"

Zorn smirked. "When I'm done with my interview I'll make that determination."

"Hurry the hell up, then, I have to get back on the street," Ty bit off.

Deciding to speed her along, he leaned as far forward as he could, setting his hands palm open on the table and splaying his fingers across the smooth Formica. "I'll tell you what, Officer, why don't you go down to the squad car that Officer Michaels transported that little shit in, and take a look. It wouldn't require more than two brain cells to see for yourself Rivera knocked himself around. There's lots of DNA." Ty pushed hard against the tabletop, his muscles bulging under his contained temper. "And then take a look at his wrists. Any cuts or bruises from the cuffs? No, because they weren't on when I fought with him."

Zorn dug in. "Sergeant, how many color-of-authority violations would you say are in your file?"

"Zero."

She pulled out several thick manila folders from a shiny new briefcase she had set on the floor when she marched in a half hour ago. Quickly she shuffled through the top one. "December of last year, officer-involved shooting, pistol whipping the suspect."

She slid the paper to the side and picked up another one. "Two years ago, assaulting a state witness."

She grabbed another sheet of paper and read. "Just three months ago, conduct unbecoming an officer, involving a female witness."

Ty swept his hand across the desk, sending the files scattering to the floor, their contents skittering along the soiled tiles. He quickly processed and dismissed the fact that his action had no effect on her. She sat ramrod straight, her eyes blazing at him.

"I can give you a dozen more scenarios just like those, Officer Zorn, and if you care to look past the bullshit charges you'll see not one of them stuck. Not even when the rat bastard IA officers involved doctored evidence *and* statements."

Ty stood. She remained seated.

"Go on and do your worst, sister, go after a fellow officer whose only guilt is trying to do his job." His voiced lowered in warning. "Go on and falsify reports, tamper with and manipulate witness statements. Go on and do it, and God help you when it comes back to bite you in your pretty little ass."

Ty glowered down at Ponch, who seemed content to let him defend himself. "If you want my piece and badge, tell me now. Otherwise, I'm out of here."

Ponch shook his head no and Ty almost winked. Ponch's dark brown eyes glittered in merriment.

"Sergeant Jamerson!" Officer Zorn shouted, coming to her feet. "You cannot walk out of this interview until I say you can."

Ty sauntered up close to the IA shark. He had to hand it to her, she didn't flinch when he invaded her space. The only clue to her agitation was the quick heave of her ample breasts straining against the top button of her jacket. He stopped inches from her and sucked on his candy. She raised her chin a notch, but even in her modest heels, the top of her head just came to his nose. He grinned, exposing teeth.

"Say it's over, Officer Zorn. Say it's over or I will."

Philamina Zorn felt her stomach sink. She sure as hell couldn't muscle the six-foot-three sergeant to her will. His size aside, his corded muscles strained beneath the black T-shirt and his form-fitting jeans. Expert that she was in defensive tactics, she wasn't going to fool herself about who would come out on top if they went hand to hand. This was her first IA case and she was about to blow it.

She took a deep breath and slowly exhaled. The contempt she read in the sergeant's green eyes was enough to quell the hardest of criminals. While she considered herself hard as nails, she was no criminal, just a good cop hell-bent on seeing the letter of the law served.

His contempt was mirrored. It was rogue cops like the one standing so arrogantly in front of her that brought the pride of a PD down. She'd seen it all the years her father proudly served, and she also saw it take his life. She'd be damned if she was going to let this guy slip through the cracks.

"Sergeant Jamerson. We can do this the easy way or the hard way, and frankly, I don't give a damn which one you choose." She squared her shoulders as wide as they would go and moved so close her breasts brushed against the hard plane of his chest. In tandem their eyes widened at the contact. Phil leashed her body's inadvertent reaction, ignoring the tightness in her nipples and the way her skin warmed.

She smiled seductively, secure in her ability to draw him out. Softly she finished. "Because in the end, Sergeant Jamerson, the truth will win." Her heart fluttered when he growled and reached out to grab her.

Ponch jackknifed out of his chair. "Don't do it, Ty, don't give her a reason."

Ty's hands halted in midair.

Ty spoke low, in almost a whisper. "Go ahead, lady, push me. Push me and see how hard I can push back."

"Are you threatening me, Sergeant?"

"I never threaten." He pointed to the scattered files on the floor. "Take those with you and go do your homework like a good little investigator and remember, even the most seasoned turned up nothing. Not one complaint has ever been substantiated."

The heat between them became stifling. He didn't back down and when he lowered his hands, his chest brushed her nipples again. She flinched. This man was dangerous. Dangerous in an exciting blood-racing way.

"There's always a first time, Sergeant, and your time is nearly up."

He grinned wickedly, his even white teeth flashing like those of a predator. He bit down on the piece of candy, the cracking sound shattering her resolve. As his pant leg brushed against the back of her left hand, he softly blew in her face and said, "That's not all that's nearly up."

Stopping her involuntary flinch, she gasped. "Sergeant Jamerson!"

"Lady, I'm just a proactive cop. Very proactive."

CHAPTER ONE

Three years later
County Task Force HQ, vice squad office

"I ask for one lousy female and I get another grunt dug up out of who the hell knows where!" Lieutenant Ty Jamerson slammed down the file he held on the nearest surface, which happened to be his desk. Glaring at Jase, who'd had the misfortune to hand him the file, Ty grunted in male understanding. He wouldn't kill the messenger. After years of working together, Jase knew it, too. He grinned back good-naturedly.

"Maybe we can dress him in drag," Jase offered. "Get him some falsies and get him up onstage." He laughed heartily. "Now that'll draw every creep outta the woodwork."

Ty ran his fingers through his shoulder-length hair. He'd be glad when this assignment was over. The last three years in vice had taken its toll on him and his team. They needed to come up for air soon, or they'd morph into the seedy underworld counterparts they sought to put away.

"Serious up, Jase," Ty chastised. "We've lost one of our own. It's balls to the walls now." The high energy in the room accelerated.

"She's just missing," Reese said.

Ty glanced across the room at Reese, another brother in blue and his longtime point man.

Ty slammed his hands down on the desk. "Just missing? Just missing for two weeks? What about the other two, the ones who've been missing for months? I'll bet my retirement those ladies are either dead or worse. Shipped off to some third-world sheik for his amusement."

Ty stalked the short space of the stuffy room, his frustration nearly out of control. He spun around and stopped, glaring at both of his men. "I told those brass assholes we needed an experienced officer, not some fresh-faced male rookie six months out of the academy." He looked down at the scattered file on the desk. "Now they can't even bother to read my request form. I need this"—he grabbed the file and looked at the name tab—"Phil Zorn like I need another one of you dickheads."

As he turned away he stopped in his tracks, realization

dawning, then grabbed the file and opened it. His eyes scanned the information. "Shit!"

He tossed the file back onto the table, and the door to the small office opened. Three sets of eyes widened, and one set narrowed.

Philamina's heart plummeted to her knees. This was a mistake, she thought. Not even close to what she'd put in for. Two men she did not recognize smiled—no, leered—the other, the one who she hadn't stopped thinking of the past three years, scowled.

She felt like a sacrificial lamb who had just walked into a den of hungry wolves. She swallowed and steeled her nerves. Her last three years in IA hadn't taught her to shrivel up and die. No, she'd learned a few things about survival, even among these beasts.

Phil contemplated Ty's tall muscular frame, his long dark hair, and the severe cut of his short goatee. He looked every bit the hard-ass he'd sold to the grunge underworld of vice. Her heart picked up an unsteady pace. No way was she going to let him see how he affected her. She smiled, exuding confidence. "So, you made lieutenant. I thought for sure you would be hosing down kennels at the pound by now."

"I thought for sure you would be riding a meter cart handing out unwarranted parking tickets." Ty's cock twinged. He admired her tall slender form. Couldn't help it. She still came across prim and proper in a sleek navy pantsuit, but now experience, and no doubt anxiety, gave her soft features some depth. Her eyes, that unusual shade of dark blue, no longer held that hungry, I-want-to-get-the-bad-cop gleam. No, something else replaced that first flush of bravado he'd found so disconcerting three years ago. She'd grown up some, and the new mature lady cop before him unnerved him more than the innocent firebrand.

"What's the rat squad want with vice?" Despite the hum his body produced at her entrance, he wanted her out of his office and out of his life. He had no room in either for a distraction like her.

"Officer Zorn reporting for duty, sir."

Ty swore under his breath. Neither Jase nor Reese wasted a minute in welcoming what Ty had specifically asked for, an experienced female officer to go undercover. In their zeal to welcome her, they bumped into each other.

"Sergeant Reese Bronson at your service."

Ty scowled when Bronson kissed her hand.

"Knock it off, Bronson, she's a cop, not the frickin' queen of England." He moved in and pushed Bronson aside. "You're mistaken, Zorn, your services are no longer required here."

She wasn't having it. She stepped into his space like he had done to her so many years ago. The fire burned hot in her eyes now. He liked it.

"Sorry to disappoint, Lieutenant. You requested an experienced female, and so you've been assigned one."

Ty ignored the soft musky scent of her anger. "I never have and never will work with a rat."

The words hit her hard in the face; he almost felt sorry for her when she blanched.

"I'm not now nor have I ever been a rat, sir. I followed my job to the letter of the law. If you happened to get caught in the crossfire, that's on you."

Ty's fists slowly opened and closed. He'd see about this. "Excuse me."

He flung the door wide and exited the office, his finger punching the sheriff's number on his cell phone.

"Bellicheck."

"Sheriff Bellicheck, Lieutenant Jamerson, sir."

"Make it quick, son, I'm on my way into a meeting."

"One word. Zorn. As in Philamina Zorn, an IA rat!"

"That was more than one word. What's your problem?"

"I requested an experienced X for my undercover operation and I get a letter-of-the-law rat. How the hell am I supposed to work with the Wicked Witch of the West? She'll be writing my guys up for spitting on the sidewalk."

"Look, Jamerson, she's all we could come up with. She's single. No kids, no family to speak of. She's perfect for this operation."

"But, sir, my men can't work knowing she's keeping book."

"She's out of IA. I give you my word, nothing you or your men do will be used to incriminate you, so long as you produce.

I want the person responsible for kidnapping Officer Marten and those other two women. Use Zorn, she's no shrinking violet. Now stop your bellyaching and get back to work."

"Sir, I—" The drone of a dead line reverberated in Ty's ear. "Son of a bitch." He slapped his cell closed and prowled back into the office to find his two men gallantly entertaining Officer Zorn. Her eyes shone with excitement and her straight white teeth startled him in their brightness. Shit-fuck-damn!

"It looks like I have no choice but to have you on the team, Officer Zorn." He moved closer and lowered his voice. "But be warned. If it were up to me, we'd be slapping a skirt on Vaughn here and having him shake his ass for dollars."

Phil stepped toward him. Her case against him three years ago fell apart, but she was determined not to let this case get away from her. "Consider me one of the guys, Lieutenant, and I assure you I will produce results."

Ty smiled. "Oh, you'll produce all right. Let me fill you in on the case you'll be working."

Philamina didn't like his tone or the way his dark green eyes glittered. Reese snorted and Jase stood quietly grinning. Why did she feel like the joke was on her?

CHAPTER TWO

"How do you know for sure these girls didn't willingly check out of their current lives for something better?" Phil moved closer to the storyboard, examining the faces of the two missing dancers and Officer Marten. The dancers looked barely old enough to be out of high school, and Officer Marten, twenty-two and just out of the academy, looked like a poster child for *Teen* magazine. Maybe she'd had enough, but hadn't had the balls to face her quick-tempered lieutenant.

Phil eyed Ty and swallowed hard. She'd never admit it, but the man pushed her buttons, causing her to react, instead of respond in her normal, carefully reined demeanor. "Young people are impetuous, they throw caution to the wind to chase silly dreams." Something Phil would never do. When you lost control you gave the winds of fate latitude. Follow the plan, play by the rules, and keep focused. It worked so far and she had no intention of changing.

"Here's a few facts, Zorn." He leaned his fists on the desk and leaned toward her, looking her directly in the eye. "Forty-two percent of all strippers are stalked. Twenty-nine percent are sexually assaulted. By those two stats alone, your theory has holes." He pushed back from her and stood up straight.

"Each of these ladies was doing what she wanted. Never a word about taking off to see the big bad world on their own."

"But the letters they leave are clear, coherent, and in their own handwriting."

"Coerced. No doubt about it, in my mind."

Phil shot Ty a look. "Why? Because *you* say so?"

Ty's eyes narrowed, Jase coughed, and Reese covered his mouth with his hand and looked down at his feet.

"It's painfully obvious to me, Officer Zorn, you have no instinct for this line of work. If you did, you'd know just by the plain fact that three women are missing from the same club under the same circumstances something is off."

Phil's face warmed. If she hadn't been so eager to make him look rash, maybe she would have considered those glaring facts. She wasn't impetuous, or a grandstander. She was cool, calm, and collected, always diligent in her facts before making a judgment.

"Okay, I'll give you that," she said.

"Thanks, you've made my day."

Jase cleared his throat. "Um, children, can we get back to the case?"

Ty threw him a narrowed glare and turned his attention back to Phil.

"Motive?" she asked before he could launch an attack.

"My guess is if they aren't dead, white slavery."

The fine hair on the back of her neck spiked and a chill ran down Phil's arms, causing the fine hair there to rise. Visions of girls bound and gagged scared to death and wishing for death instead of the repeated rapes by faceless men made her sick to her stomach.

Phil glanced at the three smiling faces on the board. "Do we have any suspects?"

Jase answered. "No one specifically at this point, but lots of regulars we're watching, and two we're looking at hard."

Phil nodded, her brain mentally compartmentalizing the information. "How about someone close and personal, a fellow worker?"

Ty swiped his hand across the bottom of his face. His frustration was evident. Not with her, but the case. "So far, everyone's checked out."

She opened her mouth to comment, but he put his hand up, stopping her. "That doesn't mean we aren't digging. We're digging like mad. Every damn thread so far ties up nice and neat."

Phil nodded and looked at both Jase and Reese, who

calmly regarded her. She turned back to Ty. "What about the notes?"

"While each of the good-bye letters was coherent, and in the missing person's handwriting, not one of them mentioned to coworkers, family, or friends at any time prior to their disappearance she had any intention of taking off. In fact, in Officer Marten's case, she left her cat, with no forwarding instructions."

Phil shrugged. "Maybe she didn't care enough about the cat."

"I know for a fact she treated that cat like a baby, and would have taken a bullet for it." Ty's adamancy told her something else, and inexplicably, it infuriated her.

"I thought fraternizing was against the GOs?"

Reese's hiss of air caught her before Ty's angry words. "There you go again, thinking like a rat, always putting a cop on the wrong side. What is it with you IA vermin? Didn't you learn from your old man that shit runs down hill?"

Phil slapped him. The action stunned everyone in the room, most of all herself. Silence fell hard and heavy. Her anger mushroomed. She'd allowed Jamerson to break her control. In a carefully controlled voice barely above a whisper, she said, "*Do not* ever speak to me about my father."

Anger swept Ty's face as the totality of Phil's action hit her broadside. Immediate beach time and no doubt the beginning of an IA investigation that would culminate in the stripping of her badge. Stupid, stupid, stupid.

She opened her mouth to apologize, but the words stuck

like putty in her throat. Never would she apologize for defending her father's tarnished honor. She swallowed hard and decided that wasn't what she needed to apologize for. She'd assaulted her commanding officer. She *could* defend her action and say his words provoked her, but that wouldn't fly. No way, not when it came to bulletproof Lieutenant Tyler Adam Jamerson. After his last IA, which was her first, she was told, in no uncertain terms, hands off.

She drew herself up stiff, her voice empty. "I . . . sir, I regret my action." In an instinctive gesture she reached out to him. His eyes narrowed to slits. He jerked away from her as if she had a major case of cooties.

Massaging his stinging cheek, Ty bent low and softly said, "Touch me again, lady, and mark my words, I'll turn you out like a twenty-dollar hooker on a Saturday night."

"Are you threatening me, Lieutenant?" Her gumption resurfaced as she realized he'd rather die than write her up for slapping him silly. The rank and file would get wind of it and never let him live it down.

Ty grinned. It wasn't one of his most pleasant gestures. Not that he had any. "A threat is an implied warning. I'm telling you a cold hard fact."

Phil swallowed hard and cooled it. She'd just assaulted her commanding officer, in front of two witnesses. Maybe she needed to back out of this. It was apparent Lieutenant Jamerson was unwilling to bend, and more worrisome, she seemed unable to control herself in his presence. A panicked tension flooded through her. Its wake left her shaky and afraid. "Sir, I respectfully request to be removed from this task force. I see no way we can work together."

Ty's green eyes flashed. "You have no idea, Officer Zorn, how much I'd like to give you what you want." He turned back to the storyboard and looked at the three photos taped there. "Unfortunately, we're stuck with each other. I need a female officer to infiltrate the club and draw out the kidnapper, and you seem to be the only one available."

"Is that what Marten's job was?"

Ty's head snapped up from the file he pulled from the desk drawer. His eyes narrowed dangerously and she felt afraid. Not of him, but of what Officer Marten had to endure, what she might still be enduring, and what Phil would have to do to bring the sick bastard who took her and two others to justice.

"Yes. And let's hope you're better at it." He dropped the file in his hand to the table in front of her and slid it across to her. "Your dossier. Learn it and burn it."

He proceeded to open a closed file folder on the table and pulled a business card from the flap. Handing it to her, he said, "Your contact at Klub Kashmir is Bud Olman, the head bartender. He's been instructed to hire the next set of tits that walks in off the street looking for a job."

Phil swallowed hard, *again*. "Hired, as in a *stripper*?" Hearing her question end on a high note infuriated her. A stripper? She was supposed to get onstage and take her clothes off in front of a bunch of drunken perverts and take dollar bills from their grubby hands with her teeth? Her entire body quaked in disapproval. No way. Besides, there had to be something in the GOs about an officer stripping. She cleared her throat. "Ah, sir, the general orders clearly state—"

"The GO is for normal cops under normal circumstances, Officer Zorn. Undercover has its own set of rules."

"I—ah, would you have that handbook available for me, sir, so that I know where to draw the line?"

Ty laughed sharply, his eyes danced in challenge. Crossing his arms over his chest, he leaned against the wall. "Officer Zorn, that handbook is called 'do what you have to do to get the job done.'"

She let out a breath she hadn't realized she was holding. "I find that hard to believe, sir. I refuse to circumvent the general orders."

Slowly he unfolded his arms and pushed off the wall. His features sharpened. "Officer Zorn, when undercover, do as those around you do or end up dead." Ty backed away from her. "You'll have plenty of cover. I've already infiltrated the club as floor manager. Reese and Jase have become regulars." He turned to both men and grinned again. "A cover they have no problem playing to the hilt."

"I will not strip!"

All three men grinned and looked at her as if they could see straight through to her stiffening nipples. "Olman needs a cocktail waitress." Ty's green eyes smoldered as he swept her with a blistering gaze from head to toe, then up again, his eyes lingering on her trembling chest. "Besides, you don't have what it takes to strip."

She checked herself from striking him again. "Your insults show what a little man you really are."

His smug gaze waned. He actually looked affronted. "You misunderstand me, Officer. I meant you don't have the lack of inhibitions for the job. I in no way inferred you don't have the necessary equipment." His eyes glowed hot. "To the contrary."

Said equipment warmed. "I—" She threw her hands up in the air. "Forget it, sir." She turned away from the three sets of admiring eyes, grabbed her dossier, and strode to the door, yanking it open. "If it's all right with you, I'll head downtown to get that job."

Ty watched the door abruptly shut behind her, the only evidence of the rat in heels was her lingering perfume. He inhaled it and closed his eyes, savoring the musky scent of her.

Jase slapped him on the back and Reese guffawed. "Son of a bitch, Ty, I think you've finally met your match."

Reese added, "If you don't want to play, I will."

Ty turned on them both and scowled. "She's a no play zone, boys. We have two missing strippers and a missing cop to track down, that's where we need to focus. Not on Zorn's tits or her ass."

Jase rolled his eyes. "Oh, but what a set of tits."

Reese quipped, "I'm an ass man myself, and hers looked like J. Lo's Mini Me."

Ty shook his head. He was an ass man, too, and couldn't remember one so fine as the one that had just stomped out of his office.

He ignored the twinge in his dick and the woman who inspired it. Instead, he sat down and opened the top file folder on case #862543, a.k.a. Operation Internal Affairs.

CHAPTER THREE

"Here's your paperwork. Have it turned in before you start tonight."

Phil nodded to Bud. Just like that, she filled out a sorry excuse for an application and she had a job as a cocktail waitress in a strip club.

"The house rules are printed on the back of the yellow sheet, but I'm gonna tell them to you so there isn't any misunderstanding."

Phil nodded again.

"Twenty-five percent of your cocktail tips go to the house, thirty percent of extracurricular happenings go to the house." Bud opened his mouth to continue, but Phil held her hand up.

"Um, what exactly are extracurricular happenings?" She was afraid of the answer.

"Lap, couch, or table dances."

She swallowed hard. "I—ah, that's not what I was told. I was told—"

"You want this job or not?"

"Yes, I do, but—"

"Then understand the bottom line of the club is to please the patrons. Which brings me to another house rule. If a guy wants to buy you a drink, you let 'im. Don't backtalk, and don't piss them off. If you have a beef, go to the floor manager. Mr. Masters takes care of business clean and fast."

"Bu—"

The old man set his hands on the bar and cocked a gray brow at her. "No buts. Still interested?"

"Yes." God help her.

He grinned. Reaching under the bar, he handed her a plastic bag. "Here you go. Be here by seven."

Phil stood openmouthed.

The two pieces of fabric she pulled from the bag Bud had handed her wouldn't cover more than a dinner plate, and a small one at that. "Make sure you wear heels. Stiletto type, none of those clunky old maid kind."

Shaking her head, Phil looked up at the head bartender's grizzled old face. She'd bet Bud had seen it all and then some. Despite his curt manner, there was something about his quiet directness she trusted. "Where's the rest of the outfit?"

He smiled, showing a surprising set of white teeth, his old, tired brown eyes dancing. Pulling the bar cloth off his shoulder, he began to clean the smooth hardwood of the bar top. He didn't speak for a long minute. "That's it."

Her jaw dropped for the second time. He shrugged and continued the circular motion, polishing the already gleaming mahogany to a higher shine. "Wear a G-string under it and you'll get bigger tips. If you want serious bank, bend over all the way every opportunity you get."

Her face warmed, but she slapped her mouth shut. Gritting her teeth, Phil silently cursed Ty. She could just see his laughter and the dark sweep of his eyebrows rise in a challenge.

She swallowed hard and gave the two-piece "outfit" another once-over. The top was a glorified bikini top tied at the plunging neckline. And the skirt? The short black pleats would barely cover what made her a girl. "Can I wear pantyhose?" she squeaked.

Bud stopped his circular motion and let out a long exasperated breath. "Sweetheart, the more skin you show, the better for business. You're here to make a buck, right?" He resumed his cleaning, avoiding direct eye contact. "The more you make, the more we make. That makes the owner, Mr. Z., a happy man. When he's happy, we're all happy."

She continued to stand, with the garments dangling in her hand, in quiet disbelief, wondering if she could squeeze into the contraption. "You want to wear hose," he said, apparently taking pity on her, "make sure they're the totally sheer kind with no control-top crap."

A small, no, minuscule concession, and one she'd take. Phil nodded. Stuffing the "uniform" back into the bag along with her paperwork, she backed slowly out of the brightly lit bar area. She weaved through the dozens of glossy high-top tables stacked with high-back chairs facing the stage, then stopped and gave her new workplace a slow once-over. She inhaled sharply. It reeked of booze, cigar smoke, and sex, the dancers, simply a commodity.

A hot commodity that hadn't depreciated since the Stone Age.

The shrouded sleekness of the stage silently pulled her. She allowed herself to go nearer.

At this time of day the circular stage centered in the middle of the "gentlemen's club" lay quiet. The mirrored ceiling above the centrally mounted pole gleamed ominously in the low din of light. Two more poles cornering the center pole stood sentry farther back. She looked up at the deep ceiling. Rows of lights nestled into the black cavern. She could detect different colored filters and a large spot. She guessed the bar lights would dim when it came to showtime, putting center stage in the spotlight.

Intrigued despite her qualms, Phil trailed her fingers across the wraparound sit-down bar encircling the stage and the straight-back chairs neatly stowed beneath. She imagined dancing in front of dozens of men, driving them to the brink of orgasm, and a thrill prickled through her.

She backed away from the stage, startled by her thoughts.

No way, she said silently. Had she really considered that? Never would she strip for a man in public and never for a dollar. She wasn't desperate and she didn't need the cash. Besides, she had her pride to consider, and more than pride, her modesty shuddered at the notion.

Her cheeks warmed at the thought of putting on the tiny cocktail outfit. But to strip? Naked? *Never*. The image propelled her right out of the club.

Walking out into the bright sunlight, she squinted, wondering how the hell she found herself in this situation. She'd never envisioned herself as undercover material and certainly not in this capacity. Her sole reason for becoming a cop was to get into IA and stay there, where it was safe and predictable, where she could make a difference putting bad cops away. And put bad cops away she did. She was damn good at what she did. Too good, apparently. Just as she was sinking her teeth into her next case, she was abruptly transferred.

"You need street experience, put in for something," Captain Warren had told her. Of course she'd argued. He'd argued right back, then accused her of narrow-minded tunnel vision, a trait he would not tolerate in his squad. "Get the hell out of here, Zorn, see how the real world works. Then if you still have the stomach for IA, I'll consider your transfer."

How could she be kicked out for doing her job to the best of her ability? For crying out loud, she hung out more guilty cops than four precincts combined, and she got kicked to the curb for it? Wasn't fair. She grumbled as she dug for her keys. Who the hell said life was fair, Phil? she thought.

She knew the answer, always had. But she would not stop righting past wrongs, especially when that wrong took her father's life. Moisture stung her eyes. Her father, one of Lansdowne's most highly decorated officers, brought down by a band of lying cops.

Anger swelled in her chest. Mac Zorn was a proud Christian cop, the son and grandson of cops. His distinguished career had been vilified by the Riders, an anonymous group of rogue cops.

She hadn't been in IA long enough to worm her way into the top echelon. Had she, she would have located the sealed file and discovered the identity of her father's accusers.

She headed for her safe comfy car, a late-model Taurus. Carefully she reined in her plots of vengeance. As she slid into the seat, Phil looked at the costume bag she gripped like a vise. The here and now washed through her. She needed to get into undercover mode.

Turning the flimsy outfit over and over in her hands, Phil decided she'd just see about exposing the maximum amount of skin. If she was going to play the part of a cocktail waitress at a high-class strip club, she'd make the men crane their necks all right. She smirked, and with that decision she knew she had a busy day ahead to prepare for her debut that night.

. . .

"I'll bet you next week's paycheck she doesn't show," Ty said to Jase as he pushed through the drudgery of paperwork that came with running a task force. The throb in his temple at Zorn's entrance earlier picked up momentum.

"I'd take you up on that, bro, but I can't afford to lose. I have that house payment now."

Ty grunted. "As much as I wish she'd walk back in here and say she quits and mean it, I can't see a way around using her. She fits the bill perfectly."

Jase grinned. "I bet she cleans up real nice."

Ty speared him with a glare. "She looked pretty damn good to me the way she was."

"Oh yeah, she did; now put that body in that skimpy little cocktail number, and you'll be plenty busy keeping her ass out of the hands of the paying customers."

Ty swiped his hand across his chin and blew out an exasperated breath. "Just what I need, keeping one eye on her and the other on the regular perverts."

"Hey, I'll keep my eye on her, no hardship for me."

"Keep your eyeballs to yourself. Let me worry about the floor and our newest edition."

Jase nodded. "Fine with me. I'm out of here. I need to go chill. The last few Friday nights at Kashmir's have been hopping." He slapped Ty heartily on the back. "I want to keep up."

Ty grunted a response that settled for good-bye. Just as he

turned back to the storyboard, Jase popped his head back into the room. "Ty?"

"Yeah?"

Entering the room, Jase closed the door behind him. "What are you going to do when she finds out you were the one who turned her father over?"

Ty ground his teeth and worked his jaw.

"The files are sealed. She'll never know."

Jase shook his head and opened the door. "I hope you're right, man. I'd hate to get the bad end of that."

After the door closed behind Jase, Ty swore. "Son of a bitch. I don't need this distraction." Tension clenched his body. What was done was done. He had no regrets.

Ty stood and stretched his long muscles. Wound up, he paced the small space of the task force office. Refusing to think of Mac's daughter and what she and her family had suffered, Ty stopped at the storyboard. Officer Marten's fresh-faced academy pic stared back.

He'd made a fatal mistake allowing the rookie to go undercover. Knowing he hadn't any choice didn't soften the sting of losing one of his own. They needed a decent-looking female officer and she fit the bill. Simple as that. Not to mention, Marten was smart.

Apparently not smart enough.

His gut soured. Now he had another female to worry about, this one too smart for her own good. That didn't bother him half as much as the fact that she came from IA.

He smiled wryly. If little Miz Rat thought she was going to keep book on him and his men, she had another thing coming. He'd show her how to play hardball in a real cop's world.

He turned back and scowled at the load of paperwork on his desk, his thoughts still on Zorn. If she was half the cop he hoped she was, she just might lead them to the missing dancers and come out alive.

Although the club was not scheduled to open for another hour, the subtle energy pricked Phil's skin. It pulsed, as some living thing: the chatter of the dancers, the clanking of glasses, and the blaring music as the stagehands checked the sound and light system roared to life.

She'd felt isolated the minute she entered through the back door. People buzzed around her, giving her no more attention than a stick of furniture. After checking out her surroundings, she remembered she had paperwork for Bud. She hustled out to the main bar and handed over the false documents. She stood alone for a long minute before Bud said, "Keep an eye out for a tall redhead. That'll be Tammy. She's house mom. Go to her for girly problems."

Great.

Feeling more out of her element than she cared to admit, Phil started for the backstage area. She needed to get into character or she'd get fired for being a mouse. One thing she immediately took note of were the ladies that chose Klub

Kashmir as their place of employment. They were a hard, dedicated lot. No little mice running for cover.

Candi, a one-time cocktail waitress and now featured dancer, took pity on Phil and showed her to her locker.

A locker that consisted of an open-front cubbyhole and a small attached bench with a locking lid. Nothing like the dancers' dressing room she'd peaked at on her way in. No, her little corner of the club didn't sport large locking lockers, expansive clothes racks for costumes, or a private shower.

"That's where us showgirls go, sweetie," Candi informed Phil when she craned her neck toward the brightly lit makeup bar. "You want to dance, honey?"

Phil shook her head. "No, I just want to make enough to pay my rent and get by."

Candi dug her two-inch neon blue nails into her tiny sequined purse and pulled out a pack of gum. She offered it to Phil, who declined. The blonde shrugged and deftly unwrapped two pieces and popped them into her mouth, noisily chewing. "So, honey, how does your boyfriend feel about you working at the Klub?" Not giving Phil a chance to comment, Candi answered for her. "Most don't like it much, but they get over it real quick when they see all the cash coming home."

Phil began what would be a string of lies. She'd gone over her cover dossier until she'd nailed her new persona. "There's no one waiting for me at home. If I disappeared into thin air, the only one to notice would be my landlord when I didn't pay rent." Realizing she spoke an almost truth, sadness

34

washed through her. The only deviation from her story was she had no landlord, it was the bank she paid her mortgage to that would notice her disappearance.

Candi patted her arm and smiled, her big, pink lips pursing. She popped her gum and shrugged. "Well, sweetie, consider me your friend. You'll find the girls here real sweet, so long as you don't swipe a client. We dancers are very territorial."

Candi's platinum blonde hair shimmered down her back as she caught her reflection in one of the numerous wall mirrors and gave herself a quick once-over. Clearly happy with her reflection, she smiled at herself. Chomping loudly on her gum, she continued, "Territorial as lions, we are."

"I'm only cocktailing, nothing to worry about from me."

Candi stopped in her tracks and slanted her head at Phil. Her petite bombshell of a body quivered and Phil thought she was going to get poked in the chest with one of Candi's bullet-shaped breasts. "Cocktailing or stripping, sweetie, with your looks, you're bound to snag a few players. They like pretty new faces."

She popped her gum again. "Whatcha say your name was?"

She hadn't. "Katharine, but you can call me Kat."

Candi nodded vigorously and popped her gum again. "I like the sound of that, Kat. Can I call you Kitty?"

Phil shrugged. "Fine with me."

Candi looped her arm through Phil's. "Well, Kitty Kat, you have a great bod and big blue eyes and your hair is so thick and gorgeous, I'm jealous. If your ass is half as tight as it looks in those jeans, plan on lots of offers tonight and *big* tips."

Phil smiled. She'd pleaded with the stylist at the local hair salon to squeeze her in and give her dark brown hair a new life, and the aesthetician to whip her skin into shape and wax what hair she didn't need for survival. The results stunned her. Joey, her stylist, couldn't pat himself on the back more, and Lynette wouldn't stop admiring her extreme makeover.

Phil had to admit when they spun her around she was shocked. But as her Auntie Kay had always told her, "You've got the bones, Philly, you just need the paint to cause a ruckus." And so she had the paint, the lighter hair, the perfectly arched brows, and bikini waxing that even wearing the skimpiest of costumes would not reveal what shouldn't be revealed. After all the pulling, cutting, and poking, Phil felt the epitome of female. She wondered what her ill-tempered lieutenant's reaction would be, and her skin warmed. Would Ty even recognize her? She smiled. She was definitely warming up to this undercover work.

"Has Tammy given you the lay of the land yet?"

"No, Bud said to go to her for girl problems. What kind of girl problems?"

Candi shrugged and popped her gum. "The girls can get nasty sometimes. She plays referee. She helps with costumes and routines, and she's a shoulder to cry on. But mostly she makes sure the rules are followed." Candi popped her gum and looked past Phil's shoulder. "Oh, there she is."

Phil turned and followed Candi's gaze to a tall, almost elegant redhead. She had the lithe body of a dancer, her pale face scored with the deep lines of a woman who'd had a hard life, yet her watery, cornflower blue eyes showed compassion. Phil looked hard at her. Her gut reaction was that Tammy didn't have it in her to kidnap anyone. She'd felt the same about Candi, but her training had taught her never to take a person at face value.

"Hey, Tammy," Candi called. "This is Katharine, a new cocktail."

Tammy slowed her hurried pace to a stop in front of Phil and smiled. Extending her hand, she said, "I've been looking for you. I've got costume issues, so I'll give you the abbreviated version of the facts of life around here." She let go of Phil's hand and angled her head. "First rule, cleanliness is next to godliness. Keep yourself clean at all times and don't overload the perfume. If you get your period, cut the string of your tampon short enough so even at close quarters it can't be seen. If you smoke, wash your hands regularly and invest in gallons of Scope. Rule two, if you're late, you pay. You're fined two dollars for every minute you're late, and we go by Bud's bar clock. I suggest you synchronize before you leave tonight. Rule three, you'll have your own locker next to the dancers' dressing room. Even if you're invited in there, it's off limits unless you dance. Rule four, if you end up on the stage, twenty-five percent of your tips go to the house. And speaking of the house, we aren't a whorehouse. Anyone pushes it, let me know, or the manager."

Tammy took a deep breath and called to a brunette dancer who came strutting from backstage in nothing more than a G-string. "I'll be right there, Misty."

She turned back to Phil. "Any questions?"

Even if she did, Phil realized now was not the time. Tammy was on a mission that didn't involve Phil. She'd play the good worker. "No, ma'am."

Tammy nodded and moved past them both. "If any come to mind, ask, don't assume. And my name is Tammy or you can call me Mom, you pick, but don't call me 'ma'am' again."

Phil couldn't help but smile. "Okay, Tammy."

The redhead hurried off, ushering the nearly naked dancer backstage.

"She's really not that hard, unless you break the rules," Candi said.

"I don't plan on breaking the rules. I need this job."

"Then you'd best get ready to get to work. In a few minutes the boss man will be coming in to make sure all the ladies showed up, and he'll be doing an inspection. He's a looker, too." Candi smiled and popped her gum. "Oh, and speaking of territory, I have dibs on him."

Phil shrugged. The thought of dating anyone who worked in this seedy atmosphere gave her the willies. Although Klub Kashmir was touted as *the* premier gentlemen's club in Lansdowne, it was what it was, a strip club. The girls were served up in the back rooms for private lap dances as effortlessly as alcohol was ordered at the bar. She shivered at the thought of dancing so intimately close to a stranger, taking her clothes off, rubbing up against him, feeling the hard ridge of his privates against the fabric of his pants, him smelling her sex.

Candi continued her quick tutorial on life as a cocktailer. "You don't have to worry about clients touching you during a lap dance. They can't. Mr. Z. could lose his license, so he forbids us to allow the clients even to breathe on us. But to make sure, there's always a bouncer standing in a dark corner of the room."

"I'm a cocktailer, Candi, not a dancer."

"That doesn't matter, honey, lots of cocktailers get asked to lap dance. Big bucks."

"You mean, one of the clients can just say they want me for a lap dance and I have to do it?"

Candi laughed, happily chomping her gum. "Sure. Why not?"

A wave of warmth permeated Phil's skin. She visualized herself dancing with her eyes closed, pretending the man beneath her taut thighs and heated pussy was her lieutenant, with no bouncer lurking in the shadows. She gasped. Oh Lord, not *him*.

"You okay, honey?" Candi asked, tightening her grip on Phil's trembling arm. "Don't be scared, these guys can't hurt you. The bouncer'll be right there, and Ty, he don't take shit from no one, not even our own people." She let go of Phil's arm and winked. "Honey, you play them poor slobs right and they'll treat you like a princess."

"Play them?"

Candi nodded and popped her gum. "Honey, it ain't called 'cocktail' for nothing. You got the tail and the cocks crow." Candi laughed. "Hey, I like that." She nudged Phil. "C'mon, jump on the cash train. You make 'em feel special, like they're the only ones in the room and you would love nothing more than to go home with them. 'Course when they ask you to, you just sweetly smile and tell them it's against company policy, but if you ever quit working the Kashmir you'd be happy to give them a call." Candi popped her gum. "'Course if you really want to go off with them, nobody has to know."

Phil nodded and felt a flash of pity for the men. Didn't they know they were being played?

"They know what we're doing, but if you're good at it? They forget fast and think with their cock, and if you're *real* good, you can empty plenty of wallets by the end of the night."

Phil smiled. The scene Candi painted was empowering. She'd never considered sex as power, but she supposed it was. Every woman in their right mind knew men thought with their little head, and so long as they did, a smart girl could capitalize on it.

Candi rambled on for a few more minutes about men, their dicks, and how in all her years of stripping she'd never met one worthy of taking home to her daughter. That is, until she met Mr. Right a month ago.

"Speaking of Mr. Right, here he comes now." Candi's voice rose in excitement. Phil turned and gasped. He might be Candi's Mr. Right, but he was definitely her Mr. Wrong.

Dressed completely in black, his tall powerful body glided effortlessly across the wide span of the club floor. His shoulder-length black hair gleamed under the harsh light. His green eyes twinkled as if he held a secret. Phil swallowed, the action tight against her dry throat. Ty's command presence was as much a part of him as was her blue eyes. She might not like the man, but her bourgeoning respect for him she could no longer ignore. The man was good.

"Hey, Ty," Candi cooed, sauntering with her look-at-my-hips-and-tits walk. It worked, too; both Phil and Ty watched her smooth firm body parts take on a life of their own.

"Good evening, Candi," Ty cooed right back.

Oh, *blech*.

Candi cuddled into Ty's broad chest and smoothed the fitted black dress shirt he wore over the plane of his muscles. "I waited for you last night."

Ty smiled at Candi indulgently, but smoothly disengaged her fingers digging between the buttonholes of his shirt. "I told you, I had work to do."

He flashed Phil a wicked grin and she felt the heat rise in her face and a hot stab of desire spike between her legs. She hadn't donned her work clothes yet, but stood in a pair of tight jeans, four-inch stiletto sandals, and a white form-fitting jersey top that hung loosely off one shoulder. Her *coup de grace?* She wore nothing beneath the top and only a G-string thong beneath the jeans. Her nipples swelled under Ty's attention, and it was all Phil could do not to shield herself from his hot gaze.

Watching his deep green eyes go from initial surprise to appreciative to downright horny, she felt a rush of satisfaction, until he finished off with calm indifference.

CHAPTER FOUR

Ty's reaction to the revamped IA officer was immediate and basic. He wanted to fuck her. And wouldn't have been particular about where, but the when part was now. He masked his surprise and chastised his cock for jumping so quickly to attention.

She was a looker all right. Long legs, narrow waist, tits sitting way up high. Her hair was now a kaleidoscope of browns, blondes, and reds, hanging long and sexy around her shoulders. Her full lips, painted and pouty, promised all kinds of deviant diversions.

Ty checked himself. She was the enemy. Plain and simple, he didn't trust her. His gaze zeroed in on her stiffening nipples, the wide areolas visible beneath the sheer white fabric of her shirt. His cock twinged hard. He was glad for the boxer briefs he wore, lassoing the buck of his shaft.

Candi cut off his view of Phil and he breathed easier. Ty glanced down at the blonde, who clung to him like a vine. While the little dancer was cute and accomplished, Ty preferred longer drinks of water, like Phil.

After disengaging Candi's blue nails from his shirt, he grinned down at Phil, who had a noticeable flush to her cheeks. Her blue eyes sparked. Whether from anger or desire he wasn't sure, and he really didn't care. What he wanted to see was that same fire in her eyes as he rode her hard to an orgasm. Ty muttered a curse. He'd spent too much damn time in this club. He wasn't a dog by nature. Although he'd remained fairly unaffected by the girls here, he found himself reacting to Phil like one of Candi's regulars.

"You must be the new cocktail Bud told me about. Why are you standing around?"

Phil opened her mouth, then closed it. Ty wondered how it would feel locking around his cock.

"I was just getting orientated," Phil said.

Candi stared at him strangely. "This is Kat." She turned to Phil and gave her an apologetic look. "Kat, this is Tyler Masters, the floor manager."

Like a trooper, Phil extended her hand. Reluctantly Ty took it. The minute he touched the smooth warmth of her skin a rush of electricity sparked his nerves. She felt it, too, her hand jerked in his, her eyes widening.

"Get dressed and get out on the floor. We're expecting a

big crowd tonight," he barked before turning on his heels and marching away.

Aware his behavior was out of line, but unable to control it, Ty cursed out loud and dared anyone who heard him to take exception. He was in a fucking strip joint and could get away with just about anything. Except doing naughty things to Philamina Zorn's luscious lips.

Bud set a bottle of water on the bar as Ty strode toward him. "It's going to be a busy one tonight, boss. Lines already forming."

Ty nodded and guzzled the cold water, wishing he could slam the chilled plastic against his throbbing cock. He couldn't remember the last time he'd sunk himself deep into a woman. His undercover work left zero time for even the most casual affair, and while he had no problem doing as the underworld did to gain their trust and settle in, he had no desire for the girls at Klub Kashmir. Call him old-fashioned, but he preferred his ladies more on the demure side as opposed to the brazen women of the club.

"Give me another round, Bud."

As he chugged down the second bottle, Ty's frustration turned to anger. He could thank his stripper mother for his distrust of women. That and a whole suitcase full of baggage.

He tossed the empty bottles over Bud's shoulders for two three-pointers.

"You never miss, do you, boss?"

Ty grinned at the old cuss. "Nope."

"Did you meet the new cocktail I hired?"

"Yeah, she's slacking backstage."

Laughing, Bud opened another bottle of water for Ty and set it on the bar. "You know, anytime you want something stronger, just ask."

Ty gave Bud a crooked smile. "I don't drink on the job."

"I hear you, just saying." Bud eyed Ty. "About the girlie I hired today. If I wasn't so desperate, I'd have told her to take a walk."

"Why?"

"She turned white when I handed her the uniform."

Ty grinned; he could imagine.

"Then she asked if she could wear pantyhose. I gave her the spiel, but I think she might not last the night. A real timid one, she is."

Ty grunted. If the old man only knew how far from the truth that statement was. Phil Zorn had the balls of a man, and while she played the librarian in IA, the sexy woman he saw backstage looked damn comfortable in her new skin.

"Want to wager, Bud?"

The old man's eyes lit up. "You're on, son. I'll bet a weekend off with pay she don't last a week."

Ty reached over the bar extending his hand. "I'll bet she makes more tips tonight than the other cocktails, and when I win, you work that weekend free of charge."

The men shook. An audible groan from Bud sealed his

fate. Turning, Ty felt like a cartoon character as his tongue and eyeballs popped out of his head.

Tall, sleek, and sexy. The name Kat fit her feline saunter. Instead of pantyhose, Phil wore a garter attached to black thigh-high stockings that ended in sexy black stiletto pumps. As she walked, her little skirt sashayed back and forth with the smooth sway of her hips. A tiny gemstone glittered in her belly button, catching his roaming eye. His body warmed as his eyes traveled up the smooth tautness of her stomach to her cleavage pushed together so tight he imagined the hot swell of her breasts locking around his cock.

He licked his lips, wanting to run his tongue between the deep valley before sucking her nipples that poked against the shimmering white fabric. His eyes continued their travel north, lingering on the smooth length of her neck, to her chin, and up farther. He wanted to suck those full lips right off her face. When they turned up into a smile, his eyes locked with hers.

Phil not only didn't shake the eye contact, but she continued her slow sexy walk right toward him. She flicked her mane of hair over her shoulder and licked her lips.

"Jesus, boss, I didn't see *that* coming," Bud muttered behind him.

Ty cleared his throat. "Neither did I."

"How about I give you this weekend? I'm not a welcher."

Without breaking eye contact with Phil, Ty said, "She tricked us both. Hang on for the ride."

Phil stopped a few feet from him. His nostrils caught the sultry musk of her perfume. They twitched in approval.

Phil smiled and raised a single eyebrow. Placing her hands on her hips, she struck a pose. "Is this acceptable, Mr. Masters?"

Ty grinned. "Turn around and I'll let you know."

He caught the flash of defiance in her eyes before she spun around. Without turning back around, she asked, "Well? Do I pass inspection? Does the back muster up to the front?"

Ty's eyes swept the smooth length of her back down to the firm ripeness of her ass. The black pleats of her skirt poked out, giving anyone who stood a few feet back a nice shot at the tightness of her upper thighs. When he failed to respond, she wiggled her ass and looked over her shoulder.

"I don't have all night, Mr. Masters."

Ty reached out to touch her shoulder, to turn her around just as she pivoted. His hand landed on her left breast. This time he didn't flinch at the contact. At least his hand didn't. He smiled leisurely, pressed his palm more firmly against her warmth, and stepped closer. Unhurriedly he trailed a fingertip around her straining nipple. She caught her breath and he felt the hard thud of her heart against his hand. Her big blue eyes widened, captivating him in their innocence. If she wasn't still a virgin, he doubted she had much experience. He wanted to be the one to tap into her. Her body language screamed uptight. Her body, though, screamed to his for contact.

He ran a finger down her waist to rest on the curve of her hip. The urge to pull her soft smooth body hard against him and torture her mouth with his lips was almost his undoing. She licked her glossy lips, the pink tip of her tongue conjuring up all kinds of sexy scenarios in his mind. Remembering where he was, he reined in his runaway desire. "If I had to pick which looked better, I'd have to call it a draw."

The thick rasp of his voice gave away his mood. Phil leaned into him. At the contact his cock thickened, the smooth line of her belly enticing him from his straining self-control.

Her sharp intake of air told him she'd felt his quickening. She surprised him by smiling sweetly up at him. Then she surprised him even more when she swept her hand up between them, smoothed it against him, then grabbed his shaft and squeezed. He hissed in a breath, his cock rearing in her hand. She quelled it by squeezing harder. Setting his jaw at a hard angle, he held his breath, resisting the urge to push her back into his office, clear his desk, and take her.

"If you continue to touch me like this, Mr. Masters, I'm afraid I'll have to file a sexual harassment charge against you and Klub Kashmir."

Bud coughed. "No, no, you don't want to do that."

Ty's jaw tightened. With supreme effort he reeled in his racing hormones.

His lips twitched in a smile. His entire body tightened with the enthusiasm of a sixteen-year-old boy anticipating his first blow job. When she abruptly released him, disappointment flooded his system.

He bent down to her ear and whispered, "Touché, Officer Zorn." Then backed off. She had balls and he was glad. He relished future sparring matches.

Ty looked over his shoulder. "Show her the ropes, Bud." Without another glance at Phil, he stalked off.

Phil couldn't regulate her breathing and her body thrummed with tension. Her nipples were as hard as the stainless-steel chairs around her and her pussy throbbed with the same driving tempo of the music. Ty's reaction to her surprised her, but hers to him stunned her.

She glanced anxiously around the brightly lit club. The stirring sound of a sleazy sax wafted through the sound system, setting the tone for the evening to come. What was it about this place that set her libido into overdrive? She'd never felt desire flood her as she had that moment she held Ty hot and hard in her hand. More astonishing, for the first time in her life, she felt no guilt associated with the desire.

Clenching her thighs, she suppressed a low moan. What the hell was happening to her?

"Bud? Can you excuse me for a minute?"

"Make it quick, the line's getting antsy."

Phil hurried to the ladies' room and locked herself in a stall. She leaned back against the smooth metal door and closed her eyes. Her entire body hummed. A live conduit. She touched her breast and gasped. A painful pleasure lit her nerve endings, the tension intense. Her pussy constricted and she had the incredible urge to slip a finger into herself. The thought shocked her. While there had been nights as a teenager when her body begged for stimulation, Phil had been too embarrassed to touch herself.

Her mother, the daughter of a Baptist minister, and her father, a born-again Christian, had made it clear to her from her early years. Masturbation was dirty and only nasty girls who had no self-control did it.

She wasn't nasty. She was good and clean and wholesome. And her father had drilled into her head the virtues of self-control. That hadn't stopped her from allowing Kyle Thompson, the high school quarterback, from putting his hands on her. Her skin shivered and the sudden heat spell Ty induced chilled. She didn't like to think of Kyle. She swallowed hard, grabbed a wad of toilet paper, and wiped the slick moisture from between her legs. Breathing deeply, she opened the stall door, quickly washed and dried her hands, and hurried out to Bud, who greeted her with a scowl.

"You're not starting out on a good foot."

"I'm sorry, it won't happen again."

She steeled herself and listened intently to what Bud told her. She followed his directions to the letter, all the while repeating her new mantra in her head: I will not respond to Ty Jamerson. I will not respond to Ty Jamerson.

For one who prided herself on such hard-ass self-control, Phil couldn't ignore the repeated twinge in her nether regions every time she heard Ty's deep voice.

As she counted out change for her book, Phil smiled. Her only satisfaction thus far was remembering Ty's massive erection. He couldn't hide that or the fact that it was she who had instigated it. It pleased her to know she had that effect on him, but even better was Ty's ignorance of what he did to her. Her cheeks warmed at the thought. She'd die of shame.

The music changed to a low, driving jungle beat, the lights dimmed around the bar, and the floor lights softly illuminated the polished chrome furniture.

Ty's deep voice grabbed her attention. "Okay, ladies and gents, we're open for business."

The set of double doors swung open and regulars and newcomers alike entered the club, stampeding for the prime seats at the wraparound bar encircling the stage. One or two men slowed enough to ogle her and paid for it by getting pushed aside.

"Hang on to your hat, honey. The moon's full and it looks like we got us some winners," Bud called from behind the bar.

She looked across the flood of bodies and met Ty's eyes. The intensity of his gaze stilled her beating heart and the magnitude of the operation hit her hard. There were lives at stake, including hers. She nodded in understanding, silently vowing not to fail.

CHAPTER FIVE

"You're going to pay for that love pat, mister, with a fat tip," Phil playfully chastised the grinning man who copped a feel every time she passed by with a loaded tray.

"You're going to pay, all right." Ty's deep voice cut through the grinding beat of the music. He hauled the man up by the scruff of his shirt. "How many times have I told you, Otis, no grab ass. I'm a floor manager, not a pimp."

"I didn't mean anything by it, I just wanted to make sure if I was going to pay for a lap dance nothing jiggled."

"That one doesn't do lap dances," Ty informed the regular.

Otis's face fell. "Now, that's too bad. She has a nice ass and I like the way she moves."

Ty eyed Phil as if ascertaining for himself the truth of Otis's words. Phil winked at her lieu, barely managing to hide a smile when he cocked his brow in surprise.

Like a seasoned vet, Phil leaned over, giving him the full Kat show, and served drinks to Jase and two other men at the table next to Otis's.

"Here you go, boys." She smiled into Jase's dark eyes and he grinned back.

"What's your name, sweetheart?" he asked.

Counting out change, Phil fluttered her long lashes. "Kat, as in *pussy* cat."

The man sitting next to Jase looked so much like a beat cop hiding in civvies he didn't need a cop sticker on his forehead to announce it. He grinned and leaned toward her. "I like pussy." When he slid his hand up her thigh, she slapped it away.

"My pussy bites strays. You don't want a case of cat scratch fever, do you?"

The man's jaw dropped and Jase snorted, thumping his friend on the back. "Tommy boy, you're barking up the wrong tree."

Tommy boy recovered with a leer. "I don't mind a little rough play."

Phil leaned in, giving the boys another free shot of her cleavage. "Tommy boy, there wouldn't be anything left but a bloody stump when I got done with you."

The smile faded from his lips. "Are you saying I can't handle you?"

Phil flashed a smug grin and stood up straight. "That's exactly what I'm saying."

Flicking her hair over her shoulder, she pivoted and held the tray up over her head, working her way through the crowd. She heard one of the men meow, and then the three of them laughed like sailors in a whorehouse. Shaking her head, Phil headed back to the bar, keeping her eyes alert and body prepared for the unexpected.

She needed to tip out for the hour. Bud told her to keep her change book light so as not to get pickpocketed by one of the clients. She figured she'd already cleared a good hundred bucks and the first dancer had yet to make her appearance. If the clients were generous and she made them feel special, she could walk with maybe three hundred bucks after tipping out the house. It didn't seem fair that the cocktailers and dancers who were doing all the dirty work should have to pay for the privilege. But in most circles, the money after tipping would be considered good. It was no wonder so many of the girls at the Kashmir put up with the maulings.

Her feet were killing her and she'd only been on the floor an hour. She looked out at the other cocktailers with respect. They went about their jobs in heels higher than hers and without complaint.

The last few hours blurred in her mind. She was not the same woman who filled out the application that afternoon. After catching a glimpse of herself earlier in the polished floor-to-ceiling mirrors, she'd blinked several times before she made the connection. The beautiful cocktail waitress in the skimpy uniform was her.

Something had happened to her when she took her first drink order and felt the first palm slide up her skirt. After shaking off the initial shock of a stranger touching her so intimately, she'd become Kat. In doing so, she allowed herself to cop an attitude in response to the unwanted petting and the innuendo, because inside the club, Kat was who she was.

The amazing part was she liked it. Not the men touching her, but the freedom Kat gave her. And the power. She didn't have to hide behind her parents' preaching. She didn't have to tell herself that nice girls didn't. Phil was a nice girl who didn't, but Kat was a naughty girl who did, and if she wanted to succeed in her cover she had to become Kat, body and soul. In becoming Kat she was able to put herself out on the floor and watch.

The unexpected perk of sensual emancipation was heady stuff. In the club, in her uniform, in her new skin, she could be and do whatever she wanted, all under the guise of doing her job. She told herself she would leave the guilt of her actions and the scintillating feelings said actions incited at the door.

Ty caught her eyes a few times, seeming to magically appear each time one of the patrons got too frisky. Jase sat with his bunch of cronies. She knew from his earlier communication that they had no idea she and Jase were undercover. Reese kept to himself, a loner, in the high, dark corner behind the bar, his eyes ever watchful.

Jase ordered JD straight up, but Bud gave him iced tea.

While his buddies were feeling the effects of their drinks, Jase stayed cold sober. She felt protected with the men around her. While she could handle herself, she knew they would have her back no matter what the situation.

The DJ called for the room to quiet and introduced Sable, the first dancer of the night.

The first moment Sable strutted onto the stage dressed as a shepherdess, Phil stood as transfixed as the men surrounding the stage. Sable was big, black, and absolutely gorgeous. Her mahogany skin glowed like polished wood.

Little Bo Peep never looked so . . . exotic.

Sable used her staff as a humping rod, and as she stripped off each of her petticoats, the wolf whistles became deafening.

"Hey!" the pervert next to Phil screamed. "Get me another round."

Phil fought down a scowl. Remembering the asshole drank the cheap beer, she nodded and hurried to fill his order.

"How's it going, Slick?" the bartender asked her.

"It's going, Bud. Give me another one of those cheap beers for my big spender over there."

She jacked her thumb over her shoulder. The old man grinned, following the direction. "I didn't think you had it in you, sister, but you work those slobs well."

He twisted the cap off a bottle, then set it on her tray. She winked at him. "I've got a lot more where that came from." She turned and sashayed back into the throng of whistling, groping, aroused men.

As she set the bottle on the table, she said, "Eight fifty."

Without taking his eyes off Sable's coconut-size breasts, the guy tossed a five at her. "I want the change, Toots," he grunted after guzzling half the bottle.

Of course he did. Guys like this drank the cheap stuff, cat-called and hooted to the dancers, then went in the john and jerked off. So much for Klub Kashmir's claim to catering to the more discriminating males. She leaned in. "Well, that's real sweet of you, mister, but you still owe me three fifty."

He flashed her a glare. "I gave you a ten." He looked back up at Sable's gyrating thighs and grabbed his burgeoning crotch.

"You gave me a five."

The man sneered, obviously not liking the fact that she was distracting him, and gave her his full drunken attention. "You ripped me off!"

Phil grabbed the nearly empty bottle from his hand. "I didn't rip you off, buddy, you ripped *me* off. If you want the rest of this bottle, cough up the three fifty."

He lunged across the table. Phil saw that train coming. She smacked him hard on the head with her tray. A strong arm grabbed her from behind and lifted her clear off her stilts and out of reach of the drunk, who had regrouped and was ready for his second attack.

Ty didn't waste a second on diplomacy. He grabbed the drunk by the scruff of his shirt and the back of his pants. As if he were taking out the trash, Ty marched to the front door, handed him off to Milo, the mountain-size bouncer, and the drunk was disposed of.

Watching it all happen so quickly and effortlessly, Phil had to admit Ty's commanding presence and fluid disposal of the asshole impressed her. The man didn't break a sweat.

Ty strode back toward her and the smile froze on her lips. His dark brows formed a V between two very angry green eyes. He was not amused.

He grabbed her by the elbow and steered her away from the crowded tables toward an alcove in the back of the club.

He turned her around and backed her into a corner.

"Rule number one. We do not brain our clients with our trays."

"But he accused me of ripping him off!"

Ty's lips twitched before they formed a hard line. "How does it feel to be accused of something you didn't do?"

Phil hissed in a breath. "That was three years ago, Lieutenant. Let it go."

His fingers tightened around her arms. When she twisted, his grip increased in pressure. "You're hurting me."

He loosened his fingers but still held her. "If you assault another client, I'll have no choice but to let you go. I can't let you beat up clients and not allow the other girls the same pleasure."

"Well, maybe you need to inform your clients they can't cheat us hardworking cocktailers."

Ty's face softened. "Phil, ah, Kat, don't take everything so literal. When in Rome, do as the Romans do."

She didn't try to ignore the hard underlying scent of the man who stood so close to her, nor the way his eyes kept dipping to her exposed cleavage and the way said cleavage suddenly grew heavy with tension. Her nipples stiffened and tingled. What had become a familiar heat flared between her thighs. "And what do the Romans do in Klub Kashmir?"

Ty grinned, flashing white teeth. "They act like Romans who do what they need to, to keep their jobs."

Phil leaned back against the hard smoothness of the wall. She was glad when Ty followed and glad Kat took over. As Kat she could admire his imposing build, the hard sinew of his arms, and Ty's undeniable maleness. Making her feel every bit a woman and feel no guilt or shame.

"And how do I go about keeping my job?" she asked.

Ty infiltrated her space so thoroughly, his heat penetrated her skin, warming it hotter. He smelled good. Clean, woodsy, strong. His chest brushed up against her. They both felt the jolt the contact elicited and they both pretended it didn't affect them. Bending down so she could be sure to hear, Ty said, "Keep strutting your stuff and cockteasing, minus the aggression."

Phil would have taken his bait as an insult. Kat took it as a compliment. Kat pressed her full breasts against Ty's chest, dragging them in slow temptation. She caught her breath when he pushed back, hiking up the friction. Her skin sizzled and her nipples strained hard against the fabric of her uniform. If he weren't so close, her knees would have buckled. He barely touched her, but being so close to him, she felt like a piece of warm putty in a sculptor's hands.

Wanting control, Phil struggled for composure. Tilting her head up, she stood on her tiptoes until she came almost eye-to-eye with him. Ty's lids hooded his dark green eyes in sexy languidness. She sucked in her bottom lip, then licked it. It gave her supreme satisfaction to watch his full lips tighten and hear the subtle hitch of his breath.

"Mr. Masters, I aim to please."

CHAPTER SIX

"Officer Zorn, are you coming on to me?"

The heat in Phil's eyes told the truth, but he wanted to hear it from her lips. He was more than intrigued—he was fascinated.

Phil shook her head, sending her hair cascading down her back. Her full breasts bobbed against the confines of her skimpy top. He visualized his hand slipping up and tugging the fabric, spilling her fabulous tits out for his hands and mouth to ravage. His blood quickened. And not for the first time that night he wasn't picky about location, only about what he wanted to do to her.

"No, sir. That would be against general orders."

He inched closer, so close he felt the lurch of her heart against his chest. Dipping his mouth to the smooth skin of her neck, he whispered, "GO doesn't apply to undercover."

He knew he played dirty the minute he ran the length of his tongue up behind her ear and nipped the soft flesh there. She moaned, arching against him. She tasted warm and sweet, like honey. His cock twinged hard. He couldn't resist running his fingertips across her taut belly and toying with her belly button jewel.

"Mr. Masters, please, I'm working."

Very reluctantly he retreated an inch, grinning at her pretend coyness. "You're working all right. Working me into a lather."

He stepped back from her and the rush of cool air reminded him he had a case to solve.

Phil got a quick grip. While she'd like to pretend that as Kat she could play no holds barred, pragmatic Phil wielded her way into the equation. She wasn't so sure how she felt about the interloper.

Ty's hands slid up her arms, then down before releasing her. In painful awareness, Phil realized his release was the last thing she wanted. That fact astounded her. It must be the hormones bouncing around the club. Somehow they'd gotten under her skin.

"Unless you want to take this a step further, outside of work, don't play with me." Ty's husky voice sent ripples of desire through her body.

Phil swallowed hard, consciously pulling herself out of the erogenous zone that was Ty Jamerson. Literally she shook herself and wondered where the hell all that sex play came from.

She was Philamina Marie Zorn, preacher's granddaughter, and while she could play Kat, it was only to those who believed she was a cocktail server at Klub Kashmir.

There was history with Ty, slight though it was, and he could hurt her. Her heart slammed against her chest. Yes, he could hurt her. Break her heart if she let him. Realization swarmed her practical mind. Vulnerability made you weak, and she needed to be strong. Strong for her own self-preservation, and strong *and* focused for the case. They had three missing women to find. She wouldn't jeopardize their lives by being caught off guard.

Ty moved back, giving her more space. She didn't need to look down to his tented crotch to know he was aroused. She'd felt him rise against her belly, and while she took a perverse pleasure in being the one to cause his erection, she also felt like a tease, and not a nice one. Not that Ty Jamerson deserved nice. But, grudgingly, she had to give him kudos for keeping his hands to himself and being on top of every horny asshole in the place who wanted to get his fingers in her pants.

"I . . . ah, sir, I was just getting into character."

Ty eyed her suspiciously, knowing she'd just fed him a line of bullshit. "Speaking of getting into character. Call me 'Ty' or 'Mr. Masters' at all times. In fact, do it off the clock until the case is closed." He grinned, the gesture lethal. "I'll call you Kat. Or when the mood strikes me, Pussy."

Kat rose to the bait. "You think you're man enough to make this pussy purr?"

Ty's grin widened. "And then some. I've got a sudden itch for some cat scratch fever."

She stepped closer, her nostrils flared, and she throbbed between her legs. If he didn't watch out, he'd find her claw marks in his back. And once she sunk them into him, she wouldn't release him, until *she* wanted to.

"Maybe you *are* man enough, but we won't find that out anytime soon."

She hurried past him, shutting him down cold. She wished she could say the same for herself. Her body flared hot with desire. Desire she'd never known she was capable of feeling, scaring her with its ferocity.

Remembering where she was and why, Phil made a quick tour of her tables, picking up orders from several men, who were grumbling because she'd disappeared for a couple minutes. The night rushed past her. And while she kept a suspicious eye cast over the ribald crowd, aside from the flying testosterone and gyrating body parts, Phil's gut told her all was as it should be inside Klub Kashmir.

One dancer after another strutted, sauntered, slid, and swam across the stage, humping the pole, air, and stage floor. The more alcohol was consumed, the looser the men's wallets became. By the end of the night, Kat counted out nearly three hundred and fifty dollars in tips.

She rubbed her throbbing feet as she turned in her tray. It wasn't worth the pain. She almost cried when she set her bare feet down on the floor, it felt so good.

She made a mental note to bring a pair of comfy tennis shoes to wear out like the other cocktails. As she rubbed her tired sore feet, she said, "You live and learn."

"I hope you do, Kat."

She looked up at Ty. "I have to hand it to the other ladies. They must have cast-iron feet. I'd give anything for a foot massage right now."

He grinned down at her. "Maybe that can be arranged."

Before she could respond, Candi bebopped over to them, chomping her ever-present gum. "How'd it go tonight, Kitty? I saw you working some of those guys. I bet you made bank."

Candi slipped her arm through Ty's and hugged his arm to her breasts.

A jolt of jealousy jabbed at Phil's gut. She didn't care for the sensation, especially since she liked Candi. She smiled genuinely. If Candi and Ty had a thing going on, she'd be damned if she'd interfere. Besides, it would no doubt save her a broken heart in the end.

"I cleaned up. I think. Three fifty less my percentage to the house. Is that good?"

Ty coughed and Candi squealed. "Wow, were you giving blow jobs on the side, honey? I only take home twice that and I'm a featured dancer."

Phil glanced up at Ty's darkened face. Her cheeks warmed. She could work this place for a decade even in Kat's skin, and still not get used to the derogatory sexual terms or the gratuitous way such acts were performed. She surmised it must be her, because she seemed to be the only one shocked by it all.

Phil opened her mouth to respond, but once again, Candi answered her question for her. "Oh, I know, you had a few lap dances."

"Well, actually, I didn't. I—" Phil looked up at a scowling Ty. "I've never done a lap dance before, I wouldn't know what to do."

Candi's jaw dropped open and her gum plopped out onto the floor. "Honey, it's just a matter of time before one of these guys pays for a lap dance. You can't go in blind." Candi disengaged herself from Ty. Patting his hand, she smiled up at him. "I have something for your new girl." Candi turned to Phil. "Kitty, you stay right there. I have a video of me dancing for a couple of bachelors last month. It's my best work to date. Pop it in when you get home, and feel free to use my moves." She turned to get it when Ty's voice stopped her.

"That won't be necessary, Candi. Kat won't be doing lap dances."

In unison both women asked, "Why not?"

Ty scowled, first at Kat, then at Candi. Quickly he hid his annoyance. "I was under the impression, Kat here had some—" He looked at Kat for some help.

Crossing her arms over her chest, Phil raised a brow. "Under what impression, Mr. Masters?"

"That you had a disfigurement."

Phil smiled slowly. "Would you like to see for yourself that

I have nothing unusual hiding under this poor excuse for a uniform?"

Ty considered calling her bluff. On an impulse, he did. He nodded and grinned at Phil's wide-eyed response. If she wanted to play with fire, she'd best learn to get burned. Lucky for his daredevil Officer Zorn, the only person left in the club area was Bud.

Phil locked eyes with her boss. She called on Kat from within and told her to do it for the missing women. Slowly, Phil turned and with her bottom aimed at Ty, she flipped up her short skirt, revealing her flawless ass. Ty's sharp intake of breath satisfied her ego. Candi gave her own commentary. "Kitty, you have a nice butt. What's the front of you look like?"

Ty couldn't wait to see. Phil spun around and flipped up the front part of her skirt. Her thighs were smooth and taut, and the slice of red material that shielded her from view did a poor job; he could see the outline of her moist lips pressed against the material. His eyes caught hers and he knew she was as hot for him as he was for her.

"Kitty, if I were a guy, I'd want to do you right now. You sure are beautiful."

"Untie the top," Ty commanded softly. Phil slid the pleats of her skirt back into place.

Slowly, she untied the knot that held the heavy ripeness of her breasts. Her nipples tingled in anticipation and much to her horror she wanted Ty to see her breasts. More than that, she wanted him to touch them.

The knot slid open. She pulled back the sheer material and turned away from Ty to Candi. Her breasts tumbled out and she caught her breath.

Candi's eyes widened and Ty cursed. "Those are real, aren't they?" Candi asked.

Gently, the dancer touched the underside of Phil's left breast. The sensation of the contact surprised Phil. Her skin was so sensitive, she felt as if a layer had been peeled off.

Phil's throat closed up as she nodded mutely. She wanted to close her top and run out the door. Even as Kat she found it excruciating baring her breasts.

Phil moved aside, allowing Kat full reign of the moment. Kat turned up the heat. She cocked her head back and over her shoulder and winked at Ty.

His eyes burned hot in his face and the flare of his nostrils reminded her of a dog sniffing the air for a mate. From the looks of Ty, he'd found the one he wanted.

Turning back to Candi, Kat asked, "So? Do they meet with your approval?"

Candi smiled as Phil gritted her teeth. Her father would roll over in his grave if he could see her now. "If I were the jealous type, Kitty, I'd hurt you right now. Your body is beautiful. I'm glad you aren't dancing; I couldn't stand the competition."

Over her shoulder, Phil cocked a brow at Ty. "Well, Mr. Masters? Is Candi's word good enough or do you want to see for yourself?"

Ty cleared his throat. "It's enough."

Slowly, Phil retied the knot to the top and turned to face him. "Excellent." Once she composed herself, she looked him hard in the eye. "So there won't be a problem with you allowing me to provide private lap dances for the paying clients, if that's what I choose?"

The muscles in his jaw worked. "Absolutely not."

Candi clapped her hands. "Oh, goody. I'll get you my video."

The minute Candi walked out of earshot, Ty ground out, "What the hell are you doing?"

Phil smiled and moved into his space. "When undercover, do as those around you do."

"I didn't mean it literally."

"Of course you did, Mr. Masters. How else am I supposed to set myself up for a kidnapping if I'm not performing? Fetching drinks won't bring attention my way."

"That doesn't mean you have to strip."

She nodded, considering his angry tone. In his burning eyes she didn't see a lieutenant's concern for one of his own; no, she saw something more powerful. Jealousy. And that stirred something sleeping deep within her. She suddenly felt like she was walking on very thin ice, ice that with one false move would crack wide open, plunging her into a black icy hole of pain and regret.

"It's not like I'm getting onstage. A private lap dance or two won't hurt."

"I don't like it."

"Too bad. Besides, the guys can't touch me, right?"

He nodded.

"Then there you go. With one of your goons in the shadows, I'll be safe."

Ty stood silent, his arms crossed over his chest, the hard line of his jaw the only clue to his anger.

What the hell did she just insist on doing? And why? Phil inhaled a deep breath and slowly exhaled. Well, there it was, out in the open. She'd just committed to performing a lap dance. Her stomach twittered nervously. Charging in and taking no names had become status quo around her lieutenant. And for someone who prided herself on painstakingly mapping out a strategy, she really needed to work on her knee-jerk reaction to her handsome boss.

CHAPTER SEVEN

Ty stood rooted to the asphalt parking lot and watched Phil drive out of the lot in her safe, practical, and most uninspiring Taurus. The complete opposite of the woman who drove it.

He had a problem, one he'd never encountered in his life. He was torn. Jesus, he felt like he'd been gut punched.

The red brake lights of Phil's car flashed as she came to a STOP sign, then disappeared into the darkness of the early morning hour.

Ty's fists clenched at his sides. When she'd exposed her body parts in the bar, his gut seized. He thought she was different.

A woman who had some class and self-respect. His mother's sunken, sallow face flashed before him. He turned back to the club and cursed out loud. His mother had raised him in the back of every strip joint from Chicago to San Francisco.

Hell, she couldn't tell Ty who his father was. Some nameless, faceless john. To this day he didn't know why she chose to give birth to him instead of having an abortion. Why, he wondered, had she kept him when she so easily aborted others? It was after the third one, the self-induced one in the flytrap apartment in Oakland, when he split the first time. He couldn't watch her kill herself any longer. Her body had long ago lost its luster of youth and she'd reduced her life to blow jobs on the side to feed her heroin habit. Guilt sent him back. He was all she had in the world. That and her heroin addiction. He should have gotten a clue when she didn't notice he'd been gone for two weeks. When he refused to pimp for her, and she called him an ungrateful bastard, he knew unless she cleaned up, she wouldn't last another six months. After repeated threats to call the cops, he got her to agree to rehab. She promised him she'd try—instead two days later he found her dead in her room with a needle stuck in her arm.

"Yo, Boss Man!" Bud called from the open front door.

Ty shook the black memories from his head and headed back into the club.

"What's up, Bud?'

"Not sure. I found this crumpled up on the bar. It wasn't there when we closed."

He handed Ty a Klub Kashmir napkin. Scrawled neatly in

black pen were two words, *Get Pussy*. Ty shrugged. Pussy abounded in the club.

"Who came by the bar after we closed down?"

Bud scratched the stubble on his chin. "No one out of the ordinary. The new girl, Kat, you, and Milo."

Mile High Milo, Ty called the Samoan bouncer who filled up the entryway. Aside from manhandling drunks, the guy had no record and the heart of a pussycat.

Ty glanced down at the napkin again. *Get Pussy.* A disturbing thought niggled at his brain. When it exploded into realization, his instincts took over. Never one to ignore his gut, Ty acted. "I'll see you tomorrow, Bud."

He hurried out the door and jumped into his truck. Kat—Kitty—Pussy. Was Kat the "Pussy" the author of the napkin wanted? A chill sprinted down his spine. He punched in the precinct number on his cellphone and demanded Phil's address. Once he had it, he floored his truck and gave dispatch orders to start the nearest unit en route.

He was about ten minutes behind her.

Phil drove too fast. The best perk of being a cop was never having to worry about speeding tickets, not that she took advantage of that fact. But tonight her feet throbbed and she'd kill for a foot massage. She couldn't wait to get home, shower, then slip between fresh sheets. Those creature comforts dominated her senses, but whispering in the back of her mind, too insistent to ignore, was the heated excitement that had ripped through her body when she bared herself to Ty.

Phil groaned and pushed her sore foot harder against the gas petal. Ty's response had been one thing—but her own hot response surprised her, and in front of a virtual stranger, no less.

What she needed was an ice-cold shower! Argh! It would take a lot more than a cold shower to cool her off.

Twenty minutes later she emerged from the bathroom, chilled and freshly cleansed of the seedy film of the club that clung to her like cheap perfume. Slowly, she rubbed the thick terry towel across her skin, taking care to dry every inch. As she rubbed the cloth across her breasts, her nipples hardened and her skin flushed, but it did nothing to quell the thickness of her blood. Instead the contact heightened her awareness of what her body craved.

Looking at her reflection in the steamy mirror, she caught her breath. She didn't recognize the hungry blue eyes that blazed back at her. She touched a fingertip to her left breast and pressed. Spikes of desire raced to her core and the now familiar heat she'd only experienced in Ty's presence flared. She closed her eyes halfway and bit down on her bottom lip. The spear of pain coupled with the spears of pleasure heightened her excitement. Boldly, her fingers trailed down her belly.

The chime of the doorbell startled her out of her self-seduction. Slipping on her robe she hurried to the incessant ringing. Who the hell was that?

"Open up, Phil!"

Her skin warmed to hot. She hurried to the front door, pulling her thin jersey robe tighter around her damp skin.

"Crap," she muttered. Every frickin' curve and dip of her body was clearly outlined by the clinging fabric. She didn't bother to look through the peephole; the bellowing voice on the other side of her door could only come from one person.

She unlocked the two dead bolts and yanked open the door.

"What is it, Lieutenant?"

He pushed past her, striding into the middle of her living room. "Sure, c'mon in."

He turned and headed down the hallway toward her bedroom. "Were you followed home?" he called over his shoulder.

She followed after him. "No. Was I supposed to check?"

He stopped abruptly in the hallway and turned around. Her nose slammed into his chest. She bounced off. "Ouch!"

Ty grabbed her upper arms and shook her. "You didn't check? Don't you know you should always have eyes in the back of your head?"

Suddenly Phil felt naïve. "I—I forgot." With the excitement and then the fatigue of the evening, she'd thrown her training out the window. Stupid. Next time that could get her killed.

"You *forgot*? Forgetting can get you killed," he said, his words echoing her thoughts.

Ty continued blasting her. "Or have you forgotten we've lost two civilians and a fellow cop? This isn't a damn desk job!"

She yanked out of his grasp. "If you keep manhandling me like you do, I'm going to have bruises up and down my arms, and the customers will complain."

Shaking his head, Ty strode into her bedroom, looked in the closet, behind the door; he did the same in the other two bedrooms, then in her kitchen and living room.

She followed him from room to room, knowing that arguing would get her nowhere. With this man, she needed to choose her battles carefully.

"Why are you here, Lieutenant?"

Ty turned angry eyes on her. She'd wake up and take notice when he showed her the napkin. "Didn't your father ever tell you, always be on the lookout?"

Her skin chilled at the mention of her father. "I told you, don't ever bring up my father again."

"Why not? Can't you face what he did?"

Phil strode to the front door and yanked it open. The sultry night air wafted in around her ankles. "Get out."

Ty leaned against the doorjamb to the living room, crossing his arms over his chest. "I'll go, but first I need to make a few things clear." His tall sleek muscles bunched beneath his tan skin. His green eyes sparkled in the low light. He reminded her of a jungle cat, predatory, and ready to pounce.

Phil's stomach churned and she knew she could call 911. She also knew Ty would stand in her hallway until he had his say. She slammed the door shut and strode past him into the living room.

She flung herself onto the sofa and crossed her arms. Ty slowly followed.

"Make it quick, Lieutenant. I'm tired and my feet are killing me."

Ty sat down on the ottoman facing her.

"What?" she demanded.

He grinned, the gesture wicked. Her blood thawed. She wanted to groan and run away. Her traitorous body was going to be her undoing. She closed her eyes and saw her mother with her hands on her hips scowling down at her:

"Philamina Marie, you were warned what would happen to you."

Phil felt all of sixteen again and remembered as if it were yesterday the repercussions of her aftergame tryst with Kyle Thompson under the bleachers. God made sure her parents knew what she had done.

"Hey?" Ty softly said, touching her foot. Phil flinched and opened her eyes.

"I don't bite, Phil."

Shaking off the nasty memories, Phil steeled herself. She could refuse her desires. She was her father's daughter, after all.

"What do you want, Lieutenant?"

Ty scooted closer till they faced each other. She curled up in a near fetal position on the sofa and Ty sat open-legged on the ottoman. If she extended her legs to the floor, their knees would touch. She backed farther into the cushions. She was tired and she didn't trust herself around him in her fatigued state.

"I want for us to be on the same page."

"We are."

He shook his head. "I don't think so. I'm concerned about your lack of street smarts. It could get you in trouble."

Phil stiffened. "I spent six months on the street before going into IA!"

Ty nodded. "Exactly, and I bet you figured you learned it all. I would have thought you'd have taken some tips from your old man."

Phil gritted her teeth. "I told you—"

"Right, don't mention Dad. Listen, Zorn. If your feelings regarding your father's case are affecting your ability to work this case, you need to fess up right now. I need to know what's bugging you."

She untangled her limbs and leaned toward him. "You of all people don't need to know about how I feel regarding my father."

"I do when it affects your ability to do your job well. Admit it, you can't forgive him."

Phil shot up and slammed her hands into Ty's chest, pushing him backward. He nearly tipped, but he grabbed her arm, using it for leverage.

Phil shook him off. "Forgive *him*? Forgive him for what? He was railroaded, set up by rogue cops like you!"

She jerked the loosened ties of her robe tighter. Ty shook his head and looked up at her. "He wasn't railroaded *or* set up. The man roughed up his beat wife, who was turning tricks!"

Phil pushed him hard in the chest again. This time she had no regrets. Ty jumped up and grabbed her by the hands. "I told you what I would do if you touched me again."

Phil kicked him, trying to twist out of his grip. Her robe loosened. She didn't care. She knew about all of his nasty skeletons from reading his files years ago in IA. "Turn me out like you did your mother?"

Phil wished with all her might she hadn't said the words. The pain that flashed across Ty's face was heartbreaking. The fury that replaced it was terrifying.

He pulled her hard against his chest. "Yeah, just like my mother. You're your father's daughter after all." He shoved her away from him.

Phil gasped. "How dare you?" She moved in on him. His eyes flashed a warning. She flashed her own. "How dare you speak lies about my father? He was swept up by the likes of you. He never touched that woman."

Ty rubbed his cheek and laughed, the sound brittle. "The big difference between the two of us, Phil, is I can admit my mother was a twenty-dollar hooker who would have done it for nothing if you gave her a fix. Your old man was a hypocrite of the highest order. While he walked around thumping his Bible, he was tearing up the sheets with a whore."

Phil's jaw dropped. Ty moved in. "You're the same hypocrite. You cover your body with those dark suits. You wear your hair tied back like a librarian. You act like you're untouchable." Reaching out, he grabbed a long hank of her hair.

She winced, expecting pain, but he ran his fingers through it, a caress instead of a pull. "Then there's the bad girl in you that you can't keep quiet." He stepped closer, his hot breath mingling with hers.

Phil's heart hammered in her throat. "Your body screams for a man, you want it, but you're too afraid to take it, afraid you might like it." His finger traced down the curve of her throat to the pulse in her jugular, now thumping against the pressure of his thumb. He pressed harder. Her blood quickened and her knees shook. The part of her that let Kat loose surfaced. She wanted to be touchable, in touch with her body, and Ty's.

She swallowed and licked her dry lips. "I tried it once, I didn't like it."

Ty grinned. "Well, then, maybe you need to try it with a man."

Phil almost smiled through the sexy haze that engulfed her. The same feeling she'd experienced touching herself after her shower surfaced, along with her yearning for the man standing in front of her.

Ty laughed low and brushed his knuckles down her throat to the V between her breasts. Her heartbeat thudded so soundly she felt the pulse of it through his fingertips. His eyes focused on her lips. "I'm right. I bet the last guy you were with shot his wad before he could get it out of his pants."

CHAPTER EIGHT

She fought for composure. "I'm sure your sexual prowess is legendary, Lieutenant. However, I didn't like being a notch on a bedpost the first time. I'm sure I'd like it even less with you." She wondered if he believed she had no interest in him. She didn't.

Ty's smile radiated promise. Phil tried to ignore it. Warning bells shrilled in her head. She knew damn well the minute she crossed that line with Tyler Jamerson she'd regret it for the rest of her life. "Besides, sir, fraternizing is a big no-no."

Ty nodded. "You're exactly correct. But as I explained earlier, in undercover we have our own general orders."

Phil smiled. "I know, 'do what you have to do to survive.'"

"Exactly." She swallowed hard. His shoulder-length hair hung loose around the angles of his face, giving him the sensual look of a dark angel. His voice lowered an octave.

"And right now, I think I need you to make it through the night."

"I doubt you need anyone, Lieutenant."

Ty moved closer. His tall frame shadowed her. Heat emanated off his chest. Her damp jersey robe steamed. Ty traced a finger through the material around her swollen nipple. "I think, Officer Zorn, you may need me as much."

Phil leaned back against the smooth hardness of the wall. "I thought you didn't like me, Lieutenant."

Ty's grin turned lethal, his eyes sparkled, and his fingers splayed against her breast. Phil commanded her body to ignore the sizzling sensations his touch evoked.

Ty moved closer still, only an inch separating their bodies. The wild beat of her heart thumped against his palm. He dipped his head down and whispered in her ear. "I don't have to like you to fuck you."

A thrill sprang from her belly, shooting to every nerve ending she possessed. Images of Ty pinning her hard against the wall, then burying himself deep within her accelerated her breath. She licked her lips.

Phil closed her eyes and tilted her head back, exposing the softness of her neck. It was all the invitation Ty needed.

Blood surged to his dick and his lips swooped down on the offering. Her warm skin pulsated against his lips. She tasted fresh, like vanilla. Phil's body jerked, then molded against his chest. The ties to her robe fell apart and the heat of her skin singed him.

His lips blazed a path from her neck to the hollow at her throat. Phil's moans incited him further. He felt supercharged, and the night's exhaustion disappeared as his body geared up for her.

Slipping his arms beneath her robe, her sultry skin felt alive beneath his hands. Her natural scent blended with her shower-applied scent, the combination toxic to his self-control.

He pushed her back flush against the wall, his hands spanning her slender waist. Bending his nose to her damp hair, he closed his eyes and breathed in her essence. "You smell good," he whispered, wondering how exciting her true woman scent would be. Just the thought of what he knew would be a soft musky scent sent more blood speeding to his cock. His hands slid farther down to the small of her back, her soft moans urging him on. His large hands palmed her firm ass cheeks. Her hips pressed against his groin and his dick swelled to capacity.

At that moment he couldn't remember wanting a woman more. He bet she was virgin tight, and he wanted desperately to find out how wet she was for him.

Keeping one arm wrapped around her waist, he slid his right hand around to her belly, trailing his fingers in languid swirls.

Philamina closed her eyes, the sensations Ty wrought overpowering her. Warm moisture slicked her nether regions, a beckoning. His fingers trailed lower past her belly button to sweep sensitively against the soft hint of pubic hair. She moaned loudly, her lips parted, her head thrown back against the wall.

"Open your eyes," Ty whispered against her cheek. As she did, he slid a finger across her hardened clitoris and she gasped, standing up on her toes. Shards of desire shattered her nerve endings. In a primal invitation, her knees spread. He slid his fingertip back and forth across her clit, rolling it across and between her moist lips, the sensation driving her higher on her toes. Her hips moved in rhythm to the slow seductive cadence of his fingers. She grabbed his shoulders and pulled herself higher against him. She wanted penetration.

Ty slid his large hand around her waist down to her bottom and splayed his fingers across its width, then pressed her against his hand. "Touch me deeper," she murmured against his chest.

The unfamiliar sound of her wanton request diffused some of the sexual haze. What was she doing?

Then Ty's long thick finger slid into her and she screamed out. The sensation was more then she expected and all that she'd hoped. She clung to his shoulders and shuddered in sexual nirvana.

"My God, Phil, you are so tight."

She opened her mouth to respond, to say something quick and witty, but words failed her. When he began a slow rhythmic slide inside of her with his finger, she about came undone.

It occurred to her somewhere in the deepest, darkest recesses of her mind that she was cavorting with a man who had little, if any, respect for her. Hell, admittedly he didn't have to like her to do what he was doing.

Phil pushed at Ty's shoulders, her self-respect overriding the scintillating sensations Ty evoked from her body. With a Herculean effort, she stopped him cold. The sudden coolness of the air that now separated their bodies was both welcome and unwelcome. Her body screamed for her to finish what they'd started, her pride screamed louder for her to get away from him as fast and, far as she could.

"You have to like me first," Phil gasped, catching her breath as she slipped away from him, tightening her robe around her trembling body. She hurried to the door and, despite her aroused state, she smiled as he rearranged the bulge in his pants. Ty's gaze bored holes into her. She flushed and stood away from the open door. "Good night."

Ty's dark green eyes blazed, his lips twitched. In two long strides he met her at the open door. He raised his hand to her face and she flinched. He smiled slowly, the look of a wolf about to devour a rabbit. As he touched her cheek, the musky scent of her sex wafted to her nose. She gasped. His smile widened. He sniffed the air near her face. He smelled her, too. "Zorn, you know it's just a matter of time."

A chill raced across her warm skin, doing little to cool it.

"Yes, sir, just a matter of time before you realize I'm not available."

Ty grinned and chuckled low. "Sure you're not." He gave

her a short salute. "I'll give you this round, but the next one will be mine." He strode past her and as she closed the door, he turned, his face serious. "Eyes in the back of your head, Zorn, even while you sleep."

Once again, the totality of the case hit home. Phil swallowed hard and nodded. This time when she double-bolted her front door, she made the rounds of her small house, making sure the only entry was by key or invasion. Her house locked tighter than most banks, Phil slid her loaded Glock under her pillow.

Warmth infiltrated her skin as she slipped between the smooth linen sheets. Yawning, she thought how much more comfortable she would be knowing Ty slept beside her.

Ty hopped into his truck and started it. His blood had not cooled. He grabbed the steering wheel, opening and closing his fingers around it. He was worse then a dog after a bitch in heat. Her scent lingered on his hand, it enveloped his senses, holding him hostage. He put the truck in gear and hit the gas pedal. He told himself she was just a female like any other. Not to be trusted, only indulged in. Twenty minutes later with Philamina Zorn still prominent on his mind, he realized he never brought up the matter of the napkin and the note written on it.

She was a damn distracting female. He wouldn't make the same mistake twice.

. . .

As exhausted as she was, sleep eluded Phil most of the night. Sexy dreams of her and Ty wrapped up in the sheets, their sweaty bodies sliding in and out of the other, dominated her subconscious. Finally she realized she wasn't going to get a decent sleep.

She brushed her teeth, washed her face, then set out for a long run. An hour later her body still craved what Ty started last night. Another cold shower proved to be as ineffective as the one last night. Instead of standing in front of the mirror and resuming her self-exploration, Phil dressed and decided to take the afternoon and hit a few boutiques Candi had mentioned the girls frequented. Her old "librarian" look, as Ty had called it, wouldn't do. Until the kidnapper was arrested, she needed to be Kat on and off the clock.

As Phil slid one skimpy outfit after another across the rack, she had to continually remind herself she needed to get past her modesty. Kat didn't possess a modest bone in her body and Phil had to live Kat's brazen persona. She took a deep breath and told herself she would not leave the store until she had a wardrobe fit for a woman who was one hundred percent in touch with her sexuality.

"Hey, Kat!"

Phil turned around and blinked at the small blonde making her way through the racks of clothes, dragging a child behind her.

Recognition dawned. "Candi?" Surprise didn't describe Phil's reaction.

Stopping close to her, Candi said, "My real name is Julie."

The petite blonde standing in front of her in tattered sweatpants and a worn Roxy T-shirt bore no resemblance to the overly made-up exotic dancer who ground and thrust her crotch in the faces of dozens of men last night. Her hair was pulled back in a lose ponytail and she didn't wear a dab of makeup, not even lip gloss. Even more surprising to Phil was the little replica standing shyly beside her.

"My daughter, Lola."

The little girl smiled bashfully. Phil's heartstrings tugged. She knelt down and smiled. "Hi, Lola, I'm Katherine. How are you?"

The child, no more than two, turned away, burying her face in her mother's legs. "She's shy. But we're working on it."

Phil stood and stepped back. Never one for idle conversation, she had to force herself to begin dialogue. While Candi didn't strike her as a kidnapper, she might be able to inadvertently lead them to one. There was no better way to glean information than lull the object of your interrogation into a false sense of security. She'd learned that tactic well in IA.

"I took you up on your advice. I'm springing for some new threads. Would you mind helping me pick a few things out?"

"Sure. I love spending other people's money."

Candi quickly warmed to the chore, pulling several pieces from different racks and putting together a formidable assortment of outfits. "Try these on for size."

Phil blushed as she zipped up the hot-pink micromini skirt and then tied the sheer white halter top around her neck.

"Let me see," Candi called. Grateful the store was empty, Phil slipped out of the dressing room. She realized her shoulders where slightly humped. Immediately she straightened them. Be Kat, she repeated over and over in her head.

"Oh, Kitty, that looks great with your skin tone." Candi looked down at Lola. "What do you think, Lola, isn't Kitty pretty?"

The little girl sucked on two fingers and nodded, looking at the floor.

Candi hugged her close and looked up at Phil, who stared at the little girl. For some reason she felt sorry for the child.

"It's because of her that I do what I do."

Phil smiled in genuine understanding. "You don't need to justify what you do to me, Candi, er, Julie. I'm not here to judge."

"I'm working real hard to make a family for me and Lola. Her dad is—well, he's not a nice man, and I've been real careful who I bring home to meet my baby."

Phil nodded and stepped back toward the dressing room. "I can understand that. You don't want to bring a jackass around your kid."

Candi smiled. "I found the perfect man for Lola and me. I'll do anything to make sure it doesn't get messed up."

Phil backed into the dressing room and pulled the saloon-style door closed. "That's great, Candi," she said with as much false enthusiasm as she could muster. She knew damn well Ty was Candi's Mr. Perfect.

Candi cleared her throat. Phil felt what was coming and was glad for the door separating them. "Look, since we're going to be working together, we might as well be straight about Ty."

Phil peeked over the door and looked directly at Candi. "What's to get straight?"

"We're a couple. And Lola needs a daddy."

Phil's chest constricted and for a minute she couldn't breathe. Then anger welled. What a son of a bitch! He was making daddy noises with Candi and her kid while less than eight hours ago he was sniffing around her.

Besides that, what about compromising the case by getting involved with bystanders? What if Candi knew something? Did Candi read into the attraction between her and Ty? An attraction Phil would drown at the first possible opportunity.

Phil decided to find out now. She slipped off the skirt and halter and tugged on a pair of distressed jeans, then pulled on a midriff tee. While more skin was covered, the lines of the pants and the tee hugged her curves, not leaving much to the imagination. She pushed the bat wings open and stepped out, looking in the mirror over her shoulder to check her ass. Casually she said, "Ty seems like the steady sort. I hope it works out for you three."

Candi's eyes softened. "He's great with Lola. She cries when he leaves."

"How long have you been at the Kashmir?"

"About six months. I had to get away from Lola's father. I needed to make good money and the Kashmir was hiring."

"I bet, especially the way the club goes through dancers. Were you close to any of the girls who were kidnapped?"

"No, not really. I'd only been cocktailing a few weeks when Star left. I didn't bother to get to know the other two."

"You don't sound concerned; you don't think they were kidnapped?"

She shrugged. "I don't know. I think the job can get to some girls and they feel like they have to vanish to shake the life."

"You don't think it's odd that the other two disappeared under the same circumstances?"

Candi reached down and picked up her daughter. "How do you know so much about them?"

"I read the newspapers, and I asked Bud a few questions. A girl can't be too careful. Aren't you afraid?"

Candi laughed. "If there is a kidnapper, what would anyone want with me? I have a kid. Too much baggage."

"Do you think the kidnapper knows that?"

Candi shrugged. "I heard all three girls were loners. No family. I have my mom and my kid. Everybody knows that. Besides—not that I really buy the kidnapper thing—*if* the kidnapper hangs out, he knows Ty'll have something to say about taking me."

"Have you seen anyone who looks like they might be the kidnapper?"

"Honey, the only thing I look at in that club is the size of a man's wallet."

"If there is a kidnapper, I want to steer clear of the guy. I'm a prime candidate to get nabbed."

As Candi rocked her little girl, her brows crinkled. "I don't get what you mean."

"I'm twenty-seven, no parents, no boyfriend, no girl-friends. Hell, not even a damn goldfish to feed. I'm the per-fect target."

"You don't have anyone who would miss you?"

"Maybe my landlord if I didn't pay rent."

Emptiness filled Phil's heart. It was true. No one gave a damn about her. If she packed up and moved, there wouldn't be a soul who'd notice enough to call the cops for a welfare check.

"Trust me, Candi, no one would give a crap if I disap-peared."

"That's sad." Candi reached out and squeezed Phil's hand. "I'd care, Kat."

Phil smiled. "Thanks." She went back into the dressing room and tried on several more outfits, her yearning for con-versation gone. Her solitary nature didn't seem to hold the same luster as it had before.

She'd never been the kind of girl to do slumber parties and giggle over boys and gossip. She'd always found ways to amuse herself. She'd been conditioned early by her parents, who felt the other children and their families' lifestyles were not conducive to theirs.

As Phil came out sporting a sexy black velvet workout suit, Candi whistled, startling her sleeping daughter into wakefulness. "You look hot," she whispered loud enough for the cashier at the front of the store to look back and smile.

Lola started to whine, and Candi hiked her up and shushed her to be quiet. "I'm going to have to go, it's past her naptime."

Phil nodded. "Thanks for the help."

"Anytime. Just follow my lead and I'll have you up on that stage before you know it."

Phil laughed. "I don't know about that. One thing at a time."

"Did you watch my tape?"

Phil's head snapped back. "The tape? Oh yes, the *tape*!" Her skin warmed as she remembered the reason she hadn't gotten around to it last night. "I started to watch it, but got interrupted."

"You have to watch it. It's easy as pie."

Lola started to whimper again and Candi gave Phil an apologetic look. "I have to go. I'll see you at the club tonight."

As the tiny dancer hurried out with a now screaming Lola, Phil called out "thanks" after her.

She grabbed up the pile of clothes she'd picked out and went up front to pay for them. Despite her apprehension when she entered the store, she felt comfortable with her choices and actually looked forward to slipping into her new skin and wearing a few of the sexy outfits.

Maybe Kat was taking over after all.

CHAPTER NINE

P hil checked her rearview mirror diligently as she worked her way through the narrow streets of her quiet neighborhood. Ty's warnings had made the necessary impression. So did Candi's confession regarding her dog of a supervisor.

Ty. No sooner had her temper subsided than it flared again. He was a dog of the highest order. Making all daddy-daddy with little Lola, and then hitting on Phil.

She gnashed her teeth. What was it about male cops not being able to keep it in their pants? With the exception of her father, she couldn't name one faithful man.

Your old man had a beat wife! Ty's words rang in her ears. "No!" she shouted, pounding the steering wheel. Her father would never do such a thing. He was devoted to her mother and their church. He was one of the proud few who held his marriage vows close to heart. Daddy had the morals of a saint.

Frustration and dislike mushroomed inside her for Ty Jamerson. Not only was he a philandering dog, he was a liar, too. She'd be sure to alert his captain to his behavior once this case was wrapped up. Cavorting with a potential witness, victim, or suspect was bad business, no matter what the cost of survival.

Phil gunned the Taurus. Her eyes flickered at her rearview mirror. Just another dark-colored truck. The streets were full of them tonight. She pulled into the club's parking lot.

Emotionally armed against the likes of Ty Jamerson, Phil smiled and grabbed her duffel bag. She was grateful for her anger. Grateful Candi told her how it was with Ty. It made it so much easier to resist him. Her smile waned. She refused to think of what almost happened with him, and refused even more vehemently to relive the sensations he elicited from her with a mere touch of his finger.

Forcing all thoughts of her surly lieutenant from her mind, Phil focused on her case. After viewing Candi's video a half-dozen times and practicing in front of the full-length mirror in the living room, Phil felt more than prepared to lure a kidnapper from the woodwork.

She looked forward to shifting gears, to becoming Kat, to checking in and surveilling not only the patrons of the night, but probing into the personal lives of the dancers. She was an investigator at heart and she loved unraveling a mystery.

She'd set aside an hour to go through several of the Kashmir employee files. Just as Ty had informed her: from the info gathered, everyone checked out. There were a few priors here and there. The basic possession charges, a couple of DUIs, and traffic violations, and while several of the girls had soliciting charges there were no convictions.

While the general workforce of Klub Kashmir was speckled with peccadilloes, none pointed to felony kidnapping. It occurred to Phil that for a business traditionally riddled with vice charges and convictions, this particular club smelled like a rose when it should reek with the stench of a Dumpster. Her instincts told her things were too neat, too tidy, too pat. She smelled a rat.

The stale smell of smoke from the previous night hit her full force as she opened the back door. The club catered to cigar-smoking men who had too much money. Even though the building was aired out daily, the lingering scent of cigars hung like a winter coat around them. Her nose twitched in distaste. The heavy perfume of the dancers didn't help matters.

As if she'd been doing it for years, Phil hustled to her locker and got down to business. From what Candi said, Saturday nights were the big money nights for the dancers and servers alike.

But the dancers were a cut above the average strip joint dancers and plied their trade well, and Bud made a decent drink. What more could a guy want?

"Milo, get those tables set up over here."

Phil's skin shimmered at the sound of Ty's deep voice. Then she snorted. What more could a man want? A man like Ty wanted it all and had no problem taking it all. Well, he had another thing coming with her. More determined to turn her blood into frost and give him the cold shoulder, Phil slipped on her stilettos. Her feet throbbed immediately.

She breathed in deeply and exhaled slowly. As she did, she slowly smiled. Her metamorphosis was nearly complete. When she stood, her shoulders squared and her hips loosened. A euphoric sensation swept through her and she laughed, the sound throaty. Yes, she was Kat now, and her claws were barely sheathed. Her eyes narrowed: Klub Kashmir, watch out.

She strutted into the main club area, ignoring Ty as she made a beeline for the bar. Wiping a glass dry, Bud smiled up at her. "Missy, if I were a betting man today, I would've lost. I thought you'd be turning in your uniform."

Phil leaned an elbow on the bar. "Not on your life, Bud. I need this job, and the bunions that come with it."

He put down the glass and hit the register, counted out fifty dollars in varying paper currency. "Thanks," she said, taking the wad from his hand. "Tonight I predict four hundred. You think I can do it?"

His old eyes glowed and he raked her with his gaze. He chuckled. "Kid, I'd say I'd be a fool to wager against you twice."

"She's a dark horse for sure," Ty said from behind her, his warm breath sliding like warm honey across the back of her shoulders.

Phil stiffened and turned. Bad move. Her breasts dragged across Ty's chest and immediately responded. She met him eye-to-eye, nose-to-nose, mouth-to-mouth. Their warm breaths mingled. She remained unaffected. Her body relaxed and she let Ty sweep his gaze across her bountifully displayed attributes. "Well, if it isn't Mr. Masters coming by to say hello."

Ty's eyes narrowed.

She twirled away from him and saucily said, "Break a leg." Then she headed out of his way just in case he decided to touch her again.

"Hey, Kat," Candi called as Phil checked her lipstick in a mirror backstage. Phil smiled. Gone was the fresh-faced mommy. The blonde bombshell was back. Candi's hair was piled on top of her head, with sequins and glitter liberally applied. A skin-tight black leather jumpsuit accentuated every sexy curve she owned. No wonder Ty liked sleeping with her.

"You look great, Candi."

Candi popped her gum. "I have something special planned." She sidled close, and whispered, "Ty doesn't know it yet, but I'm going to rock his world tonight."

Phil's stomach somersaulted. She forced a smile. "I'm sure he won't be able to wait until he gets you home."

Candi patted Phil's ass and popped her gum. "Honey, that's what I'm counting on. Wish me luck!"

"Good luck," Phil softly said.

"Here we go, ladies and gents!" Ty's voice boomed over the dance floor.

Phil hurried back to the bar and watched the men and women flood the tables and chairs. The few women last night surprised her, but tonight, easily one third of the guests were female.

Jase, accompanied by two very attractive women, hurried to the wraparound bar at the stage. Each of the ladies looked centerfold quality.

Jase winked at Phil, then whispered in the ear of the taller woman. His gaze remained on Phil as she strode his way, her tray held high, her hips swinging. Grinning, he ran his hand down the tall brunette's ass to her bare thigh. His other companion, a petite blonde, got in on the action, as well, sandwiching the brunette.

A thrill of excitement swept Phil's body. Her nipples responded.

"Do you like to watch, Kat?"

Ty's deep voice startled her. Her spine went rigid. She whirled around. "Don't come up behind me like that."

His million-dollar smile flashed. Mischief danced in his green eyes. "You didn't answer my question."

She tossed her long hair over her shoulders. He looked good. She figured he probably didn't have many bad days. His chest pushed the confines of his ribbed black nylon T-shirt. His black tailored slacks clung to his long muscled legs. He smelled clean. With his dark hair pulled back with a thin leather tie, he looked like refined danger.

Despite her iron-willed attempt, that all too familiar

quiver speared from her belly south. When he touched her arm she startled. "Afraid of the big bad wolf?" he asked, for her ears only.

She slapped his hand away. "Hardly."

He laughed low. "Too bad. I'd like to show you my big sharp teeth."

Phil looked around and found several people watching their exchange. "Stop it, people are looking."

"That's a good thing. Pay particular attention to the two ladies with Jase."

Covertly, Phil chanced a glance their way. "What about them?"

"All three kidnapping nights they were here, with the same guy. The guy has disappeared, but now they're back."

"You think they know something?"

"I'll leave that to you to find out."

Phil nodded.

As Ty turned back to other club matters, a woman called to her. "Excuse me, miss, can we get a couple of drinks over here?"

Phil turned to see who'd made the question a statement with her rude tone. Jase's brunette. Phil smiled sweetly. "Of course, ma'am. What can I get for you?"

"Two Grey Goose cosmos and a JD neat."

She nodded. Ignoring Ty, who stood grinning down at her, Phil hurried to the bar and gave Bud the order. "Two cosmos and a Jack neat." Jase always started with a real drink and finished with iced tea.

She glanced around the filling room. She spotted Reese perched in the corner. Reese was the strong quiet type. She wondered if he had a wife. She doubted it. Undercover work didn't normally allow for relationships. Not the sustaining type, anyway.

These guys were rolling stones, and no moss gathered on any of them.

As she worked her way back to Jase, he smiled his thanks and handed her a twenty. She raised her brow. "That won't cover it, sir. Thirty-six bucks."

Jase shrugged and pulled his wallet out of his pocket. He pulled out another twenty. "Keep the change, sweetheart."

She'd be glad to. Phil finished up the first round of her tables. The crowd was in a good mood. Lots of energy flowed across the floor. The drumbeat of the music blared from the speakers, matching the staccato of her heartbeat. Like a rose blooming to the morning sun, her senses opened, heightening her sense of awareness.

It was party time. Excitement of the unknown, the thrill of answering her sensual side, and the knowledge that both Ty and possibly the kidnapper had her in their sights sent her blood coursing through her veins. She couldn't kill the smile that stretched across her face, tightening her cheeks, if her life depended on it. She was on, lit, ready to rock and roll.

Phil made the second tour of her area. Her customers were drinking like water-starved camels.

Jase and his two ladies carried on outrageously and she bit

back a laugh every time she glanced their way. As she worked her tables and covertly watched for anyone or anything out of the ordinary, on more than one occasion she turned to see Ty's dark simmering eyes following her. Ignoring him, she approached Reese. "See anything unusual?"

He raised his ginger ale her way. "Just you."

"What do you mean by that?"

"You walked out of the squad room a schoolteacher and walked in here a tease."

"A tease? I'm not teasing anyone!"

"I saw you with Ty last night. Be careful there. You'll get burned."

"I could care less about that man . . . besides, I don't poach."

Reese's eyes widened briefly. "Ty's as free as the wind. He doesn't do relationships."

"Really? What about playing daddy to Candi's little girl?"

Reese's eye narrowed and he sipped his drink. "I don't know anything about that."

Phil nodded. "Not only is he a cheat, he's a liar."

"Ty's a lot of things, but I've always found him to be upfront and aboveboard."

Phil leaned against the table edge. "I guess with you he is, but then he doesn't want to get in your pants, does he?"

Reese snorted, his deep blue eyes glittered. Phil felt a reaction. He was handsome . . . the classic dark, silent type. But she read something in Reese. Integrity, an innate sense of fairness, and as dangerous as his lieu. What was it with these three? While Jase came off as a jokester, a lethal undercurrent throbbed beneath his amiable surface.

Between the three of them, there was nothing they couldn't accomplish. No one who could get by them.

She shivered. God help the man who was responsible for kidnapping the dancers. While she knew they all had a responsibility to catch the kidnapper, for the sole reason that he broke the law, when he kidnapped a cop, he made it personal. Despite what happened to Phil's father, she knew for the most part cops took care of their own. Especially the ones who lived on the edge of the law, like Ty, Reese, and Jase.

"I doubt Ty wants to get in my pants," Reese said. "If he tried, he'd find himself picking his ass up off the floor."

Phil laughed. "I'd pay money to see that!"

"Listen, keep an eye on Jase's lady friends tonight. Marten did a lap dance for them the night she disappeared."

"Ty told me they've been here on each of the nights the girls disappeared. Do you think they're the lookout for the kidnapper?"

Reese sipped his drink. "I'd bet money on it."

"What does their background check look like?"

"Pure as the driven snow. Stand-up citizens. Except for the fact that they like lap dances."

"It's occurred to me, this club has one too many stand-up Joes. Not even one bust in, what? Eight years?"

Reese shrugged. "The owner is a hard case about a clean-club."

"Go figure."

"Hey, sweet cheeks," a male voice called. "How about another round over here?"

She backed up and Reese leaned forward, his voice low. "Keep your eyes open. I have a feeling our guy is in the house."

Phil's skin crawled and Ty's words came back to haunt her. *Eyes in the back of your head, always be aware.* She'd been aware, maybe too aware, so focused on observing those around her, she neglected the paying clients. She needed to find a happy medium.

The DJ announced a two-for-one special on lap dances after the first set of dancers finished performing. The crowd roared. Phil shook her head. The rabid mentality men assumed when a pair of naked breasts were at stake amazed her. Men certainly had a fixation with them and Ty was just as bad.

She put on her tip-me smile and took several orders from a table of men and women. "Hey, Kat," one of the women with Jase called, reading her nametag. "Would you lap dance for a chick?"

The question caught her off guard. "I—I never considered that."

The woman smiled, her eyes heavily painted, her nails long and red. "I have a friend who likes to watch two girls. He tips good, too. Interested?"

"I, uh, I don't have much experience. I'm sure there's a couple of girls with more experience who would be happy to dance for your friend."

The woman's eyes narrowed as she leaned closer. "My friend specifically asked for you."

"Is there a problem?"

Ty.

Phil gritted her teeth. He was a pain in the ass. She glared at him. "No, sir, there isn't." She nodded at the woman. "Let me make my rounds and we'll talk."

As she sashayed to the bar, Ty was hot on her stilettos. "Talk about what?"

"None of your business," she said over her shoulder, heading straight for Bud. She frowned. The other three cocktailers stood one behind the other. They were slammed.

Tapping her fingers against the tray, she waited to turn in her drink orders. "It's my business if it has something to do with your work here," Ty said.

Phil refused to turn around and face him. Pig. She turned on him and flashed. "I'm here to do a job! Leave me alone and let me do it!"

"I need to know what you're doing. I need to know everything at all times."

"Apparently you like to do everyone at all times, too!" Shit, why did she just say that? She sounded like a jealous girlfriend. It galled her to hell that she wanted Ty to be an honorable man, only to discover he was the worst kind of dog on the street. If he were honorable, she could justify sleeping with him. The realization sobered her. Since when did she want sex? Since when did she care what a rogue cop who broke GOs as often as she broke bad cops thought of her?

"What's that supposed to mean?" He frowned.

Phil shook her head. "Ignore that. Just let me do my job."

He came in close. "Don't be disobedient, Officer Zorn. You won't enjoy my disciplinary methods."

Excitement speared her senseless. In the same breath she wanted to make him sweat, to make him hurt, to deny him for making her feel so wanton. She lowered her eyes and thrust out her chest. "Just how would you discipline me, Lieutenant?"

Ty grinned. "I'd start off spanking that fanny of yours until it was bright pink and you begged me to stop."

Her body parts warmed at his provocative suggestion. Stepping up to the bar, she handed Bud her drink orders but kept her gaze on Ty. "Then what would you do?"

"I'd torment you with my tongue until you promised to be a good girl."

"But, Lieutenant Jamerson. I'm not a good girl."

Ty's voice lowered to a husky whisper. "And I'm a bad, bad man."

Heat speared her pussy and Phil caught her breath. She knew he was bad, to the core. An unexpected desire to tame him took hold.

Ty Jamerson was not the type of man to tame. Maybe for

a night, two at best, then he'd be out howling at the moon for his next conquest. The thought of dominating Ty Jamerson held a thrill she couldn't shake. Too bad he was her boss. Too bad he played daddy with little Lola. Too bad, when all was said and done, that she *was* a good girl. A good girl too afraid to walk on the wild side.

Her drinks were up. "Maybe in another life, Ty, but not in this one." Raising the tray above her head, she walked as quickly past her boss as she could without dumping the drinks.

Jase's brunette friend ran her hand along Phil's thigh as she set down her tray. She flinched.

"I want you to dance for me," Jase's friend said.

Jase raised his drink. "I'd like to watch. How much, Miss Kitty?"

Fear and excitement riveted her limbs. It never occurred to her a woman would want a lap dance. "I don't know. But whatever the usual charge, multiply it by three." Phil had a feeling her time for a lap dance was going to be sooner than later, but she never expected it would be for a woman.

Besides, how could she decline? If there was even the remotest possibility either one of these women were involved in the kidnappings she would see it through. The thought of Jase, however, as a spectator or participant rattled her sense of propriety more than dancing for two women. Her brain registered the pros and cons and her modesty lost the contest. She had a job to do.

"I'll call over the GM and set it up." Jase stood. Grinning like the village idiot, he headed toward Ty at the bar.

Phil swallowed hard. Ty wasn't going to like this. She wondered what Jase was up to other than the obvious. He'd maneuvered the woman seamlessly; he was good.

Hurrying to deliver the rest of her drink orders, Phil watched Jase and Ty attempt to conceal an argument. Ty's eyes flashed and his hands fisted. It dawned on her he was telling Jase no.

Her spine stiffened. Her tray emptied, she marched up to the two men and faced Jase. "Excuse me, sir, when would you like that lap dance for your friend?"

Ty sputtered and said, "He changed his mind."

Jase's eyes darkened. While Ty was his superior, there was an easy camaraderie between the two men that belied supervisor and subordinate.

"Actually, I didn't. Kat, if you're up for it, my friend is most eager."

Kat smiled and waved to Bud. "Hey, Bud, have Tiffany cover my tables for the next fifteen minutes."

He winked. Phil turned to Ty. "Lead the way."

Ty scowled. "Fine, you two can play your little games, but I'll be the bouncer inside."

Phil smiled. "Oh, I just bet you will." As she spoke the words, she wondered why he had such a problem with this. If anyone wanted this case put to bed, it was Ty. Why not capitalize on every opportunity?

As she followed him toward the private rooms in the back part of the club, and she had a moment to think about what she just jumped into, nervousness raced through her body. She should be glad she wasn't dancing for a man. Somehow that seemed more demeaning. Man or woman, no touching was allowed. She reminded herself she was doing this for a just cause.

CHAPTER TEN

As if she stripped every night, Phil sauntered into the dimly lit dance room, a sultry smile hovering on her lips. The same one she'd practiced for hours this afternoon in front of a full-length mirror. Even while she struggled to portray the vision of a veteran dancer, her stomach flipped so tempestuously that she fought back the urge to vomit. Then, her stiletto snagged on the carpet, and Phil choked back a scream, afraid she would lose her balance and fall flat on her face. With an effort she maintained her composure.

Jase sat, arms spread out and looking a bit too comfortable, a shit-eating grin plastered across his handsome face and an amour snuggled in on each side of him. Ty scowled in the corner. Phil's gaze skittered away from him and she summoned Kat. Trepidation hacked up and down her spine like an ice pick on a block of ice and she prayed her father wasn't watching from the heavens. Swallowing hard, she forced her feet to move forward. *You can do this, Phil; be Kat, become Kat.*

"Is there special music you'd like me to dance to?" she asked softly.

Jase grinned wider. "Babe, anything you dance to works for me." The brunette swatted him and licked her lips. The blonde smiled at Ty, who continued to scowl in the corner. Phil didn't miss the glare he sent Jase's way, though. She almost smiled herself. She suspected Jase was going to get disciplined.

Phil decided she didn't care about the music, either, so she left it up to fate. Before pressing the play button on the CD changer, she turned the lights down lower.

"No touching the dancer," Ty's husky voice instructed.

While she knew technically he was supposed to be invisible, Phil felt only Ty's eyes on her. She wondered if she was supposed to strip naked. Then she remembered Candi's words her first night: *The most they expect is a thong or G-string, and pasties, anything more is a bonus. And remember, bonuses are paid with Washingtons.*

She gritted her teeth, wishing she'd had the foresight to borrow a pair of pasties from Candi. Too late now.

Pressing the tuner button, Phil took a deep breath. A slow sultry jazz riff drifted into the room from the speakers hidden in the walls. Phil closed her eyes and told herself this wasn't about her modesty or sex, or being bad, it was about finding three kidnapped women and bringing them home safe.

"C'mon, girl!" the brunette hissed.

"You're wasting our money standing there," the blonde added.

"*My money*, ladies, and she can take a minute," Jase said. Phil dared not grace him with a thankful smile. She faced Jase and his paramours. Ty stood at an angle in the corner, not ten feet from her. His face was shadowed, but she sensed his scowl, felt his disdain. He was putting her in the same category as his mother. She didn't deserve that.

The music swelled and so did her pride. She wasn't a drug addict and she wasn't a whore. She was a good girl gone bad for the night, and all for a cause. A damn noble cause at that.

She could do this. She *would* do this. And despite her acrimony toward her boss at the moment, the reality was Ty was the only man alive she would willingly dance for. She'd just pretend it was for him. Phil took one graceful step forward, then another, her hips swaying suggestively. She smiled slow and sexy, hoping if either one of the women were connected to the kidnapper someone would take her as bait. Her eyes widened as her heel dug into the thick pile of the carpet and she flew face-first into Jase's lap.

Mortified, she pushed off him and scrambled to her feet. "Oh, I'm so sorry." The heat of her blush scorched her skin. She was a fool to think she could pull this off. She was a klutz of the highest order. The matching smirks on the women's faces was not encouraging.

Ty stepped forward, but something inside Phil snapped. She waved him off. She wasn't a fool who needed rescuing.

Maybe once a long time ago she needed rescuing, but not now. She was a cop, hell, a woman, a woman who could do anything she set her mind to. Her pride shoved her good girl aside and let the bad girl loose.

"I've seen better at a peep show," the brunette said, standing up and striding toward the door. The blonde mirrored the brunette's sullen expression and followed in her wake.

Phil sprang in front of the retreating blonde, and like Delilah before Sampson, she raised her arms high up in the air, slowly undulating her hips and moving in a slow seductive swirl around the women. "Don't go, Blondie. I'll make you forget those peep shows." Phil prayed no one would detect the tremor in the back of her voice. The blonde stood still, her blue eyes glittered maliciously.

"Go ahead," the woman challenged. In a slow twirl, Phil swayed to the slow sexy music, thrusting her hips forward, stopping a breath away from the blonde's hips before pulling back. She twirled, thrust, and parried. Blondie's eyelids fluttered seductively, seemingly appeased for the moment.

From the shadows, furious, Ty watched Phil blow it. He'd hoped her stumble face-first into Jase's crotch would have been enough. But the minx was determined. He had to give her props for effort. Not only had she gotten the blonde's attention, she had everyone else's, including his.

Ty's eyes raked her long lithe body, from her red-painted toes peeking out from high leather heels to her delicate ankles to her shapely calves, then farther up to her firm thighs, where his heated gaze lingered. The flair of her softly rounded hips flexed with her movements, the belly button jewel flickering in the lowlight of the room. He remembered the velvety tautness of her skin, and his fingers ached to caress her belly.

Her full breasts swayed, beckoning him to touch.

His pants tightened uncomfortably as she undulated around the blonde, subtly pushing her back toward Jase and the brunette, who had returned to her seat. She ran her hands up her waist to her breasts, cupping their fullness in her hands and pushing them toward the trio as an offering. Ty's jaw clenched and unclenched.

Maneuvering herself between the blonde and Jase, Phil rested her stiletto-clad foot on the sofa next to Jase's arm. With a sexy dip, she dropped her ass down and thrust her pussy in his face and then pulled back. Ty imagined the hot scent of her. He frowned. Jase grinned.

The brunette's dark eyes sparkled. Licking her lips, she sat forward. Her nostrils flared and she dipped her nose toward Phil's hips. Ty's cock stiffened. He cursed. He did not want to be aroused.

Phil spun around and with her legs spread, she bent forward, pushing her tempting little ass in Jase's face and wiggled it, enticing him further. The brunette reached out, but before Ty could move, Jase pulled her hand back.

Phil's ass ground at the air. She ran her hands up the back of her smooth thighs and lifted her little skirt, showing off her tight cheeks. Ty swallowed hard and imagined grabbing those luscious cheeks with his hands, pulling them apart, and thrusting so deep into her she would scream for the entire world to hear. The tempo quickened and so did Phil's ass. She turned, her long legs gracefully moving to the music and her hands tracing her curves.

She stepped back toward Jase, and this time she placed one knee on each side of him. Her pussy was even with his face and she lifted her skirt, giving him a whiff of her innermost perfume. Ty ground his teeth as Jase's knuckles whitened, digging his fingers into the fabric of the sofa.

As Phil continued to undulate in Jase's face, she reached up and untied the front of her top. Coyly, she inched it down, showing more of her flesh. Ty strained to see a nipple. He wanted her to turn more toward him, he wanted to see all of her. From his vantage point he could tell she was dancing with her eyes closed, no emotion played across her smooth features. He wondered if she placed herself somewhere far from where she really was. He wondered if she enjoyed it. Did she fantasize that she was dancing for someone special? Him maybe?

The music drove a harder beat and Phil picked up her movements. Gracefully she pivoted, giving Jase and Ty a full view of her ass. With her back to Jase, she dipped down and rubbed her full cheeks slow and hard against Jase's lap.

Ty's mouth watered and his dick flinched hard against him. The room was suddenly hot.

"Turn around," Jase ordered.

Ty was going to kill him.

Phil spun around.

"Show me your tits," Jase hoarsely demanded.

Ty growled low, the music drowning out his protest. Before killing Jase he was going to torture him first.

Trailing her fingertips across her full mounds, Phil slowly untied the fabric restraining her breasts.

Ty held his breath.

Phil let the fabric fall from her fingertips. Like living entities, her tits sprang free. Jase and Ty both nodded in appreciation. Caramel-colored nipples topped honey-hued skin standing up firm and high.

Blood surged to Ty's groin, the bittersweet pain of wanting her and being restricted was almost unbearable.

He was about to come in his pants. Philamina was any man's wet dream.

Jase grabbed the blonde and pulled her onto his lap. Phil swirled around, presenting Ty with her back. When she started to slide down her skirt, Ty almost lost control. His reaction disturbed him. He'd stood in many a private room and watched dozens of lap dances. And while he couldn't say he'd never been aroused, it had been on a minor scale compared to the way his dick throbbed right now.

He had eyes only for Phil. He waited, wanting to see all of her, just as badly as he didn't want Jase to see any of her.

He shook his head. What the hell was wrong with him?

Over the years he, Jase, and Reese had shared informants, countless bottles of JD, and their women. Until now he had no problem with it. He scowled.

How the hell could he stop her? He licked his dry lips. His fists opened and closed at his side. Her long, lithe body moved in a slow, mesmerizing grind to the sweltering rip of the sax, and her scorching skin beckoned him to touch. He could almost feel the soft thrust of her hips beneath him.

He wanted her to stop, to dance only for him.

He couldn't force her to stop, he couldn't demand it. Hell, he was supposed to be invisible, evident only if the patron got out of hand. And by the looks of Jase, it was a damn good thing he'd insisted on chaperoning even after Jase tried to convince Ty he wouldn't let anything get out of control. *Right.* Jase wanted her about as bad as he did right now. Despite the blonde's manipulation of Jase's growing hard-on.

Phil unhooked the button to her skirt and let it slip down her thighs. She kicked it off. Turning to face him, she crossed her arms over her breasts, the movement slow, sleek, and fluid, as if part of her dance. She looked directly at Ty, her eyes hot. A small smile tugged at her lips as she bit at her lower lip.

His gut stumbled and fell. Why, the little hussy. She was playing *him,* not Jase! He resisted a smug smile in return. His blood cooled a degree. She was just like the rest. A woman using her body to torment a man, to get what she wanted. And what was it she wanted from him? He didn't know, but he'd be damned if he'd be her plaything. Anger swelled.

Ty moved farther back into the shadowed corner of the room. Patience was his friend and he'd wait into the next day to watch Officer Zorn hang herself.

Phil's heart thudded against her chest. Kat wanted to let loose, strip down to her birthday suit, and flaunt it all under Ty's nose. The thought left Phil mortified.

Jase's grin and Ty's scowl should have urged her on. Instead, Jase's eagerness to engage in extracurricular activities and Ty's disapproval set her nerves on edge. The last thing she wanted was to come between the men's friendship.

Suddenly sandwiched between the two women, Phil felt hot breath on her neck. As she slowly undulated to the thick, native drumbeat of the music, hands came from behind her. Stopping just inches away from her breasts, the hands pantomimed caressing. The woman in front of her reached back and began running her hands up and down, inches from Phil's legs. Her skin warmed and her breasts swelled. She wanted contact. She closed her eyes, grappling to control her body's shocking desire.

Opening her eyes she caught Jase's dark eyes. His brow forged hard, the planes of his face angled. Perspiration dampened his brow.

She used her body and the body of the other two women to virtually satisfy what she knew to be most every man's fantasy. Watching women make love. And in so doing, she gave herself permission to enjoy.

In unison, the blonde and brunette slipped their bras

off. Their full breasts rose high and Phil couldn't deny their beauty.

"Kitty Kat, I have a friend who would really like you," the blonde said.

Two pair of hands slipped around her waist, the touch gentle yet shocking. A sharp intake of breath erupted from one of the men behind her; Phil crossed her hand over her breasts and turned.

Even as she forbade herself to do so, she lifted her gaze to Ty. Only his eyes pierced the dark shadows of the corner where he stood.

Sharp angry eyes.

"I said no touching," Ty barked.

Abruptly the music ended. "Dance over," he said just as caustically.

Jase threw the girls' clothes at them, then rearranged his pants. A moment later they left, Jase walking stiffly. Ty and Phil ignored their departure, silently staring at each other.

Standing only in a G-string and her heels, her arms crossed over her bare breasts, Phil felt horny and vulnerable, but battle ready. She shivered as Ty stalked close to her.

"You're a whore at heart."

Holding one hand across her breasts, she slapped him with the other. This time there would be no apologies.

With the precision movement of a dojo master, Ty grabbed her hand and jerked her against him, freeing the secured hand and forcing her breasts against the plane of his chest. Her nipples, now steel hard, felt as if they would pierce his shirt, the heat between them so intense that the sprinkler system should have been going off.

Phil moaned as Ty's viselike grip held her motionless. She became aware of the throbbing lump in his pants pressing against her sensitive pussy. Looking into his eyes, she could see his pain. Before he could speak, Phil moved her hips ever so slightly against him. She heard his breath catch and lowered her eyelids to hide her triumph. He may have been holding her, but she was clearly in control.

"What is it, baby?" she whispered inches from his face. She nipped at his bottom lip. "Do you want me?" she asked, digging her nails into his back. "Do you want to slam me up against the wall and fuck me?" She bit his neck. He hissed in a sharp breath. "Do you want control?"

As Ty stood ramrod stiff, she ran a palm down his belly to his cock. His brain had no control over that head. He surged against her. "Does it hurt?" she whispered.

Resisting the impulse to pull her hard against him and claim her was the hardest thing Ty had ever had to do. Primal instinct grappled with his self-control.

He scowled hard as he pondered her questions. While the answer to each was an emphatic yes, he was completely caught off guard by her.

Phil slid her hand down his thigh, resting it there. She

pressed her body full against his. Her scent wafted up to his nostrils and her heat singed him. "If I'm nothing but a whore, what does that make you?"

He stood frozen and swallowed hard, his Adam's apple bouncing. What spell did this woman hold over him? His grip weakened. Before he could answer her, she spun away, scooping up her clothes and exited the room, leaving Ty out of breath and out of answers.

CHAPTER ELEVEN

"My friend said I'd like you."

Phil stopped her flight from Ty and looked at the man who emerged from a shadowed alcove, her instincts on high alert. Could this be their man?

"Oh really? Who's your friend?"

He smiled, the gesture reminding her of a fox. "That little blondie you just danced for."

She stepped closer to get a better look at his shadowed face. Familiarity clung to him. "Have we met?" she asked, sure they had crossed paths at some time.

He stepped closer, the flashing strobe of the ceiling lights flickering across his face. He was tall, blond, her age, his face unremarkable, but still it struck a chord. A chill skittered across her skin, the familiar feeling not a warm and fuzzy one.

"I think I would remember someone as beautiful as you."

Phil smiled and smoothed back her hair. "Thank you, Mr. . . . ?"

"Scott, Scott Mason."

That familiar buzz zapped her brain. She knew that name, she knew this person. But how? Where? Her gut told her the memory was not a pleasant one, and with that, her gut also told her this man was dangerous.

Phil extended her hand. "Mr. Mason, my name is Kat, I'm happy to meet you."

His hand wrapped firmly around hers, the contact felt disturbing. She fought her instinctive reaction to pull away. He pulled her toward him.

"The pleasure is all mine." His dark eyes glittered, his grip increasing around her hand. He stood so close to her, she could smell his bad breath. Phil blew air from her nose so as not to inhale his stale scent. How, she wondered, did the girls put up with these guys? He physically repulsed her, yet she knew she had to keep in character if she was going to pursue him as a lead.

Licking her lips suggestively, Phil asked, "What can I do for you, Mr. Mason?"

He trailed his middle finger across her palm and his smile increased significantly. "The question is, what can I do for you?"

"I'm all ears."

"I have lots of money and you have incredible lips."

"And?"

"I have this vision of them locked around my dick."

"I'm not a whore."

He still held her hand, but now his fingers traced up her arm. It was all Phil could do to allow him to touch her. "C'mon, baby, all women are whores at heart."

Recognition registered. Scott Mason. Kyle Thompson's crony and one of several boys witness to her humiliation. Her spine straightened. She needed to give Ty his name to run this guy through the system.

Did he have anything to do with the kidnapper or was he just your average run-of-the-mill misogynist perv?

Phil extracted her arm from his grip. "I'm afraid, Mr. Mason, you misunderstand my job description, I—"

"C'mon now, Kat, five hundred to make me a happy man."

Over Mason's shoulder she caught Ty's dark scowl. Like a hawk standing guard, he watched her work Mason. She was grateful for once he didn't barge in like a fireman to the rescue. Maybe he did respect her skills after all.

She turned her full attention to Scott Mason. "Be specific."

"You and me back at my place, anything goes. The sky's the limit. I'll pay you enough to take a week off from this joint."

"That would be several thousand dollars."

"No sweat, and if you're good, I have friends that'll pay more."

Kat smiled and flirtatiously touched her fingertips to her hair again and smoothed a lock. "I'll think about it."

"Don't make me wait." He turned and looked over his

shoulder to the stage where Daria, a lanky redhead, hung upside down from the central pole, dry humping the air. "There's lots of pussy to choose from."

Phil moved a half step toward him. "Why settle for ground beef when with a little patience you can have steak?"

Before she took it upon herself to commit to anything with this man, she needed to confer with her team, and get Scott Mason's stats, to see what they were up against.

To buy her some time, she ran a fingertip down his zipper flap. His less than remarkable hard-on reared. "I get out of here at two—"

He pressed her hand against his crotch. "I'll be waiting," he said, his voice harsh.

She pulled her hand from beneath his and smiled coyly. "I'm sure you will be."

Quickly, she moved away, not wanting to subject herself to any more contact. She caught Ty's eyes over the crowd and inclined her head toward the main bar.

"I'm back on the floor, Bud," she called to the old man as she stepped up to the edge of the bar.

He smiled and nodded.

"What's going on, Zorn?" Ty asked from behind her.

Phil continued to face the bar, not taking the chance to invoke suspicion from Mason if he was watching her. She'd just look like a hardworking cocktailer doing her job.

"You need to run a Scott Mason. Year of birth anywhere from seventy-eight to eighty. He might be our man."

Before Ty could respond, she grabbed a tray from the bar and headed back out to the crowed floor.

She came across Reese, dark and brooding in the corner as usual. "You really need to get out more often, Reese," she quipped.

"I get out enough."

"Sure you do." She leaned her arm against the edge of his table. "Did you see that slimeball I was chatting with earlier?"

"The skinny blond guy?"

"That would be the one."

"What about him?" Reese asked.

"Have you seen him here before?"

Reese's eyed narrowed. "I can't say that I have."

"He might be our man. He knows one of the girls Jase picked up. The blonde half of the two-girl couple who's been here each night of the kidnappings. Maybe they mark the victim and he's the bag man. When you run through the surveillance tapes, look hard for him, he might be incognito."

A chill swept Phil's bare skin. As she spoke her thoughts, there was a vital piece missing.

"He can't be our man, unless—" Realization dawned. Reese's brows lifted, and if she didn't have his undivided attention earlier she had it now. "If the MO is followed, then how would he know that, like the other girls, I have no family, no one holding me here?"

"Someone told him."

They looked at each other as solid realization dawned.

"Ask me if I want another drink," Reese grumbled. Phil realized several men had moved into hearing distance.

"Can I get you another one of those?" she asked, pointing to his empty glass.

He nodded. The music subsided a note. She leaned forward. "Our man or woman is inside, Reese."

"We suspected it, but if this guy makes a move, that confirms it."

Phil nodded, excited. The club employed almost two dozen employees, any one of them could be the link, if not *the* kidnapper. Excitement filled her. "Only someone inside the club would know each of the girls had no family."

"We've run everyone connected with the club. Even the silent partners."

"Then we go deeper. Ty's running Scott Mason, the guy who propositioned me."

"Be careful, Zorn, don't even go to the can unless you have someone with you."

"Right, I'm going to have you, Jase, or Ty stand outside the stall?"

"No, but just give the sign and I'll wait outside the door."

"I will." She stepped back from the table. "I'll be right back with that drink, mister."

"Hurry it up."

Phil quickly hit her tables, her smile dispelling the neglected men's anger. She kept her eyes peeled. As she scanned the room she saw Ty come out from the back, no doubt from his office, and set up a stance near the wide hallway leading to the front door. He nodded. Good, they should have the info they needed within the hour.

She wended her way to the bar and gave Bud her drink orders. As she made her rounds, the DJ announced the next dancer, Candi. Phil scanned the floor for Ty. He was looking at her, not Candi. He smiled a wicked smile that sent shivers up her spine before he turned to face the stage.

As the featured dancer, Candi held the rapt attention of the patrons.

The little blonde wasn't kidding when she said she was going to rock Ty's world. Like Scheherazade, Candi's veils swirled to the stage floor as she sauntered, strutted, and undulated her way down to just a G-string, her eyes never once leaving Ty's.

An emotion Phil didn't want to name grabbed her gut and twisted it. Ty stood stock still next to Milo, his arms crossed across his chest, his eyes greedily devouring Candi's voluptuous curves. As the last chord of music struck the end of the dance, the crowd went wild and men threw bills onstage.

As Candi grabbed the bills up, Phil made the mistake of looking at Ty. His eyes bored holes into her. His jaw struck a hard line. Dragging her eyes from him, she glanced at Candi, who looked at her with the hurt look of a kicked puppy.

Crap.

Why couldn't the job just be a job? Why did emotions have to surface? Feeling like she'd snatched a bottle from a baby, Phil turned and hurried to the bar.

The DJ announced last call. In forty minuets Ty and Milo would be herding the crowd out into parking lot.

She started at Ty's voice behind her. "The guy is as clean as Mother Teresa."

Quickly, she turned to face him. He looked pissed. He wanted the guy to be it, or at least a lead, as bad as she did, probably more.

"That proves nothing."

"The fact that he's been overseas for the last five months does."

"Where overseas? Maybe he was setting up buyers."

"The guy manages the Kings of Prussia, as in the European football team. I spoke to an owner and he vouched for lover boy."

"Oh."

"So you'll have to date him on your own time."

Phil hissed back a breath. "Why do you think so little of women?"

His brows creased. "I love women."

"You use women."

"Kat, your drinks are up."

Ty grabbed her arm as she turned to fill her tray. "I don't use women any more then they use me."

She looked at his hand on her arm and flashed him a glare. He removed it.

"Two wrongs don't make a right."

"Sure they do."

Phil shook her head and turned away. He was beyond saving. As she filled her tray, she wondered why she ever thought she'd be the one to save him.

Glancing at the bar clock she sighed; one more hour and she could go home. Her feet where screaming and she was tired. And, she hated to admit it, she was horny. Ty might be beyond redemption, but her body didn't seem to care much. Too bad for her body. Her brain had the final say and there was no way she would get tangled up in the sheets with the likes of him.

As she sashayed in and around her tables, serving the thirsty men and staving off their lustful gropes, her eyes clashed with Ty's more than once. Each time his heated gaze raked her body, she felt it as surely as if laser beams swept her skin.

She'd never encountered a man remotely like him. He was a paradox. Hard, boorish, and moody, yet he burned with a passion for his job, and this case, that she had yet to encounter in another cop. Not even her father. Ty had the highest conviction rate of any officer in the department. While others had higher arrest rates, many of those walked before they were formally charged. Ty's cases were solid, airtight. The DA loved prosecuting them. Ty's unshakable tenacity on the witness stand was legendary.

She glanced up at Reese, who silently saluted her. His men would follow him to the gates of hell if he asked. And through the grapevine she'd heard over the years how he'd stuck by his men when more than a few had found themselves under the scrutinizing eye of IA.

While he did wrong, skirting the law and sometimes stepping over the boundaries, he did it with the sole intention of getting the bad guy. Her IA training shuddered at the thought of anything but following the clear letter of the law. As much as she wanted to get the bad guy, she could not see her way to lying, cheating, or thieving to see a case through. Not under any condition. She didn't understand how Ty could. While she didn't condone his behavior, she respected his passion for fighting crime.

The DJ announced last call for lap dances. His voice boomed over the speakers, jerking her out of her musings. Too much Ty on the brain could get her in serious trouble.

She scanned the room for the object of her thoughts and caught him in deep conversation with Milo. He looked up and their eyes locked. Her skin warmed. He stirred her deep and she found his pull irresistible.

"I'll be out front waiting for you, Kat," Mason said from behind her, his hot smelly breath stirring her hair and her gag reflex.

She whirled around and put the empty tray safely between them. "Mr. Mason," she stuttered. "You startled me."

He pressed against the edge of the tray so hard it jammed against her breasts painfully. She moved back, but he followed.

"I'll be out front. Don't make me wait."

"I, ah, something came up, I won't be able to keep our date."

He grabbed the tray and twisted it out of her hands. Like the bully he was, he pushed her back up against the mirrored wall.

"Something's up, all right. My dick. If you're not out front in thirty minutes, you'll live to regret it."

Phil pushed back. "Threaten me again, mister, and you'll be the one who regrets it." She pushed past him, furious, and at the same time more then a little bit sad. Was this the life of an exotic dancer? Treated like a second-rate citizen? Constantly at the whim of men who because they had money and could pay for sex thought they were superior?

While she had gained a certain amount of satisfaction as Kat, it was different for her. She didn't need to do this for a living. She had options. What about women like Candi, who had a child to care for, who out in the regular workforce, without a decent education, couldn't afford to live and pay her high-priced attorney to fight for custody. The girls here were just as hardworking as the next person, and she respected the hell out of them and their talent, but the downside was what they had to put up with.

As she made her way to the bar, her eyes fell on Ty, who

was escorting a drunk who'd, by the looks of the cocktailer standing nearby, gotten out of line. Her heart thawed a degree. For someone who didn't care much for the opposite sex, he sure took care of the girls here at the Kashmir.

As she cleaned up her tables, Phil watched Candi come out of the same room where she had danced for Jase and his lady friends earlier. Candi held her clothes to her chest and kissed the man who followed her out, long and hard. Before he stepped away, the man shoved a wad of bills at Candi.

Candi looked around, making sure no one saw her stick the wad in her shoe. She glanced up to catch Phil's gaze.

Averting her eyes, Candi hurried past Phil. Although Candi was stealing, Phil felt sorry for her. Not sorry that Candi did what she did for a buck, but sorry she had to steal to make ends meet.

The owner of Klub Kashmir, Mr. Z., was a greedy bastard. In her opinion, the girls should be able to keep all of their tips.

As Phil followed Candi with her eyes, she caught Ty doing the same thing. Her blood pressure spiked. Just when she started to think of him in a better light he had to go Neanderthal on her.

Phil sighed. Lusting after Ty Jamerson was a lesson in futility. While he had openly demonstrated and even conveyed in words he wanted her, he apparently wanted Candi, too. It wasn't in her nature to share.

Besides, Candi wanted Ty. Who was Phil to mess with a ready-made family?

The lights flared on and Phil realized most of the men were gone. Once the booze stopped and the stage and lap dance doors were closed, there was no reason for any of them to stick around.

She scanned the large room for Scott Mason. He was nowhere in sight. Was he waiting out front for her? He could wait all night. Her car was parked out back. She would drive right past him and he wouldn't even know.

With the club empty, Phil hurried to the ladies' room. She stopped short when she saw Reese lurking in the shadows. "Took you long enough, Zorn," he grumbled.

"Sorry, didn't realize you had a ladies' bathroom fetish."

"Funny." Reese pushed open the door and nodded for her to follow. She did. He checked the stalls. Confident they were alone, he said, "I know Ty told you Mason was clean. But you need to be alert. Those two ladies you danced for tonight have had lap dances on the nights of each kidnapping. I'll follow you home."

"I think Ty has that market cornered. If you want to trade, that's fine. But don't think you're parking yourself at my house."

Reese grinned, the first genuine one she'd seen. He was damn good looking.

"Not even on your sofa?"

"Not even in my dog house."

"You're not a very accommodating lady."

The bathroom door slammed open and Ty burst in.

Both Reese and Phil started. Ty stopped and narrowed his eyes. "Is this a private party or can anyone join?"

Reese shrugged. "I was just letting Zorn know she needed to be extra alert tonight since those two ladies had their lap dance. I don't need to tell you the MO."

Ty looked at Phil as if she would confirm Reese's explanation. "I also told her I'd follow her home," Reese added.

"No need, I'll take care of that chore."

Reese nodded. "Good enough. Jase and I'll go over the video for the night." He nodded to Phil and exited the bathroom.

Phil stood with her hands on her hips and tapped her foot, the sound on the tile floor sharp. "Are you quite done with acting like a jealous sixteen-year-old?"

"I didn't act that way."

Phil shook her head. Her bladder called. "If you don't mind, I have to pee."

"Don't let me stop you."

"Get out of here."

"I'll wait for you outside the door."

As she slammed the stall door closed, she said, "Then go already."

When she exited the restroom, she sauntered past Ty and hit the rest of her tables. She wanted to get home and take a shower.

Her cleanup duty complete, Phil hustled back to her locker and changed into a pair of comfy sweats and sneakers. For the second time in twenty-four hours she wished for a foot massage. As she hiked her bag over her shoulder, Candi walked in.

"How'd you do tonight, hon?"

Phil shrugged. "I didn't count. But not bad."

Candi popped her gum. "I made eight hundred dollars! My ex is going to wish he never sued for custody. I'm going to buy me a shark of a lawyer."

Phil wondered if that eight hundred included what Candy hid in her shoe. She decided she didn't care. "I hope it all works out for you."

Candi moved in closer. Her eyes narrowed slightly and Phil tensed, knowing what was coming. "If that's true, then you need to back off."

Phil sighed. Under normal circumstances, she'd bristle up and tell the little dancer what she could do with her commands. But Candi touched a soft spot in Phil, or rather, the vision of little Lola's face did. The girl needed a daddy more than Phil needed to get laid.

"You have nothing to fear from me, Candi. I'm not interested.

Tired, frustrated, and now suddenly angry, Phil headed out the back door, her brain a whirlwind of colliding thoughts. Ty, the kidnapped dancers, Candi, the chance meeting with Scott Mason, and the memories that came with him.

She'd moved past what happened to her that summer night so many years ago. The nightmares had long since disappeared, but it didn't mean she'd forgotten. She would never forget. Her life lesson learned was sex on any level would be on her terms and her terms alone, because she was in control. No exceptions.

Her frustration rose. Her anger, she realized, stemmed from her desire for Ty. She wanted him exclusively and that wasn't possible.

"Kat!"

Phil hesitated at Ty's voice. Then she stepped up her pace to her car, afraid of unloading on him. She didn't want a scene. Not tonight.

Just as she opened the car door, he caught up. "I called to you," he said, out of breath.

She whirled around. "Yes, and I ignored you." She tried to go butt first into the car, but Ty grabbed her arm and pulled her out. "What the hell's going on, Zorn?"

"Why don't you tell me, Lieutenant?"

"I swear you females talk a different language. Why not speak to me in English."

"There's nothing wrong with my communication skills, sir."

He swiped his hand across his jaw. "I hate it when you get all official on me. My name is Ty, use it."

"Yes, sir." She kept her face impassive as color darkened his cheeks. Any measure of discomfort she gave him suited her just fine, and the more painful the better.

She decided to be crystal clear with him, and if he chose not to get it, then that was on him. "Look, Daddy Dearest.

What you do on your own time is no business of mine. But I'm not going to allow your extracurricular affairs to impede this investigation."

"What the hell are you talking about? I'm working this case just as hard, if not harder, than you!"

"My point exactly, sir. You seem to be working this case from every conceivable angle, which is fine, you're the boss after all, but leave me out of it."

His silence stopped her from slamming the door in his face. Instead, the way his lips twitched and his eyes danced intrigued her.

"Zorn, are you mad at me for not taking you in the dance room?"

Oh, for Christ's sake. She didn't dignify him with an answer. "Just leave me the hell alone."

"I will after I follow you home. But I have a few things to tie up. Stay put."

"Have Reese follow me."

"Too late, he's on his way to go over tape."

She remained silent.

"Piss me off and your ass is canned."

Phil remained silent and Ty finally stepped away from her car. She glanced in her rearview mirror to see him walking back toward the club.

She slammed the door shut and turned the key.

Nothing. Dammit!

She needed a jump start. She opened her car door and

looked around. A few lingering patrons milled about in the lot, no doubt hopeful to get a chance to snag one of the dancers for some of their own extracurricular activities.

She scooted out of the Taurus and lifted the hood.

"Need a jump start, Kat?"

The fine hair on the back of her neck spiked straight up. Slowly she turned around.

"Thank you, Mr. Mason, but my manager is going to get the cables right now."

"Well, then, I guess we'd better hurry."

He moved in on her so fast she was unprepared. He slammed her hard against the front right fender of the car.

"I can make you want me like you did Kyle," he said as his hand grabbed her breast and squeezed.

So he remembered her as well. She kneed him hard, but he was prepared. His knees locked. He backed away.

"I can assure you, I didn't want Kyle the way you think I did."

No, she didn't. Kyle had lured her under those bleachers with promises of love and devotion, and like a little lamb she'd followed. She couldn't have been more wrong. What followed was a free show for half the football team, of which Scott Mason was the ring leader, and a case of the crabs. From that horrible day forward she vowed never to be a victim again.

Scott laughed. He lunged and grabbed her with one arm in a viselike grip, and with the other hand he ripped her sweatshirt with a reddening tear. "That's not what he told me."

Mason's mouth gaped open as he bent to her exposed breast. The thought of him putting his mouth on her was more repulsive than she could bear. Phil let her feet go out from under her and he couldn't hold her up with one arm. He grabbed at her with his other arm as she hit the asphalt lot.

She rolled away as his grip loosened, then she was up and battle ready before he regained his momentum.

"You can't win, Phil. I work out with pro ballplayers."

"That makes you such a man."

He inched closer. It would be the last offensive move he made. Phil jumped and in a roundhouse kick, she caught him by surprise and square in the chest with her right foot.

"You miserable piece of shit!" Ty roared.

Phil's heartbeat roared in her ears as Ty grabbed the cretin up by the lapels of his jacket and punched him square in the face. The smashing sound of cartilage sickened Phil. As she winced, Ty drew back and landed another punch in the same place.

Mason screamed and a small crowd drew around the two men.

Ty hit him again. Mason flailed at the end of Ty's long arms. Phil stiffened. If Ty kept at it, he'd kill him.

"Ty, stop!" Phil yelled. As if he were deaf, Ty landed another brutal punch to Mason's face.

Ty's arm cocked back for another blow. Phil rushed forward and grabbed it. "Enough!"

Ty looked at her, his eyes a haze of fury. "Enough, Ty," she said softer. "You'll kill him."

Ty looked from her pleading eyes to Scott Mason's bloody face. He let him go.

"Did he hurt you?" he asked, his voice a low husky whisper.

Emotion welled in Phil's throat. "I'm fine."

He reached out and brushed a strand of hair from her face. "I shouldn't have left you alone."

She wanted to thank him, to tell him no one had ever stepped up for her, not even her father. He'd just preached and chastised.

Ty looked down at Mason, who groaned as he struggled to get up. "I hope you like California penal orange, asshole," Ty said.

Phil shook her head no.

Ty squinted, his eyes not understanding. Mason had money and no doubt influence among people in high places. The last thing they needed was a brutality charge to blow the case.

Ty's eyes softened as realization dawned.

He knelt down and looked at the creep eye-to-eye. "If I ever see your face around here or near her again," Ty said, his voice low and dangerous, "I'll beat you so bad, the coroner will have to go to your dentist for an ID." He shoved Mason to the asphalt. "Do you hear me?"

Blood ran down Mason's face. He coughed, sputtering blood down his shirt and jacket. He spit a wad of blood on the ground. He eyed Ty warily, but nodded.

Ty towered over him. "Now get the hell out of here. You have two minutes before I come after you."

Slowly Mason stood. Unsteadily, he walked away from them toward the back of the club.

"I need a jump start," Phil said.

Ty glanced at her, his tension broken. She was smiling, her voice sounding as cool as the morning breeze. What the hell? He turned back to the gathered crowd. "Show's over, folks. Go home."

He followed Phil back to her car. He had a new respect for the proud set of her shoulders. Maybe he'd misjudged her. Then he remembered her sandwiched in between Jase's girls. His blood surged. He'd be a liar if he admitted the sight of Phil pantomiming sex with the two women hadn't turned him on so much, thinking about it gave him a hard-on again. She held up a set of jumper cables. "I need a jump start; you the man or do I call the three As?"

He wanted to tell her what he'd like to give her, but in light of what had just happened, he suspected the last thing she wanted was to get hit on again.

"Why don't I just take you home?" That's all he'd do, he told himself. Take her home.

She struck a pose, with the hand on her hip still holding the cables. "Why don't you stop playing Tarzan and just give me the damn jump start?"

"I'll bring my truck around."

CHAPTER TWELVE

Headlights glowed in Phil's rearview mirror. For the umpteenth time that night, her emotions collided. To Ty or not to Ty.

Her body demanded she toss uptight Phil out the window and take a walk on the wild side named Ty Jamerson. Her gut promised a good time. Her brain? Ah, that stoic practical brain of hers. To do Ty equaled heartache. Yeah, her body said, so what's wrong with living a little?

She damped down her urge to speed away from him. Knowing Ty, he'd chase her until she stopped or the car ran out of gas.

Damn him! Why couldn't he leave her alone, stop pushing buttons she didn't know she had, stop pushing her physically and emotionally? He had awakened a sleeping tigress in her and while it was easy to let her reign supreme as Kat in the club, she wasn't anywhere near as comfortable allowing that bitch near Phil. Kat was insulated. Phil was vulnerable.

Phil closed her eyes for a moment at a stoplight. She wanted solitude, to figure out just what the hell had happened tonight. Too many mixed emotions swirled inside her. Pain, fury, and even a little humiliation when she remembered the sexual assault from years ago collided with the arousal and excitement of the dance room earlier. She'd buried the episode, its emotional impact and the fallout with her father afterward too much to bear. She thought she'd put it completely behind her, but with Mason's presence and her reaction, she realized she hadn't. What happened when she was sixteen was now stopping her from complete intimacy.

She opened her eyes and the light turned green. She shivered as she pressed the gas pedal. All these years she focused on everything else but a relationship, even at the most basic level with a man, because she knew it would lead to intimacy. Intimacy that terrified her. She glanced at the lights in her rearview mirror. And her skin warmed.

Was it time to take that step? With Ty?

She couldn't fathom the idea. In an effort to get Ty off her brain and libido, Phil's brain shifted to overdrive.

Tomorrow was Sunday and she had plenty to do. She'd head into the office and write a formal request to review her father's sealed file. Now that she was out of IA, getting approval shouldn't be a problem. Especially since Captain

Dettmer had been her father's best friend and his biggest champion when it all had gone down.

The headlights behind her blacked out as she pulled into her driveway. What the hell was she going to do with her lieutenant? Fuck him, her body screamed. You'll live to regret it, her brain cautioned.

She rubbed her eyes and wished for once her brain would shut up.

Just as she reached the door and dug out her keys, she called to the man a few steps behind her. "I don't need a baby-sitter, Lieutenant."

"I don't baby-sit, Officer Zorn."

She turned around and couldn't deny the man had presence. He walked with the sureness of a predator, his long fluid stride confident. His eyes glittered beneath the weak glow of her porch light. Her womb fluttered. Admit it, brain, you know you want him, too. But would he lose interest if he knew? Or worse, once the thrill of the chase had been brought home, would he walk? And she asked herself, would it matter?

She turned the last key in the door and pushed it open. Before she could close the door, he followed her in. "I don't need a late-night visitor, either," she said.

"Maybe not, but you need a few tips on lap dancing."

After she threw her keys on the counter, she whirled on him. "I beg your pardon. I think I did just fine."

He moved toward her, the gleam in his eyes rapacious. "It wasn't bad, but I've seen better."

Phil backed around the small kitchen table, putting it safely between them. "Jase didn't seem to think so." Her skin warmed as she remembered the passion in his eyes and the rise in his pants.

Ty paused for a millisecond, his features sharp. "Jase doesn't have the experience I have."

"Yes, I forget where you got your training."

As pain flashed across his face, she winced.

"Always the bitch, Phil."

"Always the bastard, Lieutenant."

As she circled the table, he followed.

"Did Scott Mason rape you?"

She gasped at his directness. "No!"

"Who did?"

His intuition stunned her. Her mouth opened, then closed. She couldn't tell him. She'd never told anyone what happened.

Ty moved in close to her but didn't attempt to touch her. His eyes blazed. "Who hurt you?" The ferocity of his tone stunned her.

She shook her head and turned away from him. "Kyle Thompson. I wasn't raped, not exactly. I was just stupid and naïve. Mason was a spectator."

"There's more to it than you're telling me."

Yes, but she didn't want to relive it. She wanted to erase it, to make it have no impact ever again on her choices.

"Why wasn't the episode in your psych report?"

Her heart rate increased and she turned to face him. "Because it has no bearing on my ability to do my job."

"Not your decision to make."

Phil had no comeback. He spoke the truth.

"You lied. That's grounds for immediate dismissal."

She smiled grimly. "Spirit of the law, Lieutenant. It hasn't affected my job performance."

"Tell me what happened."

Why did he care? She backed away.

"No."

"I don't want to pull rank on you, but I will," Ty said.

She glared at him. "Why can't you leave it alone?"

"Because this is impeding your job performance."

"Bullshit!"

He stepped closer. "Bullshit is right. If you want to be effective you need to loosen up, and that means lose some of your inhibitions."

"I did fine!"

"No, Phil, you didn't."

"You're a liar. I saw how you watched. I know you were aroused."

"Aroused is one thing, on the edge is another. I'm beginning to doubt you have what it takes to see this through."

Her fighting Irish surfaced. "I have what it takes, Lieutenant. If I can survive what those high school imbeciles did, I can lap dance a man to orgasm."

He smiled. "I bet you can't."

Her skin flushed warm. "I bet I can."

"Prove it." His smile widened to a grin. "I'll be happy to be your test dummy."

She laughed. What more did she need to prove to herself she was capable of intimacy? She was out of the club, out of Kat's skin, alone in the safety of her own house with a man who turned her on and inside out. "I bet you would, sir. But I'm sure there is something in the GOs about a subordinate lap dancing for a superior."

"I told you, Zorn, there are no GOs in undercover. Do what you have to."

"All right, Lieutenant Jamerson. I bet you I can make you come just by dancing. Not touching."

"I bet you can't."

"Let's make this interesting, sir. I'll dance for you, here and now. If I make you come, you keep my little failure to disclose traumatic incidents to the shrink our little secret."

"If you don't, I follow you into your bedroom, where you'll make it happen on my terms."

Phil shivered at the thought, the excitement at the prospect stuttering her breath pattern. Either way, for her it was a win-win. The excitement turned into anxiety. What if she couldn't go through with it? What if her self-imposed celibacy and fear of intimacy had become so ingrained, she couldn't loosen up enough? It was different at the club, which was just a job, a means to an end. Here, now, it was about want. She glanced at Ty beneath her lashes. He kept his distance, almost gentlemanly, giving her the space she needed. She lost some of her anxiety. *If* she were capable of overcoming her fear of intimacy, it would be with Ty.

"A few ground rules."

Ty smiled. "I would expect nothing less."

"You will do what I say. No touching, not even once during the dance. Give me your word."

"You have it."

She knew in her heart if she lost the bet, all she had to do was tell Ty no and he would respect it. He would sneer, he would entice, but in the end he would back off.

Question of the night was: Would she?

CHAPTER THIRTEEN

"Give me a few minutes to shower, cowboy."

Phil hurried back to her room and Ty smiled as he walked into the family room and settled into the comfortable recliner. He might be one horny dog, but he was a master of control. His self-control was one reason he'd managed to stay alive so many years undercover. He never, *ever* allowed his impulses or emotions to direct his decisions.

What Phil didn't know was he had no intention of narcing on her. Her secrets were safe with him. His smile changed to a scowl. Her pain had been apparent when he questioned her about Mason. If the prick was here or his fucking friend Kyle Thompson, he'd give them both a taste of some real pain. Ty Jamerson style.

He realized now just how sexually vulnerable Phil was. She had some issues, and for that reason alone he'd do his damnest to go slow and not push. He'd let her set the pace, and what happened, happened.

He grinned. Patience was his friend and he knew he'd need a lot of it if he was going to get the sexy Philamina Zorn between the sheets.

Like a kid getting ready to raid a candy shop, Ty rubbed his hands together and settled back into the supple leather chair. He'd wanted in her pants the minute Phil Zorn walked into the interrogation room three years ago, and tonight, at least part of his recurring dream was about to come true.

The slow sultry beat of a jazz riff drifted out from hidden speakers, the lights dimmed. His blood surged. He rearranged himself in the chair. He was already hard and he'd yet to lay eyes on her.

"Close your eyes," Phil commanded from the shadows.

"What's the point of your seducing me if my eyes are closed?"

"Do it, now."

Playing hardball was she? He closed his eyes and his dick throbbed.

He smiled at the sound of a match being struck. He smelled sulfur and listened to the music flow. After a moment, he sniffed the subtle scent of vanilla and cream. Candles.

"Open your eyes."

The subtle lighting illuminated objects in the room in a low glow. He felt Phil's presence behind him. He turned to look.

"Ah, ah, sir, face forward."

Following her order, he turned back. He closed his eyes again and took a deep breath. He exhaled and opened his eyes.

"Get, ready, Lieutenant, I'm going to rock your world." Her minty breath caressed his ear from behind, the warmth of it slid across his neck as softly as a silk veil. His blood quickened. His dick saluted her premonition.

"Rock on, Phil."

The music swelled and a smooth cool length of fabric flitted in front of his eyes, momentarily obscuring his view. She twirled it around his head, moving to the front of him.

His eyes widened. Her dark hair was piled on top of her head and she wore a tailored business suit, the skirt much too short for protocol.

Black lace garters held up sheer black thigh-high silk stockings. Long black gloves encased her arms past her elbows, almost touching the short sleeves of her suit vest. She wore stiletto heels and a smile. She wielded a silk scarf in a sexy playful arch around her body, drawing it across her breast and down along her hips.

She smiled into his eyes and licked her lips. Setting her jaw, she threw her head back, offering a view of the smooth creamy skin of her throat. She stood so close he could see the slow, regular beat of her pulse.

She leaned forward, the vest gaping open, giving him a first-class look at her tits.

"You wanted to fuck me the first time you saw me three years ago, didn't you?"

"Right there on the table, spectators and all."

She swayed seductively in front of him. "I knew you did. I saw the way you filled your pants. I thought you were going to pop a snap."

She twirled away, dragging the scarf around his throat, then pulling it quickly away. He grabbed the end of it, halting her retreat. "You just might get to see me pop a button yet."

Phil glanced down at the burgeoning mound in his lap. She bent low and ran the scarf across it. "Why don't you spare yourself the pain?"

Grinning, he unbuttoned the top button of his slacks. Phil smiled and bent over him, rubbing the length of her palm against the fabric shielding his cock. The contact sent shock waves through his groin. He caught his breath.

"You're breaking the rules already, Zorn. No touching."

"I'm not touching you, I'm touching your pants."

He reared in his seat, giving her more than a handful.

"You need to stay in your seat, sir."

"Why do you get to break the rules?"

"Same rules apply as in the club. You can't touch the dancers, in any capacity."

Ty sat on the recliner.

As much as he wanted to enjoy all of Phil's sexy attributes, he knew to do so would make him lose the bet. And losing wasn't an option.

He had his pride, his rigid self-control, and if he caved, he'd look weak. Besides, either way he won.

What he wanted more than winning was Phil hot and wet beneath him of her own volition. He smiled. She twirled, moving away from him, and taking her warmth and sultry musky scent. Then her eyes locked with his. Something moved deep inside him. With each swirl and step he felt her loosen. Was it because she felt comfortable with him, maybe even trusted him to respect her sexually? Or because she was just as competitive as he was? Either way, he had to give her props. She was far more relaxed and fluid here in her home then in the dance room.

If he was going to win this bet, he needed to think of something other than the way he craved those hot sexy legs wrapped around his waist as he drove into her. Or her arching her back and crying out as he sucked her nipples and ravaged her slick pussy with his fingers.

Ty groaned. He needed to turn off the erotic pictures in his mind. He settled back into the chair and relaxed a modicum. He stared straight ahead and replayed in his head the last baseball game he had watched. When that didn't quell the hot throb of his dick, he moved on to his fantasy football picks for this year.

He tried to keep his eyes focused on the stereo on the other side of the room. It immediately lost its appeal. His gaze was pulled back to the tempting siren before him.

She held his dick hostage and there wasn't a damn thing he could do about it. In a slow sexy peel, she pulled one of her gloves off with her teeth. She draped it over his shoulder, and

KARIN TABKE

he could still feel her body heat in the fabric. He sucked in a deep breath and held it. Even from a few feet away, her sexy scent infiltrated his senses. Slowly, he exhaled.

She moved gently to the slow pulsating beat of the music, her flared hips circling and undulating as if a man rested between her thighs. She trailed her fingers up from the hem of her skirt, outlining the curve of her hips only to dip down between her thighs. She closed her eyes halfway and rocked against her fingers, moaning softly. His cock throbbed and all thoughts of baseball and fantasy football fled his mind.

"I'm all wet for you, sir."

Not trusting his voice, Ty swallowed and nodded. Twirling around, she presented her very fine ass to him, then she bent over, running her hands down her stocking-smooth legs. Her skin radiated heat, which he felt like a blast against his face. He squirmed in his chair.

The music picked up a deep throbbing drumbeat. Phil's hips rotated to it, the jaunt and thrust meant for only one thing. Titillation.

"Come here," Ty commanded. She smiled slyly and worked her way toward him.

"Here I am, sir. How do you want me?" Her slender finger unbuttoned first one button of the vest, then a second, then a third. He waited, breathless, for her breasts.

When she laid the vest over his other shoulder, his breath expelled in a long rush. The black lacy bra that sought to hide her charms did an ineffective job. Her skin glowed; she'd oiled herself for him. In the low light of the candle, her honey-colored skin shimmered like a mirage, the fine hair on her arms standing straight up. She was as turned on as he was.

"Unbutton your pants all the way, sir."

Gladly, Ty obliged. Phil swayed and twirled, running her hands along the full swell of her breasts. "Take them off."

Ty kicked off his boots and pulled down his pants. His boxers did little to hide his raging erection.

Phil swayed and moved around to the back of the chair. "I have something hot and moist for you, sir, something so hot you'll scream."

Ty's body temperature spiked. When she poured warm honey-scented wax down his chest, he just about came. He gritted his teeth, his breath hissing between his teeth, and rose halfway out of the chair.

She bent low and whispered in his ear. "I haven't even started with you. Now take off your shorts."

Ty hesitated, the heat of the wax infiltrating his skin, cranking up his body temperature. "You're the one who's supposed to strip."

"And so I shall, but the deal was for you to follow my instructions to the letter."

Ty slipped off his shorts and Phil gasped. He was beautiful. His cock jutted up proud and full, arrogant. The thought of him planting himself between her thighs sent a riveting shiver across her skin. Her reaction gave her courage. She could do this. Hell, she *was* doing it. She felt no anxiety, no panic, no need to run.

"Touch it," she breathed against his ear.

Not moving one muscle from behind him, she watched, mesmerized as his large tanned hand wrapped around the burgeoning shaft. He hissed in a breath at the contact and his cock jumped against his hand. "Oh, sir, that is so tempting. I want to touch it, too."

Still keeping sensuous time with the music, Phil moved around to the front of him. Planting her legs, she swayed seductively, shimmying down toward him. "Move your hand," she commanded, "slowly, up and down."

He complied.

A warm sheen of perspiration coated his skin. She moved as close to him as she could without touching, blowing her warm breath across the broad head of his cock. He felt the beginnings of an eruption. He squirmed in the chair. "Stop," he ground out.

She placed a hand on the armrests on either side of him. "I haven't started."

"You're violating the rules."

Phil reached down beside her and picked something up from the floor. Then she leaned over his chest, her warm breath creating havoc with his heated skin. Her full breasts swung temptingly close to his lips. For a brief second, he closed his eyes and inhaled.

His breath exploded when the lightest of touches circled the head of his dick, then trailed around and down his shaft. His eyes shot open.

Phil traced a purple feather along his rigid cock and around his balls.

She smiled innocently up at him. "*I'm* not touching you, sir."

Sitting back on her haunches, Phil eyed him. "Take off your shirt."

Once again, her commanding tone shot what little blood was left in his brain to his cock.

Phil smiled and twirled away from him. Her ass rocked to the beat of the music. She pulled down the side zipper of her short shirt in a slow slide. Not skipping one beat, she slid the skirt down those long legs he'd fantasized about till it reached her shoes. Nonchalantly she kicked it off, the fabric landing on his face. He pressed it to his nose, inhaling the strong scent of her sex. He lowered it and their eyes locked.

She wore a black satin G-string beneath the garters. She stood in front of him, her legs straight, her hands on her hips. Her skin glowed from the oil and his dick flexed.

"Show me your tits."

"I'll show you mine if you show me yours."

"You first."

Phil slipped one of the straps down and then the other. Ty held his breath. She had full lush breasts. Anticipating the sight of her nipples intrigued him more than catching any criminal. He licked his lips. She sauntered closer, her hips swaying suggestively. Her hands covered her breasts and slowly she pulled the lacy fabric down. With her hands covering her mounds, she unhooked the front snap and let the garment fall to the floor.

"Do you want to touch them, Lieutenant?"

Not trusting his voice, he nodded.

Phil leaned toward him, her soft scent intensifying. Pushing her hands together, she offered them to him, the glowing mounds just inches from his lips.

Ty groaned and his hips undulated toward her. He nearly lost it when she pinched her raspberry-colored nipples, exciting them to stiff peaks. He licked his lips and wanted more than anything to touch them.

Rubbing her palms against her nipples, Phil laughed softly. "Your turn."

Ty didn't waste a second. He pulled his shirt over his head. His knuckles scraped across one of her taut nipples. Phil choked back a gasp, and Ty came up out of his seat.

Phil backed up. Warm moisture flooded her aching pussy. Biting back a moan of want, she turned from Ty. She wanted him in a bad way, so bad she was willing to tone down the act so he could win the bet then. Her competitive nature flared. She didn't need to win or lose a bet to feel the long thick length of Ty Jamerson between her legs. All she had to do was ask. Did she have the courage?

Once he settled back into the chair, she swayed toward him. She placed her heeled foot on the armrest next to him, her scent wafting out. His nose twitched.

"You're soaked," he whispered.

"Yeah, and in a minute you'll be, too."

"I'm not even close."

She ran the feather up his shaft again, then up to round his hard nipples. "Really?"

She released the feather and it fluttered to the floor. "I think . . ." She undulated her pelvis in front of his face, her full breasts bobbing softly nearly against his skin. Trailing her right hand down to her panties, Phil slipped her middle finger between the fabric and her skin. She moved closer to him. "You like the smell of me." Her hips moved in an inviting roll an inch from his nose.

Her left hand trailed up her thigh and slipped beneath the fabric from below. Coyly, she pulled it slightly to the side, reveling her moist lips. She continued to pull the fabric down, exposing more of herself to him. The thrill of such an intimate act urged her blossoming sensuality forward.

Her inhibitions flew out the door, her liberation on fire. With Ty it was easy.

"Isn't that pretty?"

"Beautiful." This time his voice cracked. Sweat beaded his forehead and she looked down. His hands fisted at his sides. A small clear bead of liquid dripped from the tip of his penis.

She slipped a finger into herself and moaned. Her brazen

action shocked her. Even more shocking was how sensitive and swollen she was and how intimately she felt in touch with her body. The excitement of Ty watching compounded the sensations. "Oh God, sir, I wish it was you." She meant it.

The music drummed on and her body fell into the rhythm. In a quick, natural movement, Phil rubbed her straining clit. Her excitement mounted. "Touch yourself, sir," she breathlessly commanded.

A strangled moan erupted from Ty and Phil opened her eyes to find him obliging. The sight of him almost knocked her over. "Faster," she breathed. As his hands pumped, her fingers delved deeper, her juices hot and thick. Her hips rode her hands, and she imagined it was the cock so close to her. She knew from Ty's hardened features that he was imagining himself buried inside of her to the hilt.

Their breathing became a hard, labored cadence, and Phil felt a rising swell in her belly. Her fingers moved faster, her breaths shorter, shallower. From beneath hooded eyelids she watched Ty's hand pump harder. Just as he erupted, she cried out, pleasure ripping through her pussy to her womb, exploding to every nerve ending, the intensity unlike anything she'd ever experienced.

CHAPTER FOURTEEN

Phil's knees buckled under the intensity of her orgasm. She sunk to the floor beside the recliner, breathing heavily. Her body spasmed and she licked her dry lips. She'd never experienced one before.

Ty's hard breaths touched her cheek. She looked up at him, and he grinned. "You win."

She smiled back. "I'd say we both did."

Ty ran his fingers through his hair and leaned back against the chair. Phil couldn't help looking at his penis. His cum shimmered over the still-full organ and pooled on his hard belly.

She's been prepared to win the bet. Leaning back, she grabbed several tissues from the box she'd set on the floor behind the recliner. She set them on top of his cock, a little more forcefully than necessary. She wanted to touch him, but didn't dare. The size and strength of him scared her.

Ty slid his hand over hers, pressing it against him. He was semihard and warm.

"It doesn't bite, Phil."

She looked up to find his dark green eyes on her. She smiled sheepishly and pulled her hand away. "I hope not."

As he cleaned himself up, Phil grabbed her shirt and vest and quickly dressed.

As if he were discussing the weather, Ty asked, "Was that your first orgasm?"

Phil choked as she buttoned the last button of her vest.

Ty laughed. "I knew it!"

She came around to face him and stood with her hands on her hips. "How?"

"By the shocked look on your face."

Glancing down, she bit her lip. Ty stood and reached out to touch her shoulder. "It's nothing to be ashamed of."

Ashamed? She frowned. That wasn't what she felt. She was still reeling from the force of the orgasm, yet she felt strangely unsatisfied.

Her hands dropped from buttoning her jacket. She'd gone further then she imagined she could and with no embarrassing scenes. Cocking her head, she looked at Ty. She wanted some more of him.

Ty's eyes traveled her face, as if searching the thoughts that rattled around in her brain. "Do you want more?"

She felt the heat rise in her cheeks. He smiled and traced a fingertip across her collarbone. Swallowing hard, she wanted to nod yes, but she couldn't bring herself to do it.

Ty bent his head to her hair and inhaled. "You smell good." Slipping his hand behind her neck, he held her gaze captive with his eyes. "I won't hurt you, Phil."

She swallowed hard.

"I know what stop means."

She licked her dry lips. He was willing to let her call the shots, to go as far as she was comfortable going. Her blood revved and her pussy twitched.

She wanted to feel the hard power of him against her, but she also knew she would be in total control. He was giving her the perfect opening.

Stripping the vest off and setting it aside, Phil nodded. She was amazed at how easily, in spite of her past, she enjoyed playing the sexy siren role. This time she was no sniveling ninny allowing a few assholes to demoralize her. No, Ty was many things, but he wasn't a bully when it came to sex.

Sex with Ty, she instinctively knew, even on her limited level, was a good thing. She wanted to *feel*. Even if it was just a taste.

"Same rules apply, Lieutenant. With an exception this time. *I* can touch you." She pushed him back into the chair.

He nodded and she swallowed hard. He was still naked. She couldn't help a glance down at his belly. His cock twitched and began to refill. Excitement shot through her veins.

Before she straddled the chair, she walked away to put another CD into the stereo. She hit the play button and the soft jazz riffs eased out into the room. She turned to face Ty. This time she wasn't coy.

Sauntering slowly toward him, she smiled seductively when she stopped in front of him. Slowly, she eased herself onto his lap. He surged against her sensitive nether lips. Her breath hitched in her throat, her oxygen thinned, the raw power of him almost unnerved her.

His woodsy scent mingling with the lingering scent of his semen amplified under the heat of their two bodies. It turned her on more than any other scent she could recall.

In a slow grind, she slid across Ty's rejuvenated cock. The heat and the fullness of him excited her. Her nether lips swelled and for one brief second she considered just sliding the thin fabric of her panties over and allowing him access.

She hesitated. As much as she wanted to, she wasn't ready.

Ty's knuckles glowed white as he grasped the armrests, perspiration beaded his forehead.

"Zorn, I'm going to write you up for this."

She nipped at his corded neck and brushed her full heavy breasts across his chest. "Under what section? Seducing a superior?"

"Yes."

"If I'm going to be disciplined, make it a *bad* report."

She licked his neck, tasting the saltiness. He groaned, pushing his hips up into her. Moaning, Phil pulled back enough to look at his tense face, the green of his eyes glittering with passion.

"Did you like that?" he hoarsely asked.

She nodded.

He rubbed her there again and Phil nearly swooned. He felt so good. The ache in her sex was becoming unbearable. Just let him in, she told herself, just to feel the head of him. An inch wouldn't hurt, would it?

She threw her head back, exposing her throat, and moaned, the sound feline.

It was too much for Ty. He dug his hands into her thick hair and sank his teeth into her throat. They surged against each other on impact. Phil felt her control slip and the only thing she wanted at that moment was Ty deep inside of her.

Her back arched and her breasts pressed into his bare chest. Ty slipped one hand around her waist and stood, taking her with him. He sprawled them down onto the floor, taking the brunt of the impact.

His lips burned hot against her throat, his teeth biting, his lips sucking. She arched against him again, her back coming off the floor.

Her long legs wrapped around his waist and Ty groaned.

"You don't play fair, Zorn."

"I never said I would, sir." She nipped at his bottom lip. He jerked away.

He growled and sunk his teeth into the curve of her shoulder. "Tell me what you want," he said hoarsely against her skin.

"Don't hurt me," she whispered.

"Never," he said, his teeth laving her jugular.

Electric shards of excitement zipped through her. His touch ignited a sleeping tiger, and while she was fascinated by it, it also terrified her. She pushed him over, rolling on top of him. Entwining her fingers through his, she raised his hands over his head, holding him captive. She liked being on top and she liked the power she wielded over Ty, even if it was only through sex.

She dipped her mouth to his and again he jerked away. "Why don't you like your mouth touched?"

The question caught him off guard. His eyes widened, then narrowed. "I'm not into intimacy."

She ground her mound against his full erection. "And this isn't intimate?"

"It's not the same."

Kyle Thompson's seduction flashed back. There was no kissing, no caressing; in her mind, it wasn't even sex. She was simply an outlet for his ejaculation.

A sudden ridiculous truth hit her sideways. "I've never been kissed by a man." Or a boy, not even a dry peck on the cheek from her father. She slapped her hand over her mouth. She hadn't meant to say it out loud.

Ty's face flashed surprise and . . . something else? Pity?

In that instant the spell was broken; she felt like a fraud, a little girl trying on Mommy's shoes and finding the heels too high to stand in.

She rolled off him and stood up. She didn't want his pity, and if he didn't want her to kiss him that was fine, too. She didn't need it, either.

Phil sat for a long time in the same recliner where Ty had. All traces of him were gone, except the tissues in the trash. Curled up in a fetal position, she couldn't shake her feelings of foolishness.

Was she a pity fuck? Did he feel like he had to work through her sexual issues to get her on track with her job? At least he wouldn't report her failure to report to the PD shrink. If he did, she'd have her walking papers before she could explain why she hadn't released that information.

She pulled a throw from the nearby sofa and wrapped it around her body. Shivering, she remembered his hot gaze, his hot caresses, and his unwavering word that he would stop. Her mood smoothed. Maybe she was overreacting. Maybe Ty wanted more from her than her full focus on the case. She smiled. Maybe he wasn't as big an ass as she first pegged him for.

Yawning, Phil chucked the throw and made her regular rounds of securing the house before she padded down the hall to her bedroom.

She set her alarm for 10:00. With the lives of three women at stake, she couldn't in all good conscience take a day off. There was plenty of paperwork and research she could do. She wanted to look at the employee files with a fresh eye.

Maybe the guys missed something. She'd also submit her request for her father's files.

It wasn't until after the first light fingers of dawn filtered through her window that sleep found Phil.

As Phil poured over the employee files at her old desk in IA, voices from the hallway drifted in. Who the heck was coming in on Sunday?

"I'll meet you in interrogation two, Lieutenant. Your rep should be here shortly," a familiar voice said from the far hallway. Captain Dettmer?

"What can't wait until tomorrow?" Ty's deep voice asked. He didn't sound happy.

Ty? Rep? Here? On a Sunday?

What the hell was going on?

Phil stood as Captain Joe Dettmer breezed into the squad room. His eyes immediately locked on her startled ones.

"What the hell are you doing here, Zorn?"

"Work, sir."

"Why here and not downstairs at your task force office?"

"Faster computers, and, well, I have a formal request of you."

"What is it?"

She hadn't planned on asking him face-to-face. It wasn't protocol, but what the hell. "I'd like to view my father's sealed IA file."

The old cop's bushy eyebrows slammed together in thought. Dettmer was old school; he went by the book and he took no prisoners. He and her father were cut from the same cloth. Two of the few who refused to succumb to the corruption that riddled law enforcement these days. She respected the hell out of him and was grateful he still stopped by occasionally to see how her mom was holding up.

"Mom sends her regards." A lie, but hey, maybe it would sweeten the pot.

"How is Vivian these days? I haven't seen her in a few months."

She swallowed a spurt of anger. How was her mother? As well as anyone whose husband was hung out to dry by a band of lying bastard cops covering their own asses could be. Especially since the man she loved, unable to bear the shame of it all, ate a shotgun.

"She's holding up as best she can." Another lie. The woman teetered on the brink on insanity. Phil had stopped trying to get through to her years ago. For years she played the good daughter role with her weekly visits, but they consisted of her mother rocking back and forth in the rocking chair her father bought when Phil was born and staring blankly at the wall. Now? She had to force herself. Guilt clung to her like a wet coat. She vowed to be a better daughter.

"Put your request in writing and I'll consider it." He moved to turn away, but stopped and turned back to her. "Give your mother my love, and tell her I promise to stop by this week."

He started past her when another man walked in, one

she'd had many occasions to go up against over the years. Sergeant Miguel "Ponch" Torres. Their eyes met; his narrowed to slits and he continued down the hall to the interrogation rooms.

"What's going on, sir?" she called to her captain.

He slowed his gate and stopped. When he turned, she read contempt in his eyes. "Looks like we might have a rogue cop on our hands. And you might be interested in this one."

Warning bells sounded. She knew who was down the hall. "Looks like your lieu crossed the line last night."

Her skin chilled. "What do you mean?"

"Does the name 'Scott Mason' ring a bell?"

Her skin constricted. "I know of him."

Dettmer nodded. "I know you do. Jamerson threatened to kill him last night."

Some of the tension rolled from her tight shoulders. "The guy was acting like an asshole. It was a figment of speech."

Dettmer smiled, the gesture ugly. "It was more than that. Mason's body was found this morning in the Dumpster behind Klub Kashmir."

CHAPTER FIFTEEN

"Are you telling me you've hauled Lieutenant Jamerson in as a suspect?"

Dettmer nodded. "That's exactly what I'm saying."

The blood drained to Phil's toes, causing them to tingle. Ty was a lot of things . . . but a murderer. . . . ? "Do you have a witness?"

"The body's still warm, with lots of people who witnessed his threats."

Phil's brain wracked for answers. "Time of death?"

"Coroner puts it sometime between three and eight A.M."

Her brain quickly processed the time Ty left her house. Her guess was it was sometime around 4:30.

Shit.

"Would you mind, sir, if I sat in on the interview?"

He considered her request for a long moment. "Fine.

Maybe you can read between the lines since you've been working with the man and have the experience."

"Exactly what I thought."

As they started for the interrogation room, Dettmer added, "I brought in Tony Mossa."

Oh, shit.

She'd met Tony. He wasn't nicknamed "Hardcore" for nothing. He always got what he wanted from cops who thought they were unshakable. She'd taken several seminars from him and he was tops. Phil swallowed hard. Come what may, she believed in her heart Ty was not a murderer.

But had he gone back to the club and run into Scott?

"What's Jamerson saying?"

"Nada. Said he'll only talk to his rep."

Smart move. Otherwise he could incriminate himself.

Sweet Mary! Was she really rooting for Ty to keep his mouth shut? She wasn't in IA anymore, but still. . . . She didn't want to see him go down for something he didn't do. Although he had the time and the means, she doubted a motive. Her gut told her Ty was not a murderer. That thought sobered her. She'd always believed in the system, except when it came to her father, and in his case a conspiracy took him down. Heads were going to roll when she was done, no doubt about it. But for now, she needed to concentrate on Ty.

When she walked into the room, his eyes widened for a scant second and then narrowed. She knew what he thought.

Ty worked his jaw. The backstabbing bitch. He should

have known the minute she could dig her claws into his back, she would. He straightened in the rigid chair.

"Officer Zorn," he said, almost sneering.

Phil nodded, her eyes hard and focused. Dettmer pulled a chair out from the table, holding it for her. She accepted and sat down. "Lieutenant."

Ponch piped up. "What's this, a gang bang?"

Dettmer shook his head and pulled out another chair. "Not at all. Officer Zorn has a vested interest in this case."

"Oh, so it's an open case now?" Ponch snidely asked.

Dettmer smiled and conceded. "Poor choice of words, Torres. Sergeant Mossa will be arriving momentarily."

No sooner had the words left Dettmer's mouth than the door opened and Tony Mossa walked into the room. The man was from the streets. A nasty scar marred his face above his left eye, accentuating his pockmarked olive complexion. Like everyone else in the room, he was dressed casually. He set his briefcase down on the floor and made his intro.

The tension was so thick in the room you could have sliced it up and served it.

Ponch turned on his tape recorder and placed it on the table. Dettmer and Mossa did the same with their own devices.

Mossa established the date, time, and who was present.

Ty didn't flinch. His green eyes flared hard and the muscle in his right cheek worked. He refused to look at Phil, afraid he might lunge across the table and strangle her. Betrayal stormed his gut. Hell, if he knew why somewhere in his heart he expected Phil to be any different from any other betraying woman. His mother had taught him well not to trust the gender. She'd never stood up for him, why the hell did he expect Phil to? And why did it bother him so much that she didn't? That she'd come to see the IA vultures strip him down to bones, one sliver of flesh at a time?

"All right, boys and girls, what's the charge?" Ponch asked. His arrogance did nothing to garner compassion from Mossa or Dettmer. Both men stiffened.

"Murder one, Sergeant," Mossa said.

Ty stiffened. Son of a bitch.

Ponch grinned, a genuine smile. "Are you serious? Who's the stiff?"

"One Scott Mason."

Ty growled. "I didn't kill that prick."

"Shut up, Jamerson," Ponch barked.

"The coroner gave an initial cause of death as blunt trauma to the head. Your client was seen fighting with him only feet from where his body was found, and plenty of witnesses will testify Jamerson threatened to kill him."

Ponch didn't flinch. Ty had to hand it to him. The guy was good. He glanced at Mossa. But the IA sergeant was good, too. Maybe even better. For the first time Ty could remember, fear clogged his arteries. He glanced down at his raw knuckles and the scrapes on his forearms, direct results of him pounding Scott Mason's face.

Mossa smiled and casually opened his briefcase. "You have defensive wounds on your hands and arms, Lieutenant," he said as if reading Ty's mind.

Ty opened his mouth to respond. Ponch flashed him a warning glare.

"Where were you between the hours of three A.M. this morning and eight A.M., Lieutenant Jamerson?"

Ponch nodded. "Answer the question."

"Home."

"Alone?"

"Just me and my buddy JD."

"That's all you're going to get, Mossa. Not another word until we have the full report." Ponch's face looked like an oversize tomato, a sure sign his blood pressure had spiked to DEFCON 1. Ty almost smiled. He'd never seen the quiet rep so stirred up.

Mossa did smile. It wasn't a pleasant gesture. "Your client can wait in jail. We're officially charging him with murder one. There was means, motive, and opportunity."

Blood froze in Ty's mind. Son of a bitch. He glanced at Phil, but she seemed as stunned by Mossa's words as he. Nice acting, sweetheart, he thought.

"I'll have him out before the ink dries," Ponch said. No sooner had the words left his mouth than the door to the room opened and two uniforms entered.

Ty fought down the urge to punch his way out of the room.

Ponch spoke up, outraged. "What the fuck are you doing?"

Mossa stuffed paperwork back into his briefcase. "Your client is under arrest for the murder of Scott Mason. He's being taken to booking. I believe he knows the way."

Ty stood. Phil sat silent. As he turned his back to the uniforms, presenting his hands, Phil erupted. "He was with me!"

Six pairs of widened eyes turned on her, jaws gaped, but no one was more surprised than Ty.

Phil smoothed her hands down her jeans, color flushed her cheeks. "Lieutenant Jamerson went home with me last night after his altercation with Mason. He didn't leave until nine this morning."

Mossa's eyes narrowed. "Officer Zorn. Your badge is on the line here."

Phil nodded. "I understand the repercussions, sir." More than her badge, she could kiss getting her father's file good-bye.

"Why are you lying for him, Zorn?" Dettmer asked. Fury underlined his question.

"I'm not, sir. We spent the better part of the evening brainstorming our case." She couldn't believe the hole she was digging for herself. She had no idea where Ty went after he left her house, but she was sure it wasn't to track Scott Mason down and kill him in cold blood.

She went with her instinct, and it was screaming "setup."

She could hear Ty now: *Letter of the law, Officer Zorn, and the spirit of the law. . . . Sometimes you have to work the rules to justify the end.*

She would not allow her undercover case to get blown to hell, and she sure as hell wasn't going to allow some twisted misunderstanding land her commanding officer in jail for something she was sure he didn't do.

Phil threw her shoulders back. "I'd be happy to take a polygraph."

Mossa nodded. "Okay, Zorn." He looked at Ty, who stood silent. "Why didn't you just say you were working, Jamerson?"

Ty remained silent. He had to hand it to Zorn. The lady had a quick mind. He'd thought of it, but he didn't think she'd go along. Miracles never ceased.

"Did you or did you not spend the night with Officer Zorn?" Mossa demanded.

"Let's clear this up here and now, Ty. Answer the question," Ponch said.

Ty shrugged and his eyes lit up. "I've never been one to argue with a lady."

Dettmer spoke up. "Until we're clear on this, you're on admin leave, Jamerson."

Before Ponch could utter a word at the absurdity of Dettmer's action, Phil piped up. "I'd advise against that, sir. The union will have your badge before the paperwork is filed."

He glared hard at her, but she went on to explain, keeping her voice neutral. "Lieutenant Jamerson has an airtight alibi. While he may, in IA's opinion, have means, and if you really stretch it, motive, to kill the slimeball, Scott Mason was alive and well the last time he had contact with Lieutenant Jamerson. I can vouch for his whereabouts. It all boils down to you having squat. The last time I checked, squat got you nothing but the union breathing down our backs and liable suits against the department. If Jamerson chooses to go public with this, there would be hell to pay." She looked at Mossa. "Besides all of that, the undercover operation he's heading up is making headway. To pull him now for something inconclusive would severely jeopardize the case."

She stood. She had them by the balls and everyone in the room knew it. "Now, if you'll excuse me, I have three missing ladies to find."

Phil hurried out of the room. She was just about to exit the front door when Captain Dettmer caught up with her. "Phil!"

Damm it. She turned to face him. "Sir?"

"Why are you covering his ass? He turned a long time ago. This is what we need to finally nail him."

Phil swallowed hard and ignored the hard thump in her chest. "Sir?"

He steered her away from the door and lowered his voice. "He's a vigilante cop. If we don't contain him, he's going to take the entire PD down with him."

Not very long ago she would have swallowed her captain's words whole. But now? She went with her gut. "Sir. Please trust me with this." She would not lie again if she didn't have to. It went against her every moral fiber. But . . .

The word reverberated in her brain and made her want to scream. Before Ty Jamerson there had never been any buts.

Now, out of IA and down in the trenches, she realized there was a pile of buts. So long as they served the sole purpose of catching the bad guy.

But was lying to her superior going too far? Even if it meant keeping a man she believed, hoped was innocent from being wrongly charged? Even if it meant keeping a rogue cop on the streets to nail the real bad guys?

Dettmer smiled, a fatherly smile. Her father had never smiled so benevolently at her. "Your old man would have taken Jamerson out in that room. *After* he took you over his knee. Be careful."

He pushed past her to the parking lot. She followed more slowly.

CHAPTER SIXTEEN

Halfway across the parking lot, Phil heard Ty call her name. She stopped, her back rigid. She could just see that smirk on his face. The one that said, "I got to you and we both know it." She pressed her lips into a hard line and strode away from his voice. Damn him anyway. It wasn't about sex, it was her going with her gut.

It was about doing the right thing.

She hopped on her motorcycle, hit the electric ignition, and strapped on her helmet. Then she kicked into gear and sped past her stunned lieutenant. Hah! Didn't think she had it in her to ride a bike? It was her only guiltless pleasure.

Racing down the road, she didn't give a damn if she was pulled over for exceeding the speed limit. She shook her head. Speeding? Lying to her superiors? Possibly getting a murderer off before he could be charged?

"Phil, you are going downhill fast," she muttered quietly.

Who killed Scott Mason? And why? Had he bothered someone else? He was annoying, rude, and a slimeball, but that wasn't grounds for someone to take him out. What purpose would that serve? Why would anyone want him dead? She tamped down the urge to nudge her way into that homicide investigation. She had enough on her plate.

She blew a red light and told herself it was okay because there wasn't a car anywhere near the intersection. The thrill of breaking yet another law electrified her. Shit, she was going rogue. Was it any wonder? She had the master as her mentor.

She turned off the main street to her neighborhood.

An hour later, Phil's house had never been so clean. Her adrenaline-charged energy could have launched an atomic bomb. She decided to shower and go back to the office and pore over files. There was nothing else to do, no one to visit. She plopped down on a straight-back chair at her small kitchen table. How pathetic was that? No one to visit. Her mother was inconsolable. It was always the same thing. Guilt washed over Phil. She needed to make more of an effort. But how? She wasn't a people person.

The ring of the doorbell startled her out of her pity party.

"Captain," she said surprised. She opened the door wider and motioned Dettmer in.

"Zorn, we need to talk."

"Okay. Let's go into the living room."

He followed behind her and she motioned for him to sit

down on the recliner. She suppressed a smile. Ty filled it out much better than the captain. While Dettmer was in shape for a man in his early fifties, he didn't carry himself with the sexy arrogance Ty did.

She rolled her eyes. Since when was arrogance sexy? Phil sat on the sofa across from her captain.

"So what brings you here, sir?"

Dettmer didn't waste any time getting to the point. "Your lieutenant is walking both sides of the law. I want you to keep a log on him."

"I—sir, I can't do that!"

"Why not?"

"I—" Why not? "I have my hands full with this case. I don't have the time to hide in the shadows and make book on my lieutenant."

"I'm not asking you to shadow him. Watch him in the club."

"For what?"

"I think he's skimming off the dancers. I have it from one of them he's coercing sex from not only her, but two others."

Phil gasped. No way. Ty kept his distance, well, except from Candi, but she didn't seem to mind. "Which one told you that?"

He shook his head. "I gave her my word I wouldn't release that information. You're going to have to trust me on this one."

Phil shook her head. "I've found Lieutenant Jamerson to

be gruff and direct, but he hasn't shown any sign of bullying the dancers into the back rooms, and I haven't heard any rumblings about him taking his own cut above the house cut."

"He's good, Phil. I worked with him years ago and watched him butcher a UC case, but he came out smelling like a rose."

Phil's brain couldn't comprehend her captain's accusations. Had she gone soft? Lost her objectivity?

"I'll keep my eyes open."

He stood and handed her the thick manila envelope in his hand. "Be careful of him, Zorn. He has a way about him that sucks people in."

She nodded. Didn't she know it. "What's this?" she asked, taking the file folder.

"As much of your father's IA as I could get my hands on without breaking GO."

"I've read the bullshit report they gave us."

"This has more."

Her heart kicked up a notch. Were the answers in her hand?

"Thank you, sir."

"Don't disappoint me, Zorn. I want Jamerson's ass."

Two hours after her captain left, Phil continued to read the thick report. Many of the pages were written by StreetSmart, the code name for a UC who shadowed her father. They depicted the mundane details of her father's daily life as a patrol sergeant. How long had he been followed?

In the file, StreetSmart stated he witnessed her father

pistol-whip a pimp for no good reason. Phil snorted. She'd bet if her father did do it, he had a million reasons.

But, she chewed her bottom lip, what he did was wrong. An abuse of his authority.

"Shit!" she said. "I'm believing this crap."

Impossible. While Mac Zorn breathed fire and brimstone, he also respected his fellow human beings, and more than that, he respected the law. God's law and the penal code. StreetSmart's comments were lies.

Phil scrolled through the reports, looking for the notes on Ruby, the woman who claimed her father beat her after he raped her. It was the only name they had been given during the trial and her father would never name her outright. That had infuriated both her and her mother. It was as if he were protecting the woman.

Maybe her real identity would be somewhere in the file. Phil shuffled through several more pages near the end when she came across a datasheet.

Bingo. Margery Flint, a.k.a. Ruby, 14865 North Capital, Apt. 373, Lansdowne.

She jotted down Ruby's last known and continued through the reports.

Most of it she knew. It all came out in the IA. She'd seen the transcripts her father was given by his attorney, but seeing it didn't mean he was guilty.

She needed to track down Ruby and ask her point blank why she lied, and who coerced it.

She got on the computer and logged into the data bank at the PD. She did a reverse on Margery's addy and came up with her phone number. She'd attempt a conversation over the phone first, then hopefully she could set up a meeting.

Her finger shook as she dialed the number. Nervous energy infused her limbs. After all these years, she was going to speak with the woman responsible for ending her father's illustrious career, which in turn provoked his suicide.

"Hello?" a low throaty voice answered. She sounded old, tired, and nicotine battered.

"Margery Flint?"

"Who wants to know?"

"My name is Philamina Zorn. I wanted to know if I could talk to you about my father Mac."

A long pregnant pause followed. "Miss Flint?"

"I have nothing to say about Mac."

"Miss Flint, please, I need to know who set him up. I want to clear his name."

"No one set him up. Mac had his demons."

"I don't believe you!"

"Stop trying to make him the saint he portrayed, and don't call me again."

Phil stood for a long time holding the phone to her ear, the dial tone droning angrily. Hot tears dripped down her cheeks. It was a lie! It was all lies! Her father was not the man they said! He couldn't be. The man she knew was honorable.

After several long minutes she hung up the phone, drained of energy and feeling punk.

She looked at the scattered files on her kitchen table and in a surge of anger swiped them with her arm, sending pages scattering all over the floor.

"No!" she screamed.

Impulsively, she ran to the foyer and grabbed her helmet. She needed to get away, to clear her head, to sort out the mess her life had become.

An hour later, feeling no better, Phil turned back onto her quiet street. She groaned under her helmet. Ty's black pickup truck was parked next to her stranded Taurus.

CHAPTER SEVENTEEN

"Go home, sir. It's my day off and I've filled my quota of off-duty police work."

"This is personal."

Phil swept past his tall figure propped casually against her front door. She jammed the key into the lock, the force veering it off the mark. Frustrated, she shot him a look that said, "Shut up or get your lights punched out." He cocked a dark brow at her and smiled leisurely. He looked good enough to eat. Damn him. She didn't want this distraction. She wanted to feel sorry for herself, alone, for a little while longer.

Without taking his eyes off her face, he reached down and took the keys from her hand. "Officer Zorn, you don't ram it in like that. You'll almost always fail in securing access."

He ran the edge of the key down her arm and across her knuckles. "For success, lubrication is desired." He grinned at her, positioning the tip of the key at the lock entrance. He slipped it in and something inside her moved. She licked her dry lips. "As you can see," he continued, "when guided by the right hand, it slips right in." He turned the key. The click of the tumbler turning echoed in her heart.

He pushed the door open and stepped back. "After you."

She speared him with a glare and shook her head, pulling the rubber band from her thick ponytail. Stalking past him into her house, she tossed her helmet on the oak table in the entryway. Using her teeth, she pulled her gloves from her hands and flung them on the sofa.

She shook her head again and ran her fingers through the soft tangles. Curious at Ty's silence, she turned to face him. He stood in the doorway. The late-afternoon sun behind him illuminated his silhouette, his legs braced as if on the bow of a ship, his hands fisted at his side. The impact of his masculinity hit her hard, a woman reacting naturally to a man.

Phil smiled, a soft kittenish smile, and sauntered toward his big frame. "Do I turn you on, sir?"

Ty cleared his throat before he spoke. "Yes."

She pirouetted in front of him. While she wanted him to do naughty things to her, her inner cop wanted inside that brain of his.

"Wanna make another bet?" She reached behind him and pushed the door closed.

"No."

She pressed closer to him. His black T-shirt strained against the wide plane of his chest. His black jeans hung snugly, accentuating the lean muscles of his thighs and his impressive package.

"That's too bad. I was going to let you win this time."

She laughed at his sharp intake of breath.

Game over. She wanted answers. "Did you kill Scott Mason?"

He opened the front door and reached down, picking up a small shopping bag she hadn't noticed earlier. But then, she had been solely focused on Lieutenant Studly. He closed the door.

"A little late to be asking that, isn't it?"

"Not really. I'm sure if you did off him you had a good reason." Her stomach growled. She walked into the kitchen and was greeted by scattered paper all over the floor. She bent to gather them up.

"What's all that?" Ty asked.

"None of your business." Quickly, she shuffled the papers into a semblance of order and stuffed them in a drawer at her computer desk. Her stomach growled again. Ignoring Ty's raised brow, she strode back to the fridge.

He strode up behind her as she opened the fridge door, looking for something cold to drink. She really needed it now. He stood so close to her, his heat scorched her neck. The fine hair there spiked and as much as she wanted to move forward to her father's killer, she couldn't get the vision of her body writhing beneath Ty's sweaty thrusting body out of her mind.

Goose bumps erupted along her arms. "Do I turn *you* on, Officer?" His breath caressed her neck.

She bent down to grab two bottles of water. Her ass rammed right into his thighs. Without missing a beat, Ty slipped his hands around to the front of her hips and pulled her hard against him. "Just what I thought. Why are we wasting time?"

She stood up quickly and wheeled around. Shoving her shoulder into his chest, she pushed him hard out of the way, then closed the fridge door. "Because, sir, I don't share, and the next guy who fucks me has to like me."

Thrusting a cold bottle in his hand, she strode past him to her desk and covered her scattered notes with the latest edition of *Cop Talk* magazine. She faced him. His expression was contemplative, as if he were asking himself whether he liked her enough to fulfill her terms.

"Are you having sex with Candi?"

"No."

"Have you?"

He grinned. "No."

"Have you had sex with anyone else at the club?"

His eyes narrowed. "Why all the questions? Did your captain instruct you to pump me?"

She shut her mouth. Ty smiled, his lips forming a tight line. "What else did he say?"

"Nothing."

"Liar."

"Did you kill Mason?"

"No, but someone sure beat the shit out of him. His face is a mess, and the back of his head is missing."

Phil grimaced at the visual. Scott Mason was many things, most of them not very nice, but he didn't deserve to die like that.

"Who found him?"

"An anonymous call to the PD."

Hmm. Smelled to her. "That stinks of a setup. Who besides me wants to see your ass hung out to dry?"

He sauntered toward her, stopping at the table. "Lots of people on both sides of the law."

"What's in the bag?"

"Open it and see. Why did you lie to Mossa?"

She set her bottle down on the table and opened the brown bag. "Lie about what? You were with me."

"Not until nine, like you said."

She shrugged. "So I got my times mixed up."

"Admit it, Zorn, your letter-of-the-law credo would have me in jail right now when you know as well as I do I didn't kill Mason."

She shrugged, refusing to admit he was right. She still hadn't come to terms with lying to her superior officer and didn't want to think about it right now.

Pushing it from her mind, Phil reached into the paper bag and pulled out a water-filled plastic bag. She held it up against the light. A fish. A pretty one. Long, deep red fins with the barest hint of purple at the tips. Beautiful. "What's this?"

"A fish."

"No shit, Sherlock. What kind and why is it here?"

Ty reached into the bag and pulled out a quart-size round bowl and a little plastic container of food. "It's a Beta, or as some call them, a Siamese fighting fish. Since you like to argue so much, the two of you should get along. He's yours."

Phil shook her head and put the plastic bag back into the paper bag. "Nope, I don't have fish. If you haven't noticed—" she gestured at the Spartan room—"I don't even have a live plant in here. I kill everything."

Ty pulled the fish back out of the bag and untied the plastic. In one quick maneuver, he poured the fish and water into the bowl. "Consider him a thank you for helping me out today."

Phil eyed the fish swimming happily around in circles. "For the record, women like sparkly thank-you gifts."

"Women want to take care of things, males specifically, so here's your fix."

"Your mother didn't." She bit her bottom lip. Why did she goad him about his mother? Was it to get a real live emotion out of him other than anger?

Ty stiffened, his jaw tightened, and his dark complexion paled a few shades. "Forgive my mistake. *Normal* women want to take care of men."

"Do you forgive her?"

Ty shrugged and opened the little container of food. He poured a few of the tiny balls into his hand and dumped them into the bowl. The fish went to town, slurping them right up. "Pig," Phil muttered.

"She was what she was long before she made the mistake of having me."

"You aren't a mistake."

Ty laughed, the sound harsh. "A lot of people out there would argue that." His eyes softened for a moment. "But thanks for the sentiment."

For the first time, Phil saw Ty as he must have been as a boy. His dark hair long and unkempt, his big green eyes hungry for love. She wondered how many times he reached out to his drug addict mother only to be rejected. Could she blame him for being such a hard case? Why should he trust anyone, women especially?

"Do you trust me?" she asked softly.

Just as softly, he answered, "No."

Her gut rippled. "Fair enough."

He smiled a half smile. "Don't take it personally. I don't trust anyone."

"I'm not your mother, Ty."

His eyes flashed before they softened. He stepped closer to her and reached out, taking a lock of her hair between his fingers. Absently, he rubbed it. He flashed her a wicked smile. "I hope not, otherwise I'd be giving Oedipus a run for his money." He brought the lock to his nose and sniffed. "While I've had dreams of wringing your pretty little neck, I dream more of sinking myself deep inside of you."

Phil gasped and pulled her hair from his hands. "Stop talking about having sex with me."

"Can't help it. You're a walking advertisement for all things carnal."

"Is it always about sex with you? Have you ever gotten to know a woman for herself first?"

He took back the lock of hair she pulled away. "I don't have time to form emotional attachments, or the inclination."

Phil stood her ground. "You talk about sex like it was shooting hoops, or eating a meal. How fun can it be if there's no emotion involved?"

"Lust is an emotion, so is desire. You don't have to have an emotional attachment to a masseuse to enjoy a massage, do you?"

"That's different."

"Why? It's touching, rubbing, stimulating."

"It's not the same, and you know it."

"The only difference is there isn't penetration."

Phil laughed. "I'll tell you what, Lieutenant, I'll let you give me a massage and we'll call it even."

Ty grinned and stroked her neck with the back of his knuckles.

She instantly warmed to the idea. She'd been dying for a foot massage. "In fact, let me jump in the shower and you can give me the foot massage of all foot massages."

"What do I get out of it?'

"The satisfaction of knowing you can touch a woman in an intimate way without penetration."

He scowled. "A lesson I hardly want to learn."

She smiled up at him, looking forward to his big hands on her sore feet. "I'll return the favor."

He grinned. "Deal."

Phil hurried back to the shower. She found herself humming as she lathered up.

It occurred to her that the only place for a good massage was her bed. The sofa was too soft and lumpy and she was afraid the kitchen table would collapse.

After toweling off, she slipped on a pair of white terry cloth shorts and a matching midriff top. She smiled. It didn't leave much to the imagination.

She went about laying out a fresh sheet on her bed and grabbed a bottle of her favorite lotion. Pulling her hair back into a ponytail, she headed back into the kitchen, where Ty stared broodingly down at her new pet.

"I'm calling him Bubba."

Ty looked up at her and cocked a brow. "Bubba?"

She nodded and said the name again. "Yep. Hopefully he'll live up to the name. Big, dumb, and harmless. And for his own good, he better be able to survive without food for days."

Ty chuckled. "It's a good thing they breathe surface air, or he might die from asphyxiation."

Suddenly, Phil liked the fact that she had someone, okay, a fish, to come home to. Who knew, if she didn't kill this one, maybe she'd get him a friend.

KARIN TABKE

She picked the bowl up and set it on the kitchen counter near the window. Soft morning sun flooded the room and this way he wouldn't fry. "I hope I remember to feed him."

"I'll remind you."

When she looked at Ty, she saw his attention was on her instead of the fish.

Setting her hands on her hips, she let Ty get an eyeful. Her nipples puckered under his hot gaze. "I have massage rules."

He smiled, his eyes trailing up her fluttering chest to her eyes. "Of course you do."

"Because I want the maximum effect of this, we're going to do it in my bedroom." His eyes sparked. She felt an answering spark inside, but continued calmly, "And, you will keep your hands below my thighs. No infractions." She stuck her hand out. "Deal?"

Ty grinned like the devil in a whorehouse. He wrapped his big, warm hand around hers and slowly pumped. "Deal."

Like a mother leading a toddler to naptime, Phil took Ty's other hand and led him down the hall. The gesture felt strangely intimate and soothing. She wasn't sure what provoked the action, but she was happy he didn't pull away.

She settled facedown on the bed, excitement pulsing through her body. It was just a foot massage, but she could barely contain her excitement as she anticipated his touch.

His weight settled at her feet, the bed dipping. She heard the squirt of lotion, and when he took her right foot into his hands and pressed his thumbs against the ball of her foot, she about came then and there. Shock waves shot up her legs, spearing her twat before running up her spine. Her nipples strained against the terry cloth and Phil had to keep herself from pressing her hips into the mattress.

"Feel good?" Ty asked, his voice deep and husky.

"Like heaven."

His fingers, long, thick, and strong, delved into her tired muscles. After several moments, she felt her other muscles loosen.

"Is your mother still alive?" If she didn't converse, she'd melt under his touch and that was the last thing she needed.

He dug his thumb between her big toe and next toe. "What's your fascination, Phil?"

Her breath caught. "I don't know. I guess I want to know what makes you tick."

He massaged her instep. Oh, that felt so good. He pulled her foot back so her leg was at a forty-five-degree angle. She felt him bend toward her toes, heard him inhale. "Vanilla." His warm breath on her skin cranked up her senses.

Her heart rate kicked up a notch and she really wished he liked her better. Focus, she told herself.

"So where were you today?"

He loosened his hold on her foot and lowered it back to the bed. "I was on my way to the zoo."

"The zoo?" she asked.

"The zoo."

"Why?"

"I promised Candi I'd take her and her kid."

Phil felt like all the air in her body had been released in one giant whoosh.

"Maybe you should go," she said softly.

His grip tightened. "You're kicking me out because I took a two-year-old to the zoo?"

Phil pushed away, wanting to completely pull away from him, angry at the jealousy biting at her. "That two-year-old has a mother. A very sexy one, I might add."

Ty pushed her hip over and around. "Not as sexy as you."

She smacked his hand away, the impression of his warm fingers singeing her skin. She didn't trust herself facing him so she remained prone. "Don't you have the slightest bit of guilt?" She hated the way her voice rose with the question, glad the pillow muffled most of it so she didn't sound like a jealous twit.

His fingers dug between her toes, the lotion sluicing them easily. She moaned, wondering how those fingers would feel slipping in and out of her. What the hell? Did she want him out or not?

"Guilt? About what? I took a kid to the zoo. What's there to feel guilty about?"

When he turned it around that way, she felt foolish.

His thumbs kneaded her instep, then her ankle, his hands working the muscles in her calf.

"You're jealous of a two-year-old!" Ty chuckled.

She wiggled her butt, wanting to pull away, but the lure of his hands on her was too strong. She'd put this to bed and if she looked the fool, so be it. Taking a deep breath, she exhaled. "Are you romantically involved with Candi?"

"I told you no."

"You said you weren't having sex with her."

"What's the difference?"

"Are you that primitive?" She turned to catch his laughing eyes. Thank God, otherwise she'd have to kick him out.

She had one last question. "But you took her out?"

"It's called information gathering. I took each of the girls out when I got into the club. Nothing romantic, just a working dinner."

His words struck a chord with her. They were getting too comfy. There was a case to close.

"Ty, we need to stay focused."

"I am, you're the one who wanted a foot rub."

True, and it felt wonderful.

"Believe it or not, bringing Bubba wasn't my only reason for stopping by. I assume you were at the PD today going though files. We need to talk about that, and a few other things." His strong fingers rubbed deep, loosening the kinks in her leg. "Weird shit is happening, Mason for one, and I also have a note from the kidnapper."

This time she made the extra effort to turn over. He pinned her with his hands.

"A note? When were you going to tell me about it?"

"I meant to show it to you Friday night, but I got side-tracked."

"What did it say?"

"He wants *you*, Pussy."

Phil caught her breath and she literally felt as if her blood drained at warp speed to her gut. "What exactly did it say?"

"Bud found it Friday night on the bar. A napkin with the words 'I want Pussy' printed on it. It was one of the reasons I followed you home that night. It's also the reason I'll be driving you home until we break this case."

His fingers traveled up her thigh, massaging slow and luxuriously. "I don't need a baby-sitter." She felt like a petulant child saying it. She was a target. Whether she wanted protection or not, it was smart police work. "Where's the note?"

She rolled on to her side, the action sliding her toward him and driving his fingers up her thigh. Her terry shorts were Daisy Duke short, and his fingertips brushed across her sensitive mound. Their eyes widened in unison and Phil bucked in response. A muscle in Ty's right cheek twitched.

"The lab has it," he bit out.

Sexual tension strained across his face. She didn't dare look down to his lap. She flipped over. If she stayed facing him, she'd allow his fingers trespass, thus making the deal null and void. She decided to address his male urge to protect her another time. "I'm sure it's someone inside."

"I think so, too. Let's compare notes."

"Too much intimate info is getting out. The kidnapper knew his targets. He knew they were loners, he knew they wouldn't be missed. Only someone inside would be privy to that type of info. I've told as many people without seeming obvious I don't even have a cat that would care if I never came home." She laughed caustically. "And it's the truth."

"You have a fish who'd care."

She wondered if the guy who gave him to her would care, as well. Her pride refused to broach the subject.

"The team would care. And, I have to admit, Zorn, you've surprised me. I thought you would have turned tail by now and gone crying back to IA."

"Your words stir me."

Ty laughed. His fingers stroked, kneaded, and massaged her thighs. Warm wetness seeped between them. How the hell was she supposed to concentrate on the case while he was making love to her legs with his hands?

"I have a file on Jase's two friends," Ty said. "I've already gone over them, but you take a look. Jase and Reese are following up on two of the employees who have changed their minds now on where they were the night of the first kidnapping."

Both of his hands now wrapped around the top part of her thigh, then trailed down to her knee. He cocked her foot again at a forty-five-degree angle. She felt his breath on her instep and fantasized about his warm wet mouth sucking her toes.

She squealed when it became a reality. Warmth flooded her body. Her hips pressed hard into the mattress, and she managed to swallow her delighted moans. She cleared her throat before she spoke, not trusting her voice.

"I don't think the kidnapper is inside. Someone in the club is cozying up to the girls, gleaning info, and then passing it along to the kidnapper. We find his mule, we find him."

Ty's tongue darted between her toes, his fingers massaging her calf. He spoke low against her skin, his whiskers chafing her. "I'll keep a sharper eye on Bud and Milo. You do the same with the girls. Any gut feelings about any of them?"

He sucked each toe, tonguing them as he did. Oh God, why didn't she make the rules more specific? He was taking gross advantage of her "no hands" clause. Did she say no lips? She couldn't remember. Had she meant not to? "I've," she caught her breath, "chatted with them all. No gut reaction." A light penetrated the sexy haze engulfing her. "I saw Candi take extra money from her lap dance last night and hide it in her shoe. You know her better than I do, what do you think?"

Ty shook his head with her toe caught between his teeth. Chills swept over her. "She wouldn't risk losing Lola."

Or you, Phil thought.

Phil squeezed her eyes shut. She could do this, concentrate while Ty sucked her toes and massaged her thighs. "I'll dig a little harder with Tammy, she's privy to all of the girls' woes."

Ty licked her instep. "She's a tough nut to crack."

The *ding-dong* of her doorbell startled them both. Who the hell was coming by at six o' clock on a Sunday? She never had visitors.

Phil swallowed hard, rolled over, and couldn't ignore the rise in Ty's black jeans. It was all about timing, and she was grateful for the interruption. Sort of.

The doorbell rang again, followed by an angry knock. She tried to smooth her disheveled appearance as she trotted down the hall. She swung open the front door.

CHAPTER EIGHTEEN

"Captain?" Twice in one day?

The older man smiled a fatherly smile. When he looked past her, she realized she was being rude not to ask him in. For a brief moment, panic seized her. Ty was down the hall and the man that wanted to out him stood not twenty feet from him.

The captain's gaze swept her disheveled appearance. She felt a sudden fierce urge to protect Ty. She'd lied earlier that afternoon for Ty. Never would she have thought herself capable of working outside the letter of the law. A new respect for Ty and his men emerged.

They weren't bad cops, just cops using what they had at hand to make a case. And now, so would she.

She smoothed her hair back and stepped back from the door. "Come on in."

He nodded and stepped into her house. "Can I get you something, Captain Dettmer?" she asked an octave higher than she needed to.

He looked at her strangely. "No thank you, Phil. I won't stay long."

Instead of the living room where Ty could hear them clearly, she steered her captain into the kitchen.

"Are you sure I can't get you something? Water? I think I have beer."

"No."

She sat down at the table and he took the chair next to her. "Sir?"

"I'm not here on official business." He patted her hand and seemed nervous, fidgety. He cleared his throat. "Look, Phil, I'm not good with emotions and words that go with it, but I promised Mac I'd look after you and your mom. I owe you an apology. I never should have asked you to do what I did. It was my ego, my ambition to nail that son of a bitch. I feel like I've failed Mac."

She felt as if a huge burden had been lifted from her shoulders. Phil smiled. Joe Dettmer had always been there for her family. "You didn't fail anyone, sir. You're a cop, you see something wrong, you want to fix it. It's what we do. Don't worry about me. I can handle myself."

He patted her hand again, then stood. "I'm glad you don't think less of me."

She stood, as well. Impulsively, she hugged him. "Never."

He smiled, his doomsday look erased. "I'm glad we're good. Now, before I go, I need to tell you to get down to the PD tomorrow and give a statement regarding Scott Mason. Showalter and Dunn are on the case, they should be in all morning."

"I'll be there."

As she shut the door behind her captain, Phil smiled sadly. If her memory served her correctly, her father's old friend had no children. Her hands slid down to her flat belly. For the first time in her life, she had a baby pang. The sensation stirred a myriad of feelings, some of them terrifying.

She shook them all off. The last thing she wanted to think about was marriage and babies. Instead, she thought of the man down the hall.

"I didn't know you and Dettmer were so close."

Ty's deep voice just inches away startled her. She jumped and turned around. "Jesus, Ty, you startled me."

He leaned against the wall at the end of the hallway, his arms crossed over his chest. His green eyes blazed. "Imagine how *I* feel."

Shaking her head, Phil played it off and hurried into the kitchen. While Dettmer had asked her to spy on Ty, it didn't mean she was going to. Guilt washed over her. She did ask him about time with the dancers. "You're reading too much into it. It's no big deal."

Ty followed her into the kitchen. "So I shouldn't read anything into the fact that my commanding officer, the same one who tried to trip me up on murder one charges, has asked one of my own officers to spy on me?"

Phil turned around and faced him. "Does he have reason to?"

Ty's jaw set in a hard line. "What do you think?"

"Don't answer a question with a question. Are you dirty?"

Ty stood silent and glowered down at her. "I don't know why, but it bugs the hell out of me that you think that of me."

Phil softened. "I don't think that, I simply asked you a question."

"Right. Simply asked me a loaded question."

He strode over to the kitchen window and looked out. "On occasion, I use necessary means to get what I need." He turned to face her, a flash of his devil-may-care attitude flaring in his eyes. "And some people might take offense to that."

"Offense is putting it mildly."

Ty shook his head. "You're either with me or against me, Phil, there can't be any in between."

Two things stood out about Ty Jamerson, two things that even a blind person could see. The man knew his job; and while he had borderline unethical means to see a case through, he wasn't a criminal, not anywhere close to those he put behind bars.

"I'm with you, sir."

"Good. Now let's get a battery for the heap of yours before the stores close."

Phil quickly changed her clothes and as she locked the door behind her, she asked a question that had been surfacing and resurfacing in her mind. She'd squashed it, but since they were in a semiagreeable state, she blurted it out. "Do you have a girlfriend?"

"No." Ty scowled as he stalked to the driveway, his long strides leaving her behind.

"Have you ever had one?"

He slowed, allowing her to catch up. "No."

"Me, either, with men, I mean. I guess we aren't missing much."

Ty cocked his head and looked hard at the woman walking beside him. He opened the passenger door to his truck. As she settled into the captain seat, he shut the door and took his time walking around to his door. They were more alike than he first thought.

Once they were on their way, he asked, "Why no boyfriends?"

She shrugged. "Father did an excellent job of putting the fear of God in me. And the few boys who had the nerve to sniff around my front door were promptly sent on their way."

"You never snuck one?"

"Once, and look what that got me."

"Ah, yes, Kyle Thompson."

"I was naïve enough to believe he was God's way of punishing me."

"Now what do you think?"

"I think I have some hang-ups I need to get past. But I'm also not into gratuitous sex."

Ty chuckled. "How about some good old-fashioned sport fucking?"

She angled her head and shot him a glare. "That's crude."

"I guess it was. Sorry."

"Why no girlfriends for you?"

"No point. Up until I was fifteen I never knew where I'd be the next day."

"What happened at fifteen?" She knew, but wanted to hear from him.

Ty shrugged, the painful memories of the day he left his mother burning hot. "You read my file."

"I read it, but it was just the facts. At fifteen your aunt Stephanie took you in after your mother died. You went to Parker High School and graduated on time, despite the fact that you had limited regular schooling. How'd you manage that?"

"I read. A lot."

"I would lose myself in books as a kid. Of course, the really juicy ones I hid."

"After I graduated high school I did a stint for a few years in the marines. It was a good match. I could never stomach staying too long in one place."

"I was surprised when I read your file, how much you've moved around."

Ty nodded and turned into the Kregan parking lot. "After this case is closed, I'm putting in for a transfer."

Her startled look echoed his own surprise. Although he'd toyed with the idea for months, he'd made the decision that instant. The inside of his skin itched and he knew the cause was the woman sitting beside him. He had feelings for her and he didn't like it.

Phil felt like a sledgehammer had hit her in the gut. Why should she care if Ty Jamerson transferred to the other side of the earth?

"Who is StreetSmart?"

Ty ignored her question until they were in the store. Walking down the aisle of batteries, Ty picked one up. "Where did you get that name?"

"You sure are good at putting a question back on someone. Who is StreetSmart?" she asked again.

"Sounds to me like a UC code name."

"It is. It's the bastard who set my father up. And I want to find him. I'm going to see Margery Flint tomorrow. She wouldn't talk to me on the phone."

Ty sighed. She was headed for heartache for sure. The decision to transfer was a good one. When she dug up the truth, she'd hate him.

"You won't get much out of Margery Flint. She was uncooperative after she made her initial complaint."

"Then why on earth did IA pursue the case against my father?"

Ty set the battery down on the counter. "Because he was guilty. She just opened the door. Mac wasn't the only cop taken down in that sweep."

"Who is StreetSmart, and how do you know so much about the case?"

Phil paid the cashier and Ty picked up the battery. "Everyone working UC knew about the case." He looked at her fiercely. "Your old man killed himself, Phil. That alone makes one curious. Everyone was talking about it."

At her gasp, Ty inwardly cringed. He didn't mean to throw the obvious in her face, but she was getting too close and he needed breathing room.

"That was mean, Ty Jamerson."

He drove the nail home. "The truth usually is."

"I know you know who StreetSmart is."

He remained silent. He would not give her any more info than he had to.

After repeated tries to get him to talk, all of them failing, Phil finally shut up.

Once back at her place, Ty got to work installing the battery. Phil left him alone.

Ten minutes later, she came out to the garage.

"Would you mind letting me take your truck for an hour?" she asked.

He cocked a brow.

"I have to go to the grocery store and I want to pick up the files from the office."

He tossed her his keys. She caught them. When she turned around and wagged that fine ass of hers at him, his head hit the hood and he cursed loud and long. She was a damn distracting female.

As he washed his hands an hour later, she pulled up. When she shrugged off his efforts to bring in bags, he ignored her. She'd bought enough food for an army.

"What's up with all this, Phil?"

Her lips pursed, she went about stocking her cabinets and fridge.

"Ah, the silent treatment."

"Are you done with my battery?"

"She speaks." He grinned. "Yep, the old Taurus runs as smooth as glass now."

Phil wiped her hands on a nearby towel, then extended her hand to Ty. "Well, thanks. What do I owe you?"

Ty's green eyes sparked, always a warning sign he was in prowl mode. He took her hand and instead of shaking it, he wrapped his long fingers around her hand and drew her toward him. "You're most welcome, Phil."

Her body stiffened. "Don't."

He moved toward her. "Don't what?"

"Don't try and seduce me. It won't work and I'm not in the mood."

The spark in his eyes died and he released her hand. Phil

shivered. As tired as she was both mentally and physically, if she had a choice with no repercussions, she'd love nothing more than to slip between the coolness of her sheets with Ty. But with Ty, there would always be repercussions of the emotional kind.

The vision of them snuggling together appealed to her as much as one of them thrashing beneath the sheets in a sexual frenzy. She was going soft on a man as hard as granite. She'd end up with a bloody stump of a head after repeatedly knocking her head against the brick wall that was his heart.

For the first time in her life, she found herself attracted to a man. Why was it to the one who crowed to the world he was only interested in hit-and-run encounters?

"Dinner."

She shook her head, dispelling the visions and thoughts of what would never be. "Huh?"

"Dinner. You owe me dinner for the battery."

"I can't cook."

He grinned and moved past her, opened the fridge, and gave the contents a long perusal.

"I can."

"On one condition," she said.

He turned, holding the door open. His long legs tightened against his jeans and even though he wasn't aroused, the bulging fabric below his waist strained. She remembered all too vividly the beauty of his cock. Her eyes trailed up the hard line of his abs, to his chest and to his face. Their eyes clashed.

He smiled slowly and she scowled. He cocked that damn brow of his.

She rubbed her forehead. "We talk shop only," she said. "I brought home all of the updated employee files. We can go back over those."

He nodded.

"I want your word you will not lay one finger or any other body part on me." Her temple throbbed miserably. She wanted no more cat and mouse. She needed to focus on the case, not continually find reasons to keep the object of her desire out of her bed.

He grinned and nodded.

"No sexual insinuations, no innuendo, no nothing. Shop talk only."

"Agreed."

Despite his agreement, she didn't like the way his eyes raked her body, halting briefly at her breasts and causing them to swell. Warmth pooled between her thighs and she had a feeling she would regret her conditions.

"Fine, good."

She made busy noises putting the rest of the groceries away. "So what's for dinner?"

"Looks like you picked up a couple of nice steaks here. Do you have a grill?"

"Out back."

An hour later, over perfectly grilled steaks and a yummy salad, they hashed over the case.

"I think," Phil began as she sipped her iced tea, "we need to shadow every Kashmir employee. One of them has to make contact."

Ty slowly chewed a piece of rare filet. "First of all, we won't get the manpower, and secondly, the contact may not be made in person. Home phone, cell phone, or computer."

"Then we get the records."

He smiled, nodded, and took a long pull of his beer. "Now that we can do."

"You take half the files with you and I'll work the other half, compiling what info we can glean so we can start pulling the records tomorrow."

"Sounds fair."

"We'll have to do reverses on the called numbers. I bet we'll have a few surprises."

Ty chewed his last piece of beef. Phil's mind wandered. As delicious as the meal was, she was miles away.

"Where are you, Phil?" Ty asked softly.

Hearing his voice, her eyes heated. She was so tired. The strain of undercover work, her grief over her father's senseless death, all wrapped around her surfacing feelings for the man sitting across the table from her—it was all almost too much to bear. She'd always done a good job of compartmentalizing her emotions. Now it seemed she couldn't get a grip on them.

Sighing, Phil pushed to her feet and cleared the table. Taking the dishes to the sink, she felt Ty's hot gaze on her back.

"I think you should go home now."

"Why don't we crank up that hot tub out back?"

The impulse to do just that almost beat out her cautious nature. Her tense muscles could use a good soak. But she wanted to get to bed early. She had a big day tomorrow.

She turned facing him, leaning against the counter. "I have an early call tomorrow morning."

"Tomorrow is your day off."

"I'm aware. But I have to go make a statement regarding Scott Mason. I want to go see Margery Flint, and in case you haven't noticed, I also have a case to work."

Ty eyed her suspiciously. "Don't go off half-cocked looking for the whodunits in your father's case. It's closed, and the people involved who are still around town will take extreme exception to you poking around."

"Thanks for the vote of confidence, sir. It's not like I'm a trained professional or anything." She turned back to the sink.

Ty stepped close to her near the sink. Scraping the dishes clean with a butter knife, she realized she was gripping it like a weapon.

"Look at me, Phil."

"Just leave me alone. Go home." She continued scraping. She felt his body heat and her anger diffused. Why the hell was it every time the man got within sniffing distance she turned into a pile of mush?

He curved his hands over her shoulders. "Put the knife down."

"You promised not to touch me."

"Arrest me."

Slowly, she turned around and faced him. "What is it?"

The somber look in his eyes caught her off guard. He looked . . . sad?

"Without trying to bully you or convince you I know more, which I do," he said, his sadness erased with a cheeky grin, "I want you focused only on the Klub Kashmir case."

"I can do both."

"You have a hot case, *now*; if you stray you could miss something."

She shook her head. "I can do both equally effectively."

Determination sharpened his features and his grip on her shoulders tightened. He let go, then stepped back from her. "I'm going to say this once and feel free to take it any way you want, but I will not repeat myself."

Phil notched her chin up so her eyes met his. She knew what was coming.

"On the record, as your commanding officer, I forbid you to work on any other case open or closed until such time as Operation Internal Affairs is closed."

She stood silently fuming.

"Do you understand?"

"But I—"

"No buts!" he roared. "Your father is dead, Philamina. And dragging up the dirt is not going to bring him back."

"My father is dead because someone set him up! Can't you

understand my need to clear him of the bogus charges and put a murderer behind bars?"

"I'm commanding you to back off."

"Then tell me who StreetSmart is. Give me that name and I'll have the person responsible for killing my father."

"End this now."

"Get out."

"Give me your word you will not pursue your father's case until we are done at Klub Kashmir."

"If I refuse?"

"Then I pull you, here and now."

She smiled slowly, the effect not meant to be endearing. "Fine, Lieutenant Jamerson, o great leader, I give you my word."

CHAPTER NINETEEN

Through the haze of sleep, Phil's skin warmed, and warmer still were the lips that licked her distended nipples, the pull jerking her hips against hard muscle. Her hands slid down a hard wall of tendons, muscle, and skin. She languished in the thrall of it.

Ty had come back, slipped into her bed, and it felt so right. Their bodies fit perfectly, his hands, his lips knowing just where to touch, suck, and titillate her body into a thrashing agonized frenzy. His big hands cupped her breasts and she hissed in air, his teeth laving her nipples before sucking them like a starved babe. His hips pressed against her and the long hard heat of his cock stabbed her belly. She burned red-hot for him. Opening her thighs, she welcomed him, needing the satisfaction of consummation.

"I wanted this the minute I saw you, Phil," he whispered against her lips, his tongue tracing the sensitive bottom lip.

"Make love to me, Ty." She arched against him, wanting the sublime pain of him engorging her aching void.

An alarm trilling like a locomotive screamed through her mind. She shot up out of bed and looked for Ty . . . but he wasn't there. She was alone, just as she'd been all night.

Breathing heavily, she pounded the offending mechanism with her fist and nearly cried in frustration. It wasn't the first time she'd had the dream. Each time she came closer and closer to Ty filling her.

She flung off the covers and stomped into the bathroom for a cold shower.

Phil buried her lifelike dreams and concentrated on getting an early start, her promise to Ty dust in the wind. It would take only an hour out of her day to get to Margery and ask a few questions. No harm, no foul.

Amazingly, she felt guilty. She shrugged it off. They'd rehashed the kidnapping case until her brain swelled and went numb. She'd come up with a decent list of information after Ty left last night. She'd e-mailed the list to Ty and she'd give it her undivided attention when she went into the task force office after giving her statement and her interview with Margery.

Besides, she told herself, she needed mental time away from the club. And what better way to spend her time than honing her investigative skills on another case?

. . .

Phil sprinted up the concrete stairwell to Margery's apartment.

Just as she knocked, the door opened. "Who are you?" Phil asked the surprised young woman. There was no way this woman was the haggard blonde in Margery Flint's booking photo. But there was a definite resemblance.

"Who are *you* and why are you here?" the woman threw back.

"I'm Officer Zorn, Lansdowne PD. I came to speak to Margery Flint. Is she home?"

The woman shook her head. "No, she isn't."

"Is that unusual?"

The girl eyed Phil contemplatively, then shrugged her shoulders. "She called last night, upset; she said she needed to speak with me. Here I am, and she's gone."

"Did she go to work?"

"She works nights down at the Cutty Sark. She should be home, she never gets up this early."

Phil scowled.

Concern laced the girl's words. Phil figured she wasn't a day over eighteen. "Do you mind if I take a look inside?"

The girl hesitated. "Mom doesn't have much."

Ah, a daughter. Did she know Mac?

"I only want to take a look. No tricks."

She stood back from the door. "Okay. I'm Mindy, by the way, Margery's daughter."

"Nice to meet you, Mindy." Phil twitched her lips into a smile, then walked past her into the small, dowdy apartment.

It was true that Margery Flint didn't have much in this life. The sparse furniture might have showed signs of life two decades ago. But everything was neat and in its place. Plants thrived in the little window in the kitchen. Phil wondered how people managed that. With the exception of Bubba so far, everything died at her hand.

The bedroom wasn't much larger than a walk-in closet, the bed neatly made. Nothing appeared disturbed. The bathroom was orderly.

"It looks like she just left. Any idea where to?" Phil asked, turning to Mindy. The girl wrinkled her nose and stepped toward the small table. Running a finger across the battered Formica, she said, "It's strange that Mom would be gone at this time of the morning."

"Maybe she got a phone call from a friend?"

"Mom had no friends."

Maybe, Phil thought, she scared her off yesterday with her phone call. While Margery Flint had little in this world, if she skipped town she would have taken her few possessions. Or maybe, someone insisted she leave.

"Do you remember about eight years ago your mom was involved with a cop named Mac?"

Mindy's eyes clouded and she wheeled away. "That was a bad time for my mom. She never liked to talk about it. Neither do I."

"I understand your reluctance, Mindy, but that cop was my father, and I don't believe the lies told about him. I need to know what really happened."

Mindy shook her head. "I'm afraid I can't help you, Officer. Now if you don't mind . . ." She walked to the door and opened it. "I'd like you to leave."

At the door, Phil tried again, but Mindy's lips clamped shut. Phil pushed her card into Mindy's hand, her cell phone and home number scratched on the back. "Call me, please, if you change your mind."

Mindy said she would, but her eyes evaded Phil's. As she left, Phil knew she wouldn't hear from her.

Where the hell was Margery? Was she so scared of reliving what happened that she took off? Phil decided to go by the Cutty Sark and chat with the owner, see if she showed up for work last night. Hell, for all she knew, the woman went on vacation. Doubtful.

The Cutty Sark was closed on Mondays. Dammit.

She glanced at her watch. It was just as well. She needed to get her butt over to the PD and give her statement, then head to the task force office.

Showalter and Dunn took her statement without any hassles or innuendo. For that she was grateful. She suspected it was her IA ties that kept the boys muzzled. While she might not be in that brotherhood at the moment, she still had contacts.

After she left the dicks to their homicide case, she headed down to the dungeon, also known as task force HQ.

She wasn't surprised to see the Three Stooges, Ty, Jase, and Reese, sitting at their desks, shooting the breeze. All three of them shut up the minute she walked in, and in a flurry of action found the paperwork on their desks suddenly interesting.

"Boys," she said. Jase looked up from his desk and grinned so wide she thought his mouth would split.

"Girl," he said. A wave of heat flooded her skin as she remembered the way he filled his pants when she danced with his two friends. "Nice moves you got there, Zorn."

Her eyes darted to Ty and his grin rivaled Jase's. Reese, stoic as usual, barely showed signs of life, except for the gleam dancing in his dark blue eyes. She glowered at all three of them.

"I'd like to see you strap on a G-string and pasties and dance for a living."

Jase chortled. "I'll leave that to you, Phil. You're a better man than I am."

She guessed that was a compliment. "Don't forget it."

Throwing Ty a heated glare, she sat down at the only desk left with an available computer in the room. Cutbacks in the PD showed everywhere. It was a wonder Lansdowne managed to staff one precinct, let alone four.

"I have some work to do myself, so if you guys don't mind, pretend I'm a fly on the wall."

"Sweetheart, if you're a fly, then I'm a hungry bullfrog." Jase laughed. "That means—"

"I know what that means, Sergeant."

"So long as you have police business regarding your current case, have at the computer, Zorn. Otherwise, go home." Ty's tone told her he doubted she stopped by for the Klub Kashmir case.

"I have plenty of work to do pertaining to Operation Internal Affairs."

He nodded. "Then get on it."

She worked her jaw, clenching and unclenching her fists, and set her briefcase and handbag down. She glared at Ty's back.

She didn't know why he was being such a prick, and she didn't much care, but she'd be damned if she'd engage him in front of his men.

"Did you get my e-mail?" she asked Ty, not looking over her shoulder.

"I got it. We're waiting for the phone dumps and working on subpoenas for entering the hard drives."

She turned around in her chair and faced him. Three sets of eyes rested on her. "How long do you think that'll take?"

"Maybe this afternoon. I wrote up the warrant last night and faxed it over to Judge Shapiro. Shouldn't be a problem."

"Did you include the Kashmir phones and office computer in that subpoena?"

Ty's eyes narrowed. "Did you ask that because you believe the snitch would be stupid enough to crap where he or she works or because your captain told you to?"

Philamina literally felt the heat shoot from her chest to her neck, then to her cheeks. "Did anyone ever tell you, Lieutenant Jamerson, that you are a prick?"

"On several occasions."

Jase coughed.

"We added the phones to the dump," Reese said, "and the Klub Kashmir hard drive in the subpoena."

"Thank you, Reese, for your professional response."

He nodded and shot his lieu a glare. Phil didn't spare Ty another look. Instead, she shut down her computer. Gathering her briefcase and bag, she stood. "I have nothing more to do here." She turned to Reese. "If you need manpower to seize the hard drives, let me know."

"The geek squad handles that, but I'll keep your offer in mind."

Ty smiled smugly as he watched the door close behind Zorn's fine ass. Served her right. She gave him her word she'd set aside her father's case. She'd pay for breaking it.

He swiped his hand across the fine stubble on his chin. His harsh treatment went deeper. He wanted distance. Needed it. And he didn't know any other way to push her away than the obvious.

"I think you finally met your match, old man," Reese said. He smiled at his commander and shook his head. "That woman has more piss and vinegar than most."

Jase grinned and stretched out in his chair. He propped his feet up on his desk, crossing them at the ankle, and leaned back, locking his fingers behind his head. "Yep, yep, yep, looks like old StreetSmart has a problem."

"I have no problem. You two have too much time on your hands."

"Sorry, man. I can see it in your eyes."

Ty shrugged, stood, and flexed his biceps. "Lust, my man, pure and simple."

Reese snorted. "Uh-huh, whatever you want to call it, you have it bad for her. Can't say I blame you. She is one prime piece of femininity. Worthy of at least a few weeks of my time."

Ty scowled at his man. The thought of Phil and Reese twisting up the sheets bothered him. What bothered him more was the fact that it bothered him. Another reason for him to put distance between them. "Be my guest." Ty choked on the words. "But get in line."

Reese's eyes narrowed.

"Pulling rank on us?" Jase asked.

Ty nodded, sat down at the computer, and brought up a file. "Whatever it takes. She'll be around long after I transfer out of here."

"Yeah, and hating on all of us when she finds out who you are."

Ty shrugged, but his gut twisted. "She'll find out soon enough."

His silence curtailed further conversation.

• • •

Not for the first time in the three years she'd owned her house, Phil felt a wave of loneliness as she locked the door behind her. Despite her lieu's rude behavior a half hour ago, she grudgingly admitted she missed his presence in her house. Aside from her, no one else had spent so much time in it.

It looked like she'd scared him off, why she didn't know. She probably even killed the damn fish he gave her.

She pretended it wouldn't matter, but just the same, Phil hurried to the kitchen and breathed a sigh of relief. Bubba was alive and swimming. She gave him two tiny balls of food.

As he sucked them up like the glutton he was, she smiled. Maybe she could keep something alive after all. Her hamster died the day after she got it for her tenth birthday. Her mother hadn't minded in the least. It took an act of Congress to get her to allow such "vermin" in her house in the first place.

Mother didn't care for anything furry, feathered, or scaled. Hammy the hamster lasted twenty-four hours. After Phil cried for a week, her father brought home a replacement: a little green turtle. Knowing turtles loved the sun, Phil set Hermy in his little water bowl on the sill of her bedroom window. By the time she got home from school that day, Hermy was turtle soup. Both her parents told her she was not blessed with nurturing skills. After Hermy, she believed them.

Inadvertently, her thoughts trailed back to Ty. What the hell crawled up his ass this morning? Was his rudeness his way of saying he'd cooled toward her? Or . . . shit! Did he know about her visit to Margery Flint's apartment?

Worry etched sharply across her gut. She paced the kitchen floor.

He could have fired her on the spot. She sucked in a deep breath. Her temporary lapse in judgment went against her moral fiber. Her zeal to see her father's name restored could prevent her from finding a kidnapper and possibly a murderer.

How much stupider could she be? Taking a deep breath, she calmed herself down. If he was going to fire her, he would have done it already. Relief infused her. He didn't know.

She looked absently around her clinical kitchen. With the exception of Bubba, there was no warmth. The walls were white, the floor white, the appliances white. The place needed some color, some life. Maybe she'd buy a plant. A live one. Start easy. A cactus.

She stepped over to Bubba's bowl and lightly tapped it with her nail. "Hey, big guy, do you want a girlfriend?"

The little fish surfaced and blew a bubble. "I'll take that as a resounding yes."

Phil showered, nibbled at an apple, and basically puttered around the house. Every time she walked into the kitchen, her eyes went to her desk and the drawer that held the files Captain Dettmer had given her.

She told herself it was okay to pore through them again, especially since she was in wait mode for the info on her current case. Technically, today was her day off, so she was free to pursue her personal pursuits, like her father's case.

Her emotional ping-pong graced her with a headache. She

took two aspirins. Long after the sun set her head still pounded. She felt trapped, anxious, like a full-grown cat restricted to one of those little cages in an animal shelter.

She had such cabin fever she was on the brink of calling her mom and asking if she could stop by. A visit was way past due, and maybe, just maybe, her mother would talk to her now about her father, after so much time.

Her cell phone rang. Phil glanced at the display—incoming call, no number. "Hello?"

"Officer Zorn?" The woman's voice quaked.

"Yes, who is this?"

"Margery Flint."

Phil's heart jumped against her throat.

"Thank you, for calling, Miss Flint."

"Meet me in an hour under the Case Street overpass and Old Minion Road."

"I—"

A dial tone droned in her ear.

Exactly an hour later, Phil pulled up on her bike at the corner of Case and Old Minion. She killed the engine and took off her helmet. The whiz of traffic overhead disturbed the night's stillness. Only one streetlight, several hundred feet down the road, illuminated the area. Weak, gray light streamed from all corners. Not a car in sight. Where the hell was Margery? Was she in the right spot? She knew she was, she'd heard Margery loud and clear.

In answer to her question, high beams flashed ominously ahead of her and an engine roared to life. She double damned herself for riding the bike down, and more for breaking her word to herself.

She'd been set up.

Phil pressed the electric ignition button. The engine sputtered. She pressed it again. She looked up. Tires squealed ahead of her.

"Shit," she hissed.

Instinctively, knowing she wouldn't make it out of the car's path even if she did get the bike started, Phil jumped clear of it. The vehicle picked up speed and Phil knew Margery wasn't behind the wheel as it careened toward her. There was no time to jump back on the bike and try to start it, so Phil ran for one of the concrete girders.

The car raced closer, too close. As she rounded the girder the car sped past, the side mirror catching her elbow. She screamed in pain and rolled to safety. The car made a full one-eighty, tires squealing. It came to an abrupt stop. The engine revved, then it started back for her. Phil pulled out her Sig and pulled off several rounds.

Bullets thudded into the steel. Tires squealed again. The car swerved, then straightened, and sped past her. She rolled, trained the gun on the tires, and pulled off three more rounds, spending her magazine. Dammit!

Slowly, she stood brushing herself clean of debris. From a

nearby booth, a phone rang. Ignoring the sting in her right knee and the throb in her right elbow, she limped to the phone booth. "Where is Margery?" she demanded, her breath forced.

A deep male voice altered by an electronic device answered. "That's your only warning. Back off."

"Who is this?"

For the second time, a dial tone droned in her ear.

CHAPTER TWENTY

" have a dancer out tonight, Kat. I need you to fill in."
Micki Donaldson the stage manager wasn't asking.

Phil swallowed hard, gripping the phone so tightly her fingers tingled. "Um, I—"

"Look, Kat, I need you to step up to the plate. I have two dancers out sick and you're my only option. Turn me down and you're fired."

Phil's fight instinct took hold; she couldn't be fired if she refused to dance! But this wasn't about her and her pride. Nor was it about semantics or labor laws. This was about catching a kidnapper and probable murderer. Realization sprung deep in her gut. Like seeing a puzzle piece and knowing exactly where it fit, she knew the person who killed Scott Mason was also the person responsible for taking the dancers. And the killer was linked to the club.

"No problem, Micki. What do I need to do?"

"Good answer. Put a gimmick together and bring your own music. Be ready to go on by ten." Once again, a dial tone droned in Phil's ear. She was starting to get a complex.

For several long minutes, Phil contemplated her situation. She was bruised and sore from her incident Monday night. And try as she might to lay low, the past two days she'd been repeatedly interviewed by the Laurel and Hardy heading up Mason's homicide case. When she'd gone back to the PD on Tuesday, she caught sight of Ty in the hall once. Just a glance of him sent her hormones rampaging, dammit. When she wasn't making a statement at the PD, she spent time on the computer. The PD had a program that could cross-reference the phone numbers from the cell phone and home phone numbers they had pulled. So far nothing of interest, although there were several interesting numbers Milo frequented and paid dearly for. They all began with 1-900. Bud was a good son, calling his ninety-year-old mother daily at the Cedar Hills retirement home. It was more of the same for everyone else.

The warrant for the hard drives was proving to be an effort in futility. Shapiro wasn't having any of it. Their hands were tied. You couldn't shop a warrant. Once a judge refused, your ass was toast.

"I want more probable cause," Shapiro had said. *Grrr.* Give them the damn warrant and she bet they could find all kinds of PC.

She paced the kitchen floor. She was beginning to wear a wedge in it.

Phil felt angry, frustrated, and worse, horny.

The nighttime dreams of her and Ty sweating up the sheets seeped into her waking thoughts. Every day she fought the urge to call the man, tell him to get his ass over here and take care of her.

She needed a dildo.

She also needed a gimmick and to learn the art of stripping in less than six hours.

Ty's eyes locked on Phil the minute she strode into the backstage area. Blood careened straight to his dick. Her ass looked tempting as hell beneath the snug denim cradling it, and the white tank top she wore revealed the sexy curve of her breasts. He'd spent considerable time over the past couple of days plotting how to get between her legs. Repeated visions of him fucking her hard from behind tortured his waking and sleeping hours. So much for his distance methods. He convinced himself that once he had her, he could move on.

"Hey, Ty," Candi said, her full breasts all but revealed in the tubetop she wore. She sidled up close to him, resting her hand on his back. Unbelievably, he felt no reaction. His gaze darted back to Phil, who was chatting with the stage manager. Had Phil spoiled him? The two women laughed, Phil went into the dancers' dressing room. He scowled.

Candi's roving hand slid down his fly. His hard-on flared.

Nope, not completely ruined by Phil. "I'm happy to see you, too," Candi crooned, standing up on tiptoe and pressing her offerings against his side. He couldn't help the groan of frustration that followed or the way his hips bucked against Candi's well-trained hand. "Let's go to your office, Ty, and I promise I'll take good care of this beauty."

Grinding his teeth, Ty swept Candi's hand away. "This isn't the place or time."

He strode past her toward the dressing room. "When will be the place and time, Ty?" she asked, following close behind him like a trained dog.

He heard her words, but they didn't register; he was too intent on locating Phil.

Candi touched his hand. "When, Ty?"

Scowling, he turned to face her. "When what?"

"When will be the time and place for us?"

It took Ty a minute to register what she meant. "There *is* no 'us,' Candi."

Micki strode out of the dressing room, her cell phone stuck to her ear. She gave Ty a cursory nod as she whisked by. If his suspicions were correct, there'd be no arguing with that dragon. He let her pass unaccosted.

"What do you mean, there's no us? What about Lola?"

Candi's voice rose several octaves, the sound irritating.

Mentally, Ty shook himself. He didn't have time for this. There was only one reason for Phil to be in the dancers' dressing room. No fucking way!

"Look, we'll talk about all of that later. Right now I have work to do."

"Can we meet later and talk, Ty? Maybe at my place?"

As he walked away from her, his eyes trained on Bud chatting with a new cocktailer, he said over his shoulder, "Maybe."

So Bud had hired a new cocktailer and two dancers called in sick. And no Phil. Ty glanced around the crowded room. They were a rowdy bunch, and not typical of the club.

"Looks like redneck night at the carnie," Jase said, sidling up next to Ty at the bar. Ty grunted and nodded imperceptibly at Jase's latest persona. Looked like he just stepped off a reggae bandwagon. Blond dreads and three days' worth of beard covered his face. He sported a colorful knit cap, tie-dyed polo to conform to the collar dress code, and skintight leather pants with sandals completed the island look.

Ty nodded. "Yeah—looks like murder is good for business. Not a vacant seat in the house."

Ty swept the room for Reese and found him tucked in a corner, hunkered down under a black Stetson. He'd didn't doubt Reese wore a pair of shit kickers. Give him a six-shooter and a gun belt and he could play the rogue marshal. Ty turned back to face the bar, confident his men had eyes everywhere.

"Where's your new cocktailer, Kat?" Jase asked.

Ty grunted. "Dressing room."

Jase chortled. "You telling me she's dancing?"

"It would appear so."

Jase grinned so wide Ty could have parked a Mac truck in

his mouth. "What a player." He nudged Ty. "Now that's taking one for the team."

He clicked his short shot of tea against Ty's bottle of water. "Here's looking at you, I mean, Kat."

"Fuck you, Jase."

As the night careened forward at a hot-fevered pitch, Ty's gut went on alert. The first dancer slipped and fell during her routine and the crowd jeered her. The next dancer couldn't quite pull off her dance, at least not to the satisfaction of the rabid men. Few women paid for the evening's entertainment. It was almost exclusively male and they wanted blood, or, in this case, pussy.

Milo approached him several times, singling out the troublemakers. Although Ty disposed of them, it didn't seem to matter. As soon as he kicked out the front-runners, more idiots surged forward, taking their place. Bud's quiet resolve and professionalism vanished, the old man's lines deepening in his face. The cocktailers complained about groping attacks and foul requests. The tension inside the club grew explosive. Ty hoped to hell no one lit a match.

After sending off two drunks in a taxi, Ty stepped into an eerie silence. His eyes swept the dark stage. His heart thudded in his chest and he waited like every other male in the place. He wanted to see this as bad as the guy standing next to him.

A shrill whistle echoed through the club, the sound resonating off the walls. The patrons erupted in panic. Ty stiffened.

"Raid!" someone yelled.

The spotlight flashed red and the whistle shrilled again, followed by the wail of a siren. Strobe lights flickered across the stage and fog from the dry ice machine spewed low, clouding the red-and-white flashing lights. The whistle shrilled three more times.

"Stop! Police!" the DJ screamed over the sound system.

Nervous laughter tittered across the room and chairs scraped as men sat down again. But Ty felt the expectation. The fog separated and the red-and-white strobes hiked up their speed, and through the mist the DJ called to the crowd, "Whatcha gonna do, bad boys?"

Phil strutted onto the stage in thigh-high black leather boots, black fishnet stockings attached to viewable garters, fitted beneath a little blue skirt complete with duty belt. A nightstick and cuffs dangled from the black leather. She wore a black SWAT vest and a police hat. And covering the top part of her face was a black velvet mask. Ty's dick jerked hard along with every other cock in the room. He swore vehemently.

She cracked the whip in her right hand, standing straight with her legs spread, her chest out, daring the crowd to come near.

"The badder the boy, the better the chance Siren will cuff you and make you her slave," the DJ taunted.

The place erupted and the song "Bad Boys" thundered through the speakers.

More than a dozen men rushed the stage and Ty hurried

down to make sure none of them climbed onstage or touched Phil. As she wagged her hips and swayed to the driving beat of the music, Ty forced himself to watch the crowd instead of her.

Reese and Jase were already up in front. Even though he knew they were there for Phil's protection, it bothered him. She turned, presenting her back to the crowd, and bent forward to give everyone in the room a great shot of her ass. She wiggled it, wagged it, and rolled it before straightening and half-turning to face the crowd. Her full red lips pouted, then she smiled and turned. As she strutted, swayed, and thrust at the crowd, she slid off one leather glove in a slow taunting strip. She dropped it on the stage and continued to the edge.

Son of a bitch, she was going to get hurt. Ty pushed through the crowd, stopping just shy of the edges of the stage. Siren's eyes locked with his. She smiled seductively and sunk to her knees, her eyes never wavering. She parted her knees and moaned, her tongue darting out to lick her red lips. Her right hand slid down her belly to rest between her thighs, and in a slow deliberate movement, her hips undulated as if a man rode her deep and hard.

Throwing her head back, Siren rode out an imaginary orgasm. As she came, her eyes caught Ty's and held them for one breathless heartbeat, electrifying him to his core.

He was going to have her. That night.

In a slow sexy charade, Siren stood up, her body swaying like Delilah for Sampson. Her long fluid limbs shimmered effortlessly under the flashing lights. Ty was close enough to smell her sultry intoxicating perfume.

Her smile promised torture.

She began her seductive strip, boldly strutting across the stage, daring any man to take her. Peeling one piece of clothing off with agonizing deliberation that whetted every man's libido to bursting, Siren teased and tormented.

Ty's temper soared. The crowd loved it. Phil was down to her G-string, garters, and bra. The music drummed and the crowd surged forward. They wanted to see all of her.

The tension thickened, the crowd grew louder, and Siren's hips gyrated harder. Ty's concern heightened. He caught Milo's gaze and cued him to get up to the front.

As Milo stepped in front of a man, blocking his view, the drunk made the mistake of pushing Milo in the back. It caused the giant's forward inertia to continue forward with three hundred and fifty pounds of driving force. The crowd was so thick, Milo's bulk stopped after only a few feet.

Siren rubbed her ass up and down the pole as if it were every stiff cock in the house. Ty cursed. Siren's eyes never wavered from Ty's.

Bending over, she unhooked one of the garters while wagging her ass at the rabid crowd, then rolled the stocking down her leg until the top of her boot stopped it. She unzipped the front of the leather, revealing her long shapely leg. Kicking off the shoe, the flimsy stocking fluttered to the floor after it. The men erupted wildly. Bills flew from wallets to the stage and more followed when she undid her garter belt and revealed her other leg.

Siren slipped on a pair of heels, dancing only in stilettos, a G-string, and bra. Her skin glowed with a sheen of perspiration, her smooth muscles moved in perfect synergy. She was the most exquisite female he'd ever encountered.

And during her entire dance, she only had eyes for him.

Ty gulped and yearned to have that gyrating body beneath his as he pounded into her. Like every other man in the room, he waited with bated breath for her to take off her bra. She swirled and swayed, grabbing the pole and arching her back into a C as she hung onto it. Her free hand trailed across her cleavage, down her flat belly to her hip. As she came up from her downward spiral, she reached up to the front snap of her bra.

Despite the driving beat and volume of the music, every man in the room caught and held his breath. Except one asshole. Unable to control himself, he jumped up onstage. Just as Siren leapt forward and caught him in a leg sweep, sending him on his ass, a dozen other men surged onstage. Ty leaped up and grabbed Phil, pushing her toward the back of the stage and into Micki's frightened arms.

Then all hell broke loose.

CHAPTER TWENTY-ONE

Ty shouted to Reese to call 911. Bedlam reigned for less than ten minutes before every person, other than employees, was escorted, dragged, or kicked out of the club.

By the time Phil put on her street clothes and elbowed her way to the bar, Ty and the boys in blue had cleared out the rioters, but reporters had swarmed like vultures over road kill, in Phil's mind, not much of an improvement. They were probably lying in wait for something like this.

Both she and Ty made every effort to stay out of camera distance. Phil smiled when Jase shuffled by, smoking a cigarette like a joint and mumbling to himself. He played the stoner well.

Micki hurried up to her, Tammy hot on her tail, and yelled over the low din, "Nice job up there, Kat. Plan on permanently filling that spot. I'll let Bud know he needs another cocktailer." She handed her a bulging paper bag. "Here's your booty call for the night."

Phil raised her eyes to Micki's. "My take?"

"Yep, I cleared the stage for you. You get what those losers throw at you, you know."

She'd forgotten about the wads of bills thrown onstage.

"Don't forget, your spot is ten o'clock. By the way, I like the mask. Good gimmick."

Micki gave her a thumbs-up, then pushed her way past several uniforms toward the old bartender.

Phil blinked. Just like that? No choice, just "you're on at ten"?

"Are you all right?" Tammy asked.

Phil nodded. Yes, she was. She'd been terrified to get up on that stage, but seeing Ty, focusing on him, and knowing he would protect her, made it easy to dance.

"You did a great job, Kat. See you back onstage tomorrow night. Welcome to the dressing room." Tammy squeezed her hand before she hurried past her.

Phil shook her head and groaned. Her elbow stung from her near-death experience and her feet were once again throbbing. But she'd be damned if she'd barter for a foot rub with Ty. She shivered, seeing in her mind the way he watched her dance. He had her undressed before she slid off her first glove. Candi had told her to make eye contact with one or two guys and pretend like she was dancing only for them, so they'd cough up their whole wallet. Choosing Ty had been instinctive, for a lot of reasons. She didn't want to admit it because that would mean she had feelings for him. Feelings she desperately wished she could ignore.

The mask was a last-minute decision, one she was grateful she'd made. It gave her power and an unexpected perk. Her inhibitions flew out the window. She loved the way the men hung onto her every move. And she basked in the knowledge that Ty wanted her.

"Are you okay, Kat?" Candi breathlessly asked.

"I'm fine. Sorry you didn't get to go on tonight." She felt bad; Candi had a baby to feed, and she didn't want her stealing. She handed Candi the bag Micki had given her moments before.

"Here, Candi, for Lola."

Candi gasped and stepped back. She shook her head. "I couldn't take that."

Phil smiled and noticed how Candi's eyes kept darting to the bag. "Well, I can." She pushed the bag of bills into Candi's huge tote. "Next time I need something, you can help me out."

Candi's eyes moistened and she dragged the back of her hand across her eyes, smearing her mascara. "Thanks, Kat."

Her gaze flickered over Phil's shoulder and in a flash her demeanor flipped. Her breasts shot out and a smile lit up her face.

Phil stiffened. There was only one person that could turn Candi on so brightly, *and,* Phil silently moaned, her, as well.

She felt his body heat behind her and her skin reacted, goose bumps flash dancing across her skin.

"Look what Kat gave me, Ty. Her tips for the night."

"What a good Samaritan. Make sure the house gets its cut before you go."

Phil stiffened. Slowly, she turned around. Her nipples scraped Ty's chest. They both reacted, Phil stepping back and Ty grinning like a hyena. "The stage is back there," Ty said softly.

"You give yourself too much credit, Mr. Masters," Phil snapped.

"Do I?" He cocked that damn brow of his and Candi coughed behind her.

"Ty, are you ready?"

He scowled. "Ready for what?"

"You know, my place?"

His scowl deepened. "No, I have too much to take care of here."

With a curt nod, he strode past them both. "What a jerk," Phil muttered.

"He's not, really," Candi defended. "He's just stressed right now."

Didn't Phil know it. Accused of murder, trying to find three missing women, one a fellow officer, all the while pretending to be someone else. Her mood softened. Okay, maybe he wasn't *that* big of a jerk, but he was still a jerk.

"I'm out of here, Candi."

Phil strode to her dressing room, which was not much of a perk, but at least she had her own dressing area and clean toilet. Grabbing her duffel bag, she hoisted it over her shoulder and headed out the back door.

"Hold up, Kat."

Ty trotted up to her. "Where the hell do you think you're going?"

She shrugged, turned back toward her car, and started walking. The balmy night air felt cool after the stuffy heat of the club. "Home," she called over her shoulder.

Ty grabbed her arm and pulled her around to face him. "I told you I would see you home. I need a few more minutes here."

She yanked her elbow free. "I'm not a child, and I know the way." Emotions collided again. She'd felt Ty only had eyes for her tonight and she for him. Up onstage she'd felt a connection with him. His eyes never once left hers.

Her gut churned. Then there was Candi's reminder to Ty about going back to her place, which had struck her jealousy bone. Phil hated that it bothered her. She wanted to believe Ty when he said he wasn't romantically involved, but it was hard with the sexy little bombshell following him around like a lost puppy.

"Just leave me alone," she pleaded.

Hurrying away from him, Phil jumped into her car and sped away. She needed time to think, to get a grip on her emotions. Too much was happening too quickly and she wasn't sure who she was or what she stood for anymore.

When she pulled into her driveway, Ty was hot on her ass. Damn him! He must have broken speed records to catch up or his business didn't take long. She jumped out of her car and ran to her front door. If she could just get in and close the door.

She pushed open the door.

"Stop playing the good safe cop," he called to her.

She entered the house, but his words were too taunting to ignore. She whirled around, her cheeks heated. "What do you mean by that?"

Ty sauntered into the house. He closed the door and carefully locked it behind him, purposely taking his time. He smiled. He liked her this way, all hot and bothered. He was going to push her buttons all the way into the bedroom tonight.

Her chest heaved in indignation and she dropped her duffel. It landed with a heavy thud.

"I'll have you know," she stammered, "I've lied, skulked, and thieved more since I met up with you this last week than I've done in my entire life. Don't give me that 'good safe cop' bullcrap."

"You want to be bad. I see it in you every time you strap on a G-string." He moved closer. Her eyes narrowed and her chest fluttered. "C'mon, Phil, admit it, it's no fun being good."

She backed away. "Life isn't all about fun."

"You're too serious."

He stalked closer, his nostrils flaring as her sexy scent filled his senses. "Be bad with me."

"I-I can't be bad."

"Yes, you can. Bad girls have no shame. Bad girls have fun. And you were shameless onstage tonight. How did it feel?"

The pulse in her throat leaped against her skin. He ran his fingertips across her skin there. She shivered. Slipping his finger under her shirt, he nudged it down her shoulder, revealing her collarbone. He ran his fingertip across the indentation. Her nostrils flared. Her craving for this man was becoming an obsession.

"It felt good."

"It looked good. Let me make you feel good."

His proposition titillated her senses. She knew there were hundreds of ways he could make her feel better than good.

"I can play Kat for you," she whispered, "all night long."

He brushed his lips against her collarbone and she moaned. Slipping his arm around her waist, he pulled her hard against him and pushed her back up against the wall. "I don't want Kat. I want Phil. Uncensored. I want Phil's nails in my back."

Phil moaned again, arching against the hard heat of him. Her pussy throbbed and she wanted to rip the clothes off both of them.

Everything her parents told her ran through her mind. Bad girls were dirty, bad girls were shameless, bad girls got pregnant, bad girls were not respected, bad girls couldn't hold their heads up, bad girls were bad, bad, bad.

But she was a woman now, a woman who could make her

own decision on the definition of bad. She smiled. Ty was right, safe good cop was boring, no fun. It took too much effort. It was time to let her hair down and experience sex on her terms, with the man she chose. And she chose Ty, right here, right now.

Ty's mouth clamped down on one of her straining nipples, and she gasped, arching against the delicious tension of his lips. He sucked through the fabric of her shirt. "Oh, that feels so good." She didn't recognize the throaty voice as her own.

Bad girls might be everything her parents said they were and a whole lot more, but they'd forgotten a few things. Bad girls had all the fun, bad girls had orgasms, and bad girls announced it to the world. Just like Kat. Kat was bad, she wasn't troubled, and Kat didn't care. Phil liked Kat.

So what if she enjoyed sex? That didn't make her bad or good. It made her human, womanly. And for the first time in her life, she found a man who she knew instinctively would respect her sexually. He told her before he wouldn't hurt her and she believed him. She was a virgin in so many definitions of the word.

"Show me bad, Ty." There, she'd said it. She'd taken the plunge. Exhilaration flooded her body.

He growled. His hands pulled her shirt down, baring her naked breasts. He ravaged one, then the other. His passion for her overwhelmed her senses. She wanted more of him. She clamped his head to her, arching against him, wanting him there and between her legs. Jutting her hips against his, Phil moaned low, wanting him to strip her naked.

Ty's hands caressed her breasts while his mouth pillaged them. His hot breath assaulted her cheeks. "Tell me what you want."

She showed him instead, pressing her hips harder against his. He dug his long fingers into her hair, pushing her head back against the wall. His dark green eyes bore into her. His nostrils flared, his face hardened in passion. "Tell me," he demanded.

Heat flushed her cheeks. She couldn't *say it*.

"Say it," he urged.

There was the good way, "please make love to me," or there was her new bad way. "I want you to fuck me until the cows come home." Exhilaration flooded her as the words erupted from her lips. Emancipation! She felt like she could fly.

Ty's chest rumbled and his words titillated her beyond comprehension. "There isn't one cow in this damn town." He nipped at her neck, biting down on her flesh. "So you're stuck with me for a while."

"Wait!"

"What?"

"Do you like me? At least a little?"

His eyes burned hot and he smiled. "I like you enough." He cupped her breasts in his hands, thumbing her hard nipples. "Now shut up and strip."

Phil pulled her shirt off and hurried Ty along with the buttons on his. Unable to unbutton the damn thing fast enough, she pulled each side and yanked hard, sending buttons bouncing off the walls. He grabbed her against him and just when she thought he was going to kiss her, he sank his teeth into the small of her neck. She screamed. He released her and they both fought to drag the other's pants down their thighs.

Phil kicked off one pant leg, then Ty yanked off his.

In one swift motion, Ty slipped his right arm around her waist and hoisted her against the wall. Phil slid her legs around his waist. Leveling herself, she wrapped her right arm around his neck, and with her left, pushed his boxers down.

The hard heat of his cock pressed against the soft inner skin of her thigh. Fear mingled with her excitement. For a startled second, Phil wondered if she was capable of taking him all in.

"I won't hurt you, baby," Ty murmured against her temple. "Just relax." Her thighs loosened their death grip around his waist. Her hips tilted back. The broad smooth head of his penis gently pushed for entry. Her slick folds lubricated him. He groaned at the contact. Phil arched her back, shoving her breasts in Ty's face.

He lifted her slightly and thrust up into the warm wet heat of her. Phil gasped. The sleek raw power of him filling her hot aching void rendered her breathless. Her thighs clasped around his waist.

"Jesus, you feel good," Ty murmured against her throat.

She wanted to cry, he filled her so deliciously. Lord, she'd been missing out.

They stood unmoving for the longest of seconds, and Phil realized he was, with some difficulty, allowing her to stretch inside to accommodate him.

Her eyelids fluttered open, shyness overcame her, and she whispered, against his bare shoulder, "Thank you."

Ever so slightly, he moved. The action sent shock waves through her body. Her womb constricted. She wanted the moment to last forever.

"Did I hurt you?" he asked.

Shaking her head, tilting her hips against his, she murmured, "No pain."

He grinned like the big bad wolf that he was and surged inside of her. "No pain," he repeated, and then withdrew to her gasps and tightening thighs, only to thrust high into her.

Phil gasped, the only response she could give. The sublime feel of his hard hot width filling her to capacity, his strong arm around her waist holding her hard against him, his deep green eyes burning molten and the sharp edge of sex on his face warranted no other response.

Like a finely tuned piston, Ty pumped in and out of her. Phil's breaths turned into short moans of pleasure. Their bodies grew slick with sweat as friction built fast and furious inside of her.

Tension raged through her veins and she wondered why

she'd waited so long for this. Ty filled her up. She was completely woman, completely sexy, completely sensual.

He gathered her tighter in his arms. His lips singed her neck and his teeth scraped the flesh of her shoulder. His tempo increased and every nerve ending in her body burned hot and bright. He hit her deep and hard, and each time he penetrated to the hilt, she wanted to scream. Then an orgasm blindsided her and she did scream. Ty's rough shout followed as he spilled himself deep inside her.

Breathing hard and heavy, Phil hung onto Ty's neck. Their sweat-slicked bodies slid against each other as spasms wracked her body. Her self-induced orgasm the other night didn't come near to what Ty did for her. She wanted it again and again. She'd never get tired of the way he made her feel. She licked her lips. Her chest rose and fell in perfect cadence with his erratic breaths.

He nuzzled her slick throat and licked her salty skin. "Mmm, I'd take that over a piece of candy any day."

She nodded, surging against his teeth nibbling at her throat. "Yeah, not bad."

Still joined as one, Ty pulled her off the wall and carried her down the hall, his fingers digging deep into her ass. She rocked against him, liking the feel of him.

"What are you doing?" she asked, hearing her voice lazy and languid.

"We're getting a shower."

CHAPTER TWENTY-TWO

They stood in the shower. Phil kicked off the offending pant leg of her jeans.

"Ty, wait a minute."

"No."

"Yes, I can't—we can't—I don't have any condoms."

"There's one in the back pocket of my pants. But don't you think it's a little late to be worrying about that?"

"Yes, well . . ." She did a quick calculation in her head. "If the rhythm method is effective at all, we should be safe."

"Even if it wasn't, we're safe. I got snipped years ago. And I'm clean as a whistle."

Sadness swept her. Not that she wanted children with him. But that he would take such a permanent step to prevent a pregnancy. "What if you change your mind and want children?"

"I won't, Zorn. Now shut up."

"But—"

He stooped and pressed her against the tile wall. She smiled. She liked it the last time he had her back against a wall.

"Look, there are too many little bastards running around this world. The last thing I want is to add to the count."

"But what if you get married?"

"I'm not the marrying type."

He reached past her and turned the showerhead on. She startled at the hit of the cold spray of water. He grinned. "Now, I'm going to lather up that sweet body of yours before I have you again."

"Sorry, Lieutenant, it's my turn to have my way with you."

Ty's dark brows rose. He grinned like sin and stepped back, flattening his muscular back against the smooth tile. His cock thickened.

Phil swallowed hard. He was beautiful, in every raw male sense. His skin fit tightly over sleekly bunched muscles. The trail of dark downy hair that ran down from his belly button to encircle his thick shaft was so sexy she wished she could take a picture and sleep with it under her pillow.

She grabbed the bar of soap and lathered it up between her hands.

"That's an awfully impressive piece of machinery you have there, sir."

The thick heavy shaft bobbed. Ty stretched his arms out, then crossed them behind his head. His hips thrust slightly out and he looked as innocent as a baby. He didn't fool her. He'd rocked her world, now she was going to return the favor.

She sprayed his body with the now warm water. His skin glistened. She couldn't wait to get her hands on him.

As the warm water beat down on her back, she lifted her hands to Ty's head. On tiptoes, she ran her fingers through his long dark strands, massaging his scalp. He closed his eyes for a brief second and moaned softly. She smiled. "Feel good?"

"Yeah."

Running her lathered hands up his outstretched arms, she reveled in the slick feel of his muscles bunching beneath her fingertips. She palmed his biceps. Moving closer, she smelled her scent mingled with his, the mixture heady. She inhaled near his chest, loving the musky smell of their sex. She didn't question her attraction to this irresistible man, she just answered the call.

The heat of his distended cock radiated through the pulsing water, its wide head tapping against her belly. Tempting as it was, she had other plans for that luscious appendage.

She lathered his chest, lingering over his hardened nipples. Unable to help herself, she nipped at one. His hands slid down her back, and she shook them off. "No touching."

"Yes."

She stepped back and narrowed her eyes. His cock thrust up hard between them. "No. You're one pushy selfish man, Ty Jamerson. My rules this time, or you can take your toys and go home."

KARIN TABKE

His eyes glowed jade. He settled back against the tile, folding his hands behind his head once again. He flexed his biceps at her, and she knew he wanted to argue the point, but she also knew he wanted her more. And she intended to enjoy her power.

Satisfied, she stepped back between his legs and continued the slow sensuous chore of washing every inch of his body, except the thick inches he wanted washed the most. She slipped her lathered hands between his cheeks after she'd commanded him to turn around. She knew she rubbed too much, but those hard glutes in her hands felt too good to just wash once. She pressed her breasts against his back and slipped her hands around the front to his waist, making sure she came within inches of his cock. His hips undulated against the tile.

"Spread 'em," she commanded, and he assumed the position. Oh, she liked the look of his tight ass smeared with creamy lather and his arms raised above his head.

Changing her tactics, she slid one hand down between his cheeks, then under and between his legs. His balls hung warm and heavy and she cupped them. The gesture sent him to his toes. "You like that, sir?"

"Yeah," he responded hoarsely. Sliding her hand past his balls, she caressed the thick base of his cock. "I want to wrap my lips all around you, and suck you while I'm pumping you with my hands."

He growled. Slowly, she withdrew her hand, massaging and caressing every inch of him as she did.

"Do it," he said in a strangled tone.

"Hmm, maybe I will, maybe I won't."

She wanted Ty at her mercy. She wanted power over him, she wanted him to lose all control and kiss her.

The revelation startled her. Why on earth was it so important that he kiss her? Because, she told herself, it was an act of intimacy, an act he was not willing to give. And she needed this act of intimacy.

Her skin flushed and she dug her fingers into his ass. The plain truth was she wanted Ty to like her more than just enough to fuck her. She wanted him to like her enough to kiss her, enough to cross his self-imposed line. If he kissed her, maybe there was some hope for a future.

She gasped at the thought.

"What's wrong?" Ty asked, turning his head. She slapped her body flush against his back and ass. "Nothing, don't turn around." She'd revisit her feelings later. She smiled—she had a man to fuck.

Phil pushed back the shower curtain and grabbed the squat stool sitting outside, which she used to fix the constantly sputtering lightbulb on the ceiling. Setting it behind Ty, she stepped up, giving herself a couple of inches over him.

"Now, sir, I have control over you. Do what I tell you or live to regret it."

"Stop playing games, Phil."

"No games, Ty, just pure sport fucking."

Did she imagine his cringe? "Isn't that what we're doing?

Fucking for the sport of it?" she whispered against his ear. She ran her lathered hands around to his pecs and plucked at his nipples. Sinking her teeth into his neck from behind, she smiled against his glistening skin as he inhaled sharply. "Answer me," she demanded, still clutching his skin between her teeth.

"Yes, sport fucking."

Hmm, he didn't sound so convincing. She nibbled her way to the other side of his neck, sliding her hands down his taut belly, her pinky slipping across the top of his swollen head. "Mmm, I love the way you fill me up."

In a slow slide, she trailed her fingertips down the underside of his rigid shaft. "Mmm, I like that," Phil said. She wrapped her fingers around the throbbing base. He jutted hard in her hand. "Have you ever made love to a woman, Ty?"

"Is there a difference between sport and love?"

She wrapped her other hand around the long length of him and in a slow deliberate pump, she began to milk him. He filled to bursting in her hands, his skin heated, and she could feel the throb of blood pulsate in her hands.

"I think so. Making love involves emotions—other than lust."

She licked the backside of his ear and sucked in the lobe. Then with the tip of her tongue, she mimicked the pumping of her hands.

Ty's breath came harder and she felt the ricochet of its heat off the tile. "I've never loved a woman, if that's what you mean."

"Have you cared enough to kiss one?" She punctuated the question by stabbing her breasts in his back and biting down on his earlobe. His hips thrust fast and furious in her hands and she felt like she was riding an out-of-control bronco. She doubted she had any control. His body, his muscles, his flesh and bones set the pace and all she could do was hold on for the ride.

"No," he ground out. She could feel him beginning the rise. Her hands slowed their manipulation and she moved away from his back. "Slow down, cowboy, I want to ride, too."

She settled her butt onto the little stool. "Turn around," she commanded him.

He turned so fast, the thick weight of his cock spanked her cheek. She grabbed him with her right hand. "Armed and dangerous, are you?"

The warm water cascaded over him, washing away the lather. She looked up at him, her eyes mischievous, her full lips curved with a promising smile.

The next instant her hot wet lips wrapped around the head of his dick, holding him hostage. Ty thought he'd explode on the spot. Water bounced from his chest down to his belly. The sight of her luscious lips locked around his cock was almost his undoing. He thrust into the warm recess, gritting his teeth. It was sublime, the sweet pain of near bursting and knowing he had to pace himself. Her fingers held him at the base and kept him from pushing too far. He knew he was big, and his instincts told him this was the first dick she'd put in her mouth. The thought pleased him.

He smoothed her wet hair back from her face and watched fascinated, as she sucked and pumped him just like she said she would. The pressure of her lips clamping on him drove him mad. He closed his eyes, savoring her tongue as it lapped him, and her lips as she sucked him.

Her right hand slipped around to his ass and innocently between his cheeks. His hips thrust in circles, like he wanted more penetration. He wanted inside of her tight, hot little cunt. When he'd taken her against the wall he'd felt like he'd reached Nirvana. She had been so slick, so hot, and the tightest fit he could remember. Her pure passion for him astounded him. A twinge of guilt stabbed him.

Lust did not equal love, or even *like* in his book. Sex was a recreation for him. It made him feel good and so he practiced it. Sex with Phil was great. The best. He wasn't sure why it was with her, an uptight lady cop with a penchant for putting away fellow officers, but deny it he could not.

He groaned when she released him.

"Back," she commanded, maneuvering him in front of her so that she was in the corner.

Bossy one.

She stepped up onto the stool, turned around, and promptly presented her ass to him. He smoothed his palm over the sleek wet mound. Running his other hand up her taut belly, then to her full breast, he gently twirled a thrusting nipple between his thumb and index finger. Her tit pressed into his hand and her soft moans of delight filled his dick to capacity. He nibbled her shoulder and swept both hands down to her ass, parting her cheeks just an inch. He couldn't resist the urge to slide his shaft up and in between. He gritted his teeth. If he didn't penetrate soon, he'd come all over them both. "Ah, Phil, bend over."

She did just that. Before he deprived them both of the pleasure of his cock buried in her, he pulled away, but only enough to slip a finger up between her cheeks. He felt her anus tighten. "Get ready for a ride, cowgirl."

Holding her steady with his left hand around her waist, Ty bent Phil over slightly. He couldn't see what he knew would be a pretty pink cunt, but he felt it. He slipped a finger into her and her body shuddered as she constricted around it.

"Oh God, Ty."

Gently at first, he rocked into her with one finger. He had thick long fingers, fingers women loved. She was wet for him; his fingers easily slid in and out in a slow rhythmic cadence. Her hips rocked against him, her skin flushed warm.

She hung in his arm, trusting him to take her where she had never been before. In just a few thrusts he felt it, that spot all women have and few knew how to enjoy. He tapped it. Phil's body tightened and she gasped, "Oh!"

He pressed his splayed hand against her womb and tapped that spot again, this time harder. "Feel that? Wait till I slip my dick into you and hit it."

Continuing to hold her steady, Ty slid his hand down her belly to rub her tight little clit. Her body reacted as if attached to a string and he held the other end, jerking her up and down. Ty loved her body's natural unfettered response to him. All walls were down, she allowed herself to feel, and he loved the power he had to make her breath catch.

"Oh, Philamina, you have so much pleasure in your future." And he nearly came thinking of all the ways he could pleasure her.

He slipped another finger deep into her wet pussy and tapped her spot repeatedly. She screamed. Not a little scream, or even a medium scream, but a scream with both lungs. Her body constricted and her pussy muscles twitched and hugged his fingers. He grinned against her ear and whispered, "I can do better."

Gasping for air, she hung limp in his arm. Using both hands, one on each side of her hips, he speared her with his cock. The movement caused her to straighten before she bent forward again. For a long minute they hung as one, suspended in the torrential feeling of it all. "Ty," she said, moaning, "that feels so damn good."

He withdrew only to thrust high into her. He slid his right hand to her ass cheeks and slipped his middle finger between her folds. Her anus tightened. Gently, he rubbed his fingertip against it. "Open for me, Phil, I promise it will feel great." Each time her ass pushed back in her thrusts to accommodate him, her anus softened. He inserted the tip of his finger and she gasped. "Relax, sweetheart, trust me."

She relaxed when he slowed his in-and-out thrusts. "There

we go." She opened just enough so that his finger made it halfway into her. "Now, let's pick up the pace."

As his cock thrust up into her, her anus tightened around his finger, but when she thrust back, opening up for him, he pushed his finger all the way into her.

The fevered pitch crashed as an orgasm hit her so hard she nearly stumbled. Ty's strong arm kept her steady.

He bit her neck, the hard rush of his seed erupting inside her thick constricting walls. He groaned, the sensation the most sublime he could remember.

It was going to be hard to give this woman up.

CHAPTER TWENTY-THREE

"Did you like that?" Ty softly whispered in her ear.

Yeah, she liked that. A lot. Unable to form a coherent answer, Phil licked her lips and nodded. Ty's next actions surprised her. He gathered her in his arms and pushed the stool away. Her slick body slid against him. She regretted her toes touching the porcelain tub. Gently, as if she were a babe, he lathered her skin and rinsed her. He washed her hair, massaging her scalp with his long fingers. As sore as she was, her pussy tingled in response to the sensuous act. She felt him rise behind her.

"Doesn't that thing ever sleep?"

Ty laughed low. "Around you, apparently not."

"So perpetual erections aren't normal for you?"

"Not like this."

The announcement surprised her, and more, made her

feel special. She frowned. Damn, she hated wanting his approval and affection. He turned off the water and grabbed a towel from the nearby rack. She shrugged off her misgivings. She'd think about feelings and life after the cows came home. She smiled.

"What's so funny?" Ty asked.

"Not funny. I'm enjoying this too much."

"Me, too."

He toweled her carefully, making sure to cover every inch of her moist skin. He took exceptional care between her legs and the swollen flesh there.

"Sore?" he asked softly.

"A little."

He knelt down in front of her and reverently kissed her just above the dark curls shielding her swollen lips. She held her breath, the gentleness of the sensation warming her to wet. His lips traveled lower, and just as gently he pressed his lips to her sheltered clit.

"Ty," she said, moaning once again.

"What?" He breathed hot against her throbbing skin.

"I want more of you, but I don't know if I can take any more."

"I can give you other things than my dick, Phil."

As he spoke, he nuzzled her moist curls. His tongue slid against the full slit of her. She arched against his mouth. The warm wet infiltration of his tongue soothed her and aroused her in a sweet pain. Her lips clenched and her back arched.

When he sucked her clit into his mouth, and his tongue twirled around it, flicking back and forth, she stood up on her toes. She needed something to grab, so she dug her fingers into his long wet hair. He growled. His lips pressed harder against her. Slipping his hands around her waist, he dug his fingers into her cheeks. His tongue lashed out, spanking her hardened clit, the sensations it wrought skimmed alarmingly fast up her body. Her hips rocked hard against his mouth and as sore as she was, she wanted penetration. Needed it.

As if reading her mind, Ty slipped a finger into her hot slippery pussy. She gasped for air and thrust harder against his mouth.

He devoured her. What started as a slow assuaging manipulation turned into a food orgy, her pussy the gourmet dish. He sucked her clit in a rhythm that matched his fingers' in-and-out slide. Heat swept her from head to toe, her skin sizzling hot. The tension mounted, rising to a fevered pitch. Her hips rocked back and forth, faster and harder. She gave no thought to Ty or his needs. The only thing in her world at that moment was his tongue buried deep inside her swollen liquid folds. Her clit filled to overflowing, his finger tapped her sweet spot, and an orgasmic flood riveted her. She gasped out his name. Her fingers curled, pulling his hair. She felt wild, savage, and primal. A female animal being pleasured by her mate.

As the waves of the orgasms crashed through her body, each hitting harder and drawing longer to recede, she sucked in deep gulps of air, trying to catch her breath.

Ty's lips and tongue slowed their hungry offensive, as if he knew continuing his assault on her flesh would be too much.

Instead, he released her throbbing clit, and his finger slipped from her, trailing her juice along her skin where he caressed her. He pressed soft kisses to her thighs, then her belly. Then he settled his cheek against her abdomen, still holding her close.

Slowly, afraid if she moved too fast she would crumple to the floor, Phil remained still. "Ty, can we do that again later?"

He nodded against her skin. "Absolutely."

As if she didn't weigh more than five pounds, Ty stood and scooped her up in his arms. "If you want more, I need some sleep," he said.

"I've never slept with anyone before." Her statement came out childlike. Ty smiled at her.

"Me, either."

"Then I guess we're both getting our cherries popped."

She slipped her arms around his neck, liking the feel of his thick neck muscles tightening under her touch. She loved the way he took control, making her feel feminine. For the moment she had no problem with Ty taking the initiative. It was nice for once not to be on guard, not to be in control, not to be on her toes emotionally.

It would be some time before the cows came home and she aimed to enjoy every minute until they did, the consequences be damned.

. . .

Phil's bladder woke her from a heavy sleep. She was curled against Ty's side, her head on his shoulder and one leg thrown across his. Although early morning light seeped between the blinds into the bedroom, she saw by the clock on the nightstand that she'd only slept a few hours.

Ty slept on his back, his right arm curled under and around her neck, holding her close.

For a long moment she ignored the pressure of her bladder and focused her full attention on the man sleeping so soundly next to her.

In repose, the angled planes of his face softened. His long dark hair fell away from his face, exposing his classic lines. His full lips parted slightly and she noticed for the first time just how long his black lashes were.

His pulse flicked strongly against the corded muscles of his throat. Her eyes traveled back to his lips. She leaned up and brushed her lips against his, surprised at their warmth and softness.

Her blood quickened and she fantasized about him kissing her long and deep, his tongue in her mouth, his teeth nibbling her lips.

The thought and visual aroused her. Would a relationship spawn from what just happened or was this it? Did she *want* a relationship with this complex man? What would it be like to be claimed by him, as his alone? A primal excitement stirred her. She smiled. If he had any idea of the thoughts running through her head, he'd bolt as far and as fast as he could from her.

Not wanting to leave Ty's warmth, but having a need for the bathroom, she slipped from the bed to take care of more pressing matters.

Ty watched from hooded eyes as Phil's silhouetted form retreated from the bedroom. His lips burned where she had kissed him. The act instantly aroused him, the touch sending shards of electricity to his groin, making him grateful for the sheet twisted between his thighs.

He groaned and chastised himself. He wasn't on this ride for the warm fuzzies. But Phil was. Hadn't her kiss proved what she wanted? Hell, she was a woman. They liked that stuff. He, well, didn't. To him a kiss was more intimate than intercourse, and kissing wasn't an intimacy he relished sharing.

He knew Phil wanted him to kiss her. For her it would prove something. It would for him, too. It would prove he was involved, and more than physically.

He was moving on after this case, taking a job at the state department. He was tired of UC and he was tired of not having a life. He needed a breather. Hell, if he wanted, he could take a couple of years off. He had so much money banked, and the hazard pay that went with undercover wasn't anything to sneeze at, coming from both the city and the state.

He heard the toilet flush and closed his eyes, regulating his breath. When Phil's warm body slid into bed and she cuddled up to him, he couldn't stop the automatic curl of his arm around her shoulders.

He sighed. What the hell? If it made her feel good, who was he to deny her?

Phil slowly came to her senses. Warmth trickled across her nipples, the sensation luxurious and sinful. Ty's hot tongue licked at one aroused peak, then suckled it. Her senses came alive. She moaned and stretched, arching her back, inviting him to sample more of her. He licked and sucked the nipple, then trailed a hot path to her other equally aroused nipple. "Mmm," she mumbled. "What are you doing?"

"I got hungry," he said against her skin. The warm liquid sensation traveled up her neck. Her eyes fluttered open. Ty held a bottle of warmed chocolate syrup over her throat, squeezing a steady stream along the curve of her neck. "Breakfast never looked so good." His lips dove into her flesh, his teeth nibbling her throbbing jugular. She writhed against him, reveling in his hard warmth and lascivious tongue. He licked her throat clean and traveled up to her chin, where she felt a smudge of warm sticky syrup. His tongue slid across her chin, catching the bottom part of her lip.

Her fingers dug into his long hair and she pressed her breasts against him. "Eat all of me, Ty."

He squeezed syrup down her belly and in between her legs. With measured deliberate strokes of his tongue, Ty proceeded to lick every drop off of her. When he sank his face between her thighs, the warm firm thickness of his tongue slid between her nether lips, dragging across her straining clitoris with such sensuous slowness that she nearly came. He didn't touch her with any other part of his body but his lips and tongue, and he had her coming unwound.

She wanted his mouth between her legs, she wanted his cock buried so far inside of her she couldn't speak. She wanted to ride him like a bucking bronco. She wanted him to drizzle the syrup across her lips and lick it off before kissing her senseless.

She wouldn't beg for it. It would only have meaning if he gave it freely.

Ty took his time, savoring every inch of her. He brought her to climax with his tongue, with his fingers, and finally, when he slipped deep inside of her, she came undone.

The thick heavy heat of him filled her and she reveled in the power of him. She reveled in the power of their lovemaking and the power of them as one.

She begged him to make her come and he obliged. Not once but twice, before he exploded inside of her, hoarsely calling out her name.

They fell asleep, still connected. When Phil woke several hours later, Ty's side of the bed was empty and so was her house.

Just like that, he was gone.

CHAPTER TWENTY-FOUR

When Ty woke and found himself as hard as Phil's granite countertop, he knew he needed to get out of her bed and her house. His physical need for her made his skin warm, creating a violent itch. He'd never spent more than a few hours with any one woman. Sex was a physical release. Pure and simple. But during the span of one night with Phil, it had become complicated. He didn't like it. As he put on his clothes as fast as he could, he wanted to throw them off faster, crawl back into the sheets with Phil, and hold her against his chest.

Instead, he did what he always did when faced with an emotional entanglement. He took off. As he sped from her house, he fought the urge to turn around. He pounded the steering wheel. There was only one cure he knew of for what he was craving. Another woman.

His cell phone rang. Glancing at it, he recognized the number.

"Masters."

"Hey, Ty, it's Candi." She hesitated before continuing. "I was, well, we were supposed to get together and talk."

"How about my place after I close up the club tonight?"

Candi squealed. "That would be wonderful! I can't wait."

He ended the conversation and the churning feeling in his gut told him he'd just made a big mistake. His brain argued that point. He was no good for Phil and she had become an unexpected complication. The sooner he moved away from her emotionally, the sooner his objectivity would return.

He sighed and turned on the radio. "Lesson in Leavin'" blared into the cab of his truck. He turned it off. He wasn't a fool-hearted man. He was smart. He'd had a temporary bout of stupid. As far as he was concerned, he'd fixed it.

Let Phil be angry. She'd get over it and they would go their separate ways. No harm, no foul. Simple.

Phil lay awake in her bed, the feeling of abandonment burning hot inside. When she woke to her empty bed, she'd made a quick sweep of the house. Not one sign of Ty Jamerson. If she wasn't so sore and didn't have spots of Hershey's chocolate syrup sticking between her legs, she'd have sworn it was all a dream. Not even a note, with a quick "Thanks, it was great."

Grabbing her pillow from under her head, she pummeled it, squashing it up into a little square. Frustrated, she slammed her head down on it. What the hell did she expect? Flowers over breakfast in bed? Not Ty's style. He'd been upfront and honest with her. He hadn't promised her anything but the ride of her life. At least there he'd come through.

She rolled over, planting her face in the soft pillow, sniffing deeply of Ty's scent. She punched the mattress.

She rolled out of bed and hurried into her bathroom. She kicked the little stool sitting next to the tub and screamed out in pain. Her toe throbbed and she grabbed it, hopping on her other foot. "Damn you, Ty Jamerson!" She snatched the offending piece of furniture and hurled it out of the bathroom and into the hallway. "Stupid stool."

Her foot still throbbed as she turned the water on full blast and stood under it until her teeth chattered. Walking from the bathroom as she was toweling off, she heard her cell phone ring. Ty?

She hurried to the phone on the nightstand. "Hello?"

"Officer Zorn?" a woman's shaky voice asked. Familiarity niggled.

"Yes. This is Officer Zorn, who is this?"

"Mindy Flint, Margery's daughter."

"Did your mother come home?"

"No, and I'm really worried about her."

"Have you filed a missing persons report?"

"No—I, I think—I don't trust the cops."

Phil didn't remind her that she was a cop. "Why not? What happened, Mindy? Tell me what you know."

"I can't, not over the phone. Meet me at Café Solé on Mission Boulevard in an hour. Can you do that?"

"Absolutely." She didn't hesitate, not even after her close call the other night. This was different. She'd be in a public place in broad daylight.

Forty-five minutes later, Phil sat back against the wall at a back table in the grubby little diner, nursing the worst cup of coffee she'd ever had the misfortune of ordering. Normally, she took a dash of cream, but today she created her American-ized version of café au lait with the help of massive doses of sugar. She wasn't sure what was worse, the before or after.

Mindy skirted through the door like a little mouse being chased by a hungry cat. Phil stood. What the hell had her spooked?

Locking eyes with Phil, Mindy hurried toward her. "Thanks for meeting me."

"Thank you for calling me."

"You're not recording me, are you?"

"Hell no, why would I?"

Mindy shrugged and sat down. "It's what cops do."

Phil nodded. "True enough, but I'm not wearing a wire. Truth be told, my superiors have no idea I've revisited my fa-ther's closed case."

"He wasn't as bad as they made him out to be, you know?"

Unexpectedly, Phil's eyes heated up and she blinked back tears. "He wasn't bad at all. He was framed, and I know it was a cop who framed him."

Mindy nodded. "My mother would never tell me what happened. I know she didn't want to testify against Mac, but she didn't have a choice."

"Why did she lie?"

Mindy stared at a spot on the table for a long moment before she answered. "She didn't."

Phil gasped. "That's not true!"

Mindy reached across the table and took Phil's trembling hands. "From the time I was a little girl, I knew why men came around my house. I pretended that it was normal, that all little girls' moms had lots of boyfriends. It was the reason I trusted cops. Lots of uniforms came through my front door, and they always left with a smile on their face. Mom was a beat wife, plain and simple, to whoever would have her."

Phil shook her head. Denial clouded her vision.

"When Mac started coming by, it was to preach to her," Mindy continued, "to tell her there was a better way. In some ways, Mom believed him. She started turning cops away. The more she turned away, the more Mac came to visit. There was another cop who was friends with Mac. After a while he was the only one Mom let come around. Mom did other work for him. Until Mac found out."

Phil blinked. So far her father had only tried to save a lamb from slaughter. "What happened then?"

"Mac came by and he was there."

"Who was he?"

Mindy shook her head. "Mom called him Sal. He always

came by late. If I was still up, Mom made me go to my room. His voice scared me so I didn't argue."

Phil's skin cooled. Her instincts told her Sal set up her father. She wracked her brain. No Sal or Salvatore rang a bell.

"Mac came over one night and that other cop was there. He found him in bed with my mother. There was a terrible fight. The other guy left, but Mac stayed. Mom attacked him and said if he loved her he'd taker her away. She dug her nails into his face and he flung her off. She hit her head against the doorjamb. He—he cried, and told her over and over how sorry he was."

Mindy's eyes watered and she looked at Phil. "Mom told him to leave, to never come back."

Phil shook her head. Tears overflowed Mindy's brown eyes, making silent streams down her cheeks. "When he left, Mom cried, then ran after him, pleading with him to take us away, to be my dad. She told him the only reason she was in bed with Sal was because he would kill her if she didn't."

Mindy smiled through her tears.

"Mac picked her up and carried her into her room. They were in there for a long time. When Mac left that night, he told my mother if he ever caught another man in her bed, he'd kill her."

Phil gasped. No! Not her father! "I don't believe you."

"I'm sorry. After that night he came by all of the time, and the other guy my mom called Sal didn't come around again."

"Then why did he hurt her?"

"Sal came back after a while, and Mom started acting really strange. One night a couple of months later, Mac caught them. I heard fighting and things being thrown. I hid under my bed. The next thing I knew Mac was pulling me out from under my bed. He told me everything would be all right. I believed him. My mom was gone and so was Sal.

"Later the next day Mom came home. She was a mess. She wouldn't talk to me about it." Mindy coughed. "Shortly after that another cop, this one I know now was an undercover cop, came by and told Mom he'd been watching her and Mac. That Mac was running whores and he knew she was supplying him with names. Mom denied it. She wanted to know where Mac was. The cop told her he could never hurt her again. Mom insisted Mac never hurt her. The cop told her it was okay, she didn't have to lie for him, he was going to go to jail for a long time. He told her if she testified against Mac, they would drop pandering charges against her. She refused to do it. He told her if she didn't she'd be arrested and I would go to a foster home."

"Did Margery ever tell you Mac hurt her?"

"No. Mac was a gentle man. That one time he pushed her away, it was her fault. Not his. He was a good man."

"Do you remember what the cop who said he was watching looked like?"

"Tall, blond. But it wasn't natural. Long blond hair, and a short Fu Manchu–type mustache." Mindy blushed and looked at her clasped hands. "He was handsome." She looked up from her hands, her dark eyes still moist. "I'm afraid Sal has my mom."

It was Phil's worst fear, as well. She nodded and wondered why he would come back for Margery eight years after the fact. Her skin crawled. Because he knew Phil was snooping around. He was still a cop. What cop knew she was hell-bent on finding her father's killer?

Now her skin chilled. Only one name came to mind: Ty Jamerson.

If she had been gut punched by a heavyweight boxer, she could not have hurt more than she did at that moment. She'd been intimate with her father's killer. "Oh, shit," she whispered.

Confusion ping-ponged in her brain.

"Mindy, I'll do what I can. In the meantime, you have my number, call me if you remember anything else about Sal or the cop who forced your mother to testify."

Mindy nodded. As Phil walked past her to the front door of the diner, Mindy called out, running to her and grabbing her hands. "The blond cop! He liked candy. Root beer barrels! Both times he came to the house, he gave me one from his pocket."

The soft whoosh of root beer–scented breath swept across her senses, and the memory was as distinct and arousing at that moment as it had been three years ago.

Phil's blood drained. Now there was no doubt.

CHAPTER TWENTY-FIVE

On the drive home, Phil processed Mindy's information. Her heart wrung every time she thought of her father in bed with Margery Flint—Ruby, a hooker and a drug addict. She couldn't accept it, *wouldn't*. Not stand-up, decorated police sergeant Mac Zorn. Not her stalwart God-fearing father. He would never betray her mother—Mindy's memory was lax. As a fatherless little girl she must have created a fantasy world with Mac as her daddy.

Phil swiped a tear from her cheek and focused on the road. None of it mattered anyway. Because regardless of her father's guilt or lack thereof, no matter how she added it up, no matter how she shifted the puzzle pieces, she always returned to the same person: Ty Jamerson. He might as well have pulled the trigger. If he hadn't forced Margery to testify against her father, he'd still be alive.

He lied to her when she'd asked him who StreetSmart was. It was him, of course. Betrayal rankled deep. How could she have let herself get so close to Ty? All of the warning signs were there, the bells had rung loud and clear repeatedly. Why had she ignored them?

As she drove home, she wasn't sure what emotion she felt stronger, anger at Ty for his lying ways or disappointment that he was the one. She realized she hoped he would be her knight in shining armor. Instead he was the black knight, one who could never redeem himself in her eyes. Her disillusions went beyond Ty. Her father had culpability here, as well.

She felt abandoned by the important people in her life. Her father, her mother, and now Ty. What was so hard about living the truth? Now *who* is being naïve? she asked herself.

It was a big bad world out there, and she could attest to the fact that sometimes life had many gray areas.

But her father? He had been larger than life in her eyes. He still was.

Mac was a good man, who *might* have made an error in judgment. But did he deserve to die for it? No, he didn't! As her Auntie Jenny always told her, What goes around comes around. Ty Jamerson would get his and she'd be the one to make it happen.

She'd get him, all right, and tonight was as good a night as any. Carefully, she prepared.

Later as she headed out the front door, hell-bent on taking Ty Jamerson down, she slammed into a body. "Captain!"

"Evening, Zorn. Have a minute?"

She nodded and stepped back into her house.

"Something wrong, sir?" She gestured him into the living room.

"A hunch. I came to warn you."

"Warn me, sir?" She sounded like a damn parrot.

She sat down in the same chair she'd seduced Ty in. Her captain sat across from her on the sofa.

"This case you're working. I think for your safety you should resign from it."

"Resign? I can't, we're close. I can feel it."

The man looked tired, as if he hadn't slept in days. "Are you okay, sir?"

"I'm getting too old for this shit, Philamina. I'm worried sick about you. So is your mother."

"You spoke with my mother?"

He nodded. "I stopped by earlier today to say hello. She says you don't call."

Shame flooded her. "I-I will, once this case is closed."

Dettmer scooted to the edge of his seat, locking his hands together between his knees. He looked hard at her. "I don't like the fact that you've gotten thick with Jamerson. He's going down, and when he does I don't want you going down with him."

"That will not happen, sir. And don't worry about Jamerson, I have his number."

Dettmer cocked a brow. "Is there something you need to tell me?"

"No, just a hunch right now. When I get concrete evidence, you'll be the first to know."

"I don't like you working your own angle without support."

Phil stood. "I'm a big girl and a trained professional, sir. When I have something to give you, I will. Now, I don't want to be rude, but I was just leaving for work and I don't want to be late."

Dettmer nodded and stood. "Keep your eyes and ears open. Sometimes the bad guy's right under your nose."

Yeah, and didn't she know it.

"I'll keep alert, sir."

As she followed him to the door, he turned and put his hand on her shoulder and squeezed. "Your old man would be proud. Even though he didn't think much of women in uniform, you've done him proud, Philamina."

Her eyes moistened. She was going to do him one proud better. Lock the bastard up who drove him to take his own life.

"Thank you, Captain. That means a lot coming from you."

He smiled, turned, and pushed open the door. He turned back to her just as quickly. He pulled an envelope out of his pocket and handed it to her. "I almost forgot, this was wedged into the screen door."

She nodded, took the envelope, and slipped it into her oversize bag, then followed him out of her house.

Sitting in her car, she stared at the scrawled message. Her skin chilled and the fine hair on the back of her neck spiked.

Dance for me tonight or I take another one. Did the kidnapper know she was a cop?

She'd bet the napkin Ty found in the bar had the same handwriting. She hurried back into her house and put the note into a Ziploc bag. A slight movement from the counter caught her eye.

"Sorry, Bubba." She'd forgotten to feed him. The little red fish swam furiously around his bowl, his tiny mouth breaking the water. She couldn't help but smile as he gobbled up the three little orange food balls she dropped into his bowl. He was a porker and he was still alive, so there was hope for her yet. Maybe next year, if Bubba survived, she'd get him a friend.

At exactly eight o'clock, Phil strutted into Klub Kashmir. Ty hadn't called and she didn't expect him to. After all, he got what he wanted from her. So why call, to thank her? He wasn't the polite type. She tossed her bag into her locker. That was okay, because she got what she'd wanted from him, too.

"Oh my God, Kat, guess what?"

Candi rushed up to Phil, her big blue eyes shining bright, her red shiny lips stretched into a wide smile.

"What?" Phil couldn't not like Candi, it was impossible.

Candi grabbed her hands and squeezed them, then hugged them to her breasts. A little familiar for Phil, but she didn't pull her hands away. "Ty asked me to his place tonight!"

Phil knew at that moment what it felt like to get gut kicked by a mule. The violent reaction left her breathless.

Quickly, she recovered, at least superficially. She cursed silently. Why did that news affect her? It shouldn't have; she hated Ty and every lying word and action he stood for. He was the worst of the worst.

You're better than Candi any day. His words came back to slap her in the face. She's missed their real meaning then, just after he'd ravaged her against her hallway wall, but with Candi standing in front of her, happier than a pig in crap, the full meaning hit her.

She was better than Candi? Any day? What would he tell Candi tonight? She was better than Kat any day? Jesus, how had she been so stupid? Another lie from his lips to her ears.

She should warn Candi. The thought of breaking her heart almost stopped her but, she straightened her shoulders. Better have a little heartbreak now than a big one down the road. "Candi, Ty's a cheating bastard, stay away from him."

Candi dropped Phil's hands like she had a raging case of herpes. "How dare you speak about him like that!"

This was a losing battle. "Because it's the truth."

"You're just jealous he picked me over you," Candi said, not looking cute in her saccharine smugness. "I saw how you went after him, Kat. You lost, so live with it."

Candi had morphed from sweet to sour in less time than it took to glue on a pasty. Phil backed up. For the sake of the case and her own pride, she refused to argue the point. Maybe there was some truth to Candi's words. Phil shuddered.

"He's all yours. I have no interest in him."

"And he doesn't have any in you, so stay away."

Candi strode past Phil like the Queen of the Nile, all five feet, two inches of her.

Phil's hands fisted. If she detested Ty Jamerson, why on earth did she want to rip Candi's bottle blonde strands out by the roots?

She spun around, right into a hard wall of muscle and bone. Speak of the devil. She looked up into Ty's narrowed eyes. Obviously, he was no happier to see her than she him. She stepped back, not giving him the courtesy of one word. He grabbed her arm, but she yanked it away. "Don't touch me!" she snapped.

His lips broke into a smile. "Fickle, aren't you? Less than twelve hours ago you were begging me to touch you."

Phil slapped him with every ounce of muscle, anger, and humiliation she possessed. White imprints of her fingers flared on his tan cheek. A muscle twitched. His lips narrowed to a thin line.

Phil assumed a defensive position, ready to go to fists with the bastard. She wished he'd touch her, she wanted to sink her nails into his face and rip him to shreds.

He didn't move or say a word, he only rubbed his cheek and stared at her. He was somewhere else completely. Probably thinking of how many ways he was going to fuck Candi.

Then he blinked and a half smile twisted his lips, the action almost like a second thought. "I was coming to find you. You're not dancing tonight. You're back to cocktailing."

"Bullshit. I'm dancing and there's not a damn thing you can do about it." She was dancing to draw out a killer, and if she had to hog-tie her lieu and stuff him in a closet somewhere, dammit, she'd do it. When undercover, there are no rules.

"Are you defying a superior officer's command?" Ty whispered.

Phil smiled, a big one. She sidled closer to him, so close she felt the heat of his body. The same heat that drove her over one orgasmic edge, only to drive her over another more intense one. Hate him she did, and hate him she would, but she knew in her heart and her brain no other man on earth could make her feel the way he did. She'd never have the pleasure of his hot cock between her legs again, and that pissed her off nearly as much as his lying, cheating, self-serving, son of a bitch ways.

"It's official, Lieutenant Jamerson. I defy you," she whispered back.

His eyes burned molten. She stuck her arms out, presenting him her wrists. "So go ahead and arrest me."

He slipped his arm around her waist and pulled her hard against his chest. He didn't seem to mind that they stood in the middle of the club, with several people milling around them. "I'd like to do a lot more than arrest you."

"Don't feed me your lines, Ty. I know where you're going after we close up tonight."

His eyes narrowed, then widened. He released her. Her stomach twisted. So it was true. She realized she'd been hoping Candi had made it up to taunt her.

"You, sir, are a despicable character. Stay away from me." She started to move away, but remembered the note.

She dug into her bag and withdrew the plastic bag. She slapped it against his chest. "I'm dancing."

He looked at it. "Where did you get this?"

"On my front door. Now leave me the hell alone and let me do my job."

Before he could see her tears, Phil hurried past him. She was crying, like a little girl! She ran into the bathroom and into a stall, slamming the door shut behind her. She sat on the toilet and fought back the emotional flood.

Feelings of guilt, anger, and regret raged inside of her. She didn't want to feel bad for wanting Ty, for liking the way he made her feel. Why did it make her bad to enjoy another human being's body or have him enjoy hers? Orgasms weren't solely for men; women had needs, too. *She* had needs.

She hadn't realized how hungry she'd been for the physical aspect of sex until a master had showed her the way. Her skin warmed and she sucked back tears. She didn't want to ruin her makeup. She was human and had feelings and there was nothing wrong with her feelings.

She just wished to hell she didn't have them for Ty Jamerson.

Phil sucked it up. She refused to allow her emotions to clutter up her mission: Find the kidnapper and find the girls.

She had an open invitation from the one responsible, and she aimed to please. She'd dance like Delilah for Sampson, drawing the kidnapper out.

She smiled smugly. And while she was at it, she'd show Ty just what he was going to be missing out on.

CHAPTER TWENTY-SIX

"Yo, Masters," Reese called to Ty, who stood rooted to the floor, his arms crossed rigidly across his chest. Ty didn't acknowledge his man; instead, he ground his teeth and wished he'd never promised Candi dinner at his place. He'd been thinking with his dick, he'd reacted emotionally, and that really set him off. To hell with it, he was canceling on her. He wanted nothing to do with any female, least of all one he had no interest in.

Ty moved slowly to his man.

Reese grinned, the gesture unusual.

"What's the plan for tonight?" he asked.

Ty handed him the plastic bag. Reese whistled and handed it back to Ty. "A gift. Same handwriting as the other one. Our man must be feeling pretty sure of himself." Reese scanned the packed club. "He's out there. I can feel it."

So did Ty. "I don't want her to dance," Ty said, his voice barely audible.

"Why the hell not? It's the break we've been waiting for."

Ty remained quiet.

"What gives, Ty? She get under your skin?"

When Ty didn't respond, Reese went further. "I see. I don't know what the hell's going on between the two of you, but you'd better shit or get off the pot. She's not the kind of woman to jack around."

"I'm not jacking her around. Nothing is going on."

Reese laughed, the sound caustic. Ty cringed. "I see. That tells me you've already wham-bammed her in your usual gentlemanly manner."

"Shut up, Reese."

"Status quo with you. Love 'em and leave 'em, TJ."

"Look who's talking. You could give me lessons."

Reese shrugged. "Not talking about me, man, talking about you dipping your wick in the company inkwell. You know better, especially with her."

Ty's eyes narrowed. "What makes her so special?"

"Other than the obvious, there's the little matter of you putting her old man away, in case you forgot."

"I didn't forget."

Reese clamped his hand on Ty's shoulder. The men stood dead even in the height and breadth of shoulder departments and they each dragged around their own demons.

"I've got your back, man," Reese said.

"But?"

"No buts."

Reese stalked off and Ty contemplated the evidence in his hand. So lover boy wanted her to dance for him? Ty's anger rose. Why the hell didn't she just tell him about the note? Why did he have to piss her off to get the information?

He let out a long, frustrated breath. If he lived to be a thousand years old, he would never understand what made a woman tick.

He pulled out his cell phone and called in for more plain-clothes units to be inconspicuous but available. If they got a bead on the guy, he wouldn't get far once he made it out of the club.

A ribald ditty roared from the wall speakers and Ty watched disinterestedly as Sable strutted on the stage. He looked closely around. Even on a Thursday night, the club was filled to capacity, but for a full house the crowd was un-usually quiet. Especially with a dancer onstage. It set an omi-nous tone.

Ty slipped the Ziploc into his pocket and cursed Phil. His anger ebbed—slightly. He supposed waking up to find him gone with no note and no phone call, not even a "thanks, it was great," would piss off most any woman, and he knew she de-served more from him. His skin warmed and his dick tingled. Philamina Zorn was not like any woman he'd ever known.

Her wrath was formidable. He grimaced, knowing he'd feel the full weight of it before this case was closed. He told himself he did the easiest thing for them both: he could deal with her anger and she could think he was a bastard. He laughed out loud, the cynical harshness of it sobering. He was a bastard, in every sense of the word, and she deserved someone who would put her first, who would consider her feelings, someone, dammit, who would kiss her. He didn't come close to stacking up to those credentials.

His skin tingled and he felt warm and fuzzy all of a sudden. The urge to kiss those luscious lips of Phil Zorn had been hard to resist. He'd never kissed a woman, not the way Phil wanted to be kissed. The way she should be kissed. Long, deep, and wet.

His cock swelled and he cursed out loud. The case was almost over, he could feel it in his gut. Tonight was the night. All or bust, and he needed to focus.

Sable's last piece of clothing fluttered to the floor, but for a crowd so large, the reaction was minimal.

"Siren!" someone shouted.

"Siren!" another man called.

"Shit," Ty mumbled. He glanced over his shoulder to Reese, who slipped down from his perch. He turned back to make eye contact with Jase, who tonight resembled an all-American preppy.

The crowd chanted, "Siren, Siren, Siren!"

Sable huffed with what indignation she could muster, reaching down to grab up the few dollar bills bestowed on her before marching offstage.

The stage lights dimmed and the DJ's voice boomed across the room. "Gents, gents! Our sultry Siren will grace this hallowed stage in a half hour. Have a drink and enjoy the anticipation."

The crowd surged toward the stage, the chant climbing higher on the decimal scale. "Siren! Siren! Siren!"

The DJ spun a hip-hop tune. "Okay, ladies and gents," he announced, "I have a special treat for you tonight. She usually closes down the house with her sweet, sexy, and sinful sway, but tonight Miz Candi the delish diva will share her honey-dew with you now!"

The roar of the crowd waned a few octaves, and Ty breathed a sigh of relief.

The music swelled, a deep jungle beat. The lights dimmed, the strobe light flashed, and Candi made her slow sexy strut onto the stage.

Ty's eyes looked past the buxom blonde to the backstage area, hoping to catch a glimpse of the woman who'd managed to get under his skin.

The crowd wasn't mollified until Candi finally bared her pendulous breasts. They tolerated her offering.

Like Sable, Candi strutted indignantly off the stage, grabbing the few bills littering it.

"Siren, Siren, Siren!" the crowd chanted.

"Ladies and gents, back by popular demand, the sinfully hot diva of the night squad, lady of law enforcement, queen of cuffs, and the spread-eagle mistress, give it up for Siiiiireeeeeeen!"

A siren wailed, red-and-blue lights flickered across the stage and walls, a yellow light stuttered to the beat of the strobe. Dry ice crawled like a downed junkie dragging himself to his next fix, a whistle blew, and "Bad Boys" thundered through the speakers. The crowd erupted, the men hooting and screaming, fists pumping the air and catcalling.

The tension mounted, the expectation high, and Ty held his breath, waiting as anxiously as the men pressed tightly against him for a better look. And somewhere in the club a kidnapper and possible murderer lurked, having eyes only for Siren.

Long leather-clad legs strutted out onto the stage. A bull-whip cracked the floor, the snap of it giving rise to most men in the room. Her outfit tonight was leaner, sleek, with far less to take off.

Ty groaned. His job mandated that he watch the audience. With Herculean effort, he turned, presenting his back to Phil, and scanned the rabid group of men pressing hard against him toward the stage. Beneath the dim lighting, he had difficulty deciphering faces.

His gut churned and he realized there was a name for the emotion he experienced for the first time in his life: jealousy. He didn't want any man to see Phil the way he had. He wanted her for himself.

He glanced over his shoulder and watched, as mesmerized as those around him by the sexy lady who took stripping to a new level.

Deeming his presence closer to her more vital than watching the crowd, Ty moved to the edge of the stage and took inventory.

He loved the way Siren's legs went on and on, an endless luxury. He fantasized them wrapped around his head as she pulled him down to her hot soaked pussy. Ty's blood drained straight to his dick.

"Bad boys, bad boys, whatcha gonna do?"

Possessing her again became an unbearable obsession.

She shook her ass and shimmied it. She cracked the whip on the stage, the sharp sound sending rivulets of excitement through his limbs. If it was just the two of them, he'd tie her up with that whip and have her begging for mercy.

Siren's eyes glittered beneath the black mask. She hugged the pole and twirled around it upside down. Her full breasts nearly touched her chin.

She slunk to the floor and spread her legs, leaning forward, flashing a shot of her ripe cleavage. Seductively, she rolled over on the stage floor, then hoisted herself up. Bumping and grinding in a slow artful cadence, she unbuttoned the front of her leather bustier.

Ty held his breath the moment she pulled it away, exposing her breasts. The men around him panted like dogs after a bitch in heat. Siren strutted to the edge of the stage, her hips swaying sinfully to the wild beat of the music. Her eyes glittered behind the mask. She smiled at him, her gaze unwavering. She touched her breasts, pushing them together, making the mounds into smooth, sweet flesh mountains.

A man next to Ty surged against the stage, but Ty backhanded him three deep into the crowd.

Siren laughed and spun away. Ty resisted the urge to jump up on the stage and cover her from the rabid eyes of the crowd.

CHAPTER TWENTY-SEVEN

Siren worked the crowd. The woman who'd slipped into her skin was not Phil, hell, she wasn't even Kat, she was Siren, queen of the dance floor. Seductress extraordinaire, undercover cop on the hunt for a kidnapper.

She used reverse psychology on the stage. The kidnapper wanted her to dance for him, he'd commanded it. What if she danced for another? Could she anger him? Draw him out of the crowd? Or would he turn on her? Take revenge by snatching another dancer?

He'd gone outside of his regular MO. Now he was taunting. Two notes in less than a week? Siren bet he was close to losing control. She went with her gut and turned her full attention on tormenting her boss.

Swaying her hips to the grind of the music, Siren extended her arm and pointed right at Ty. She smiled beneath her mask and danced to the edge of the stage. She crooked her finger and bade him to come to her. It was so easy. Like a string was attached to his chest, she walked backward and he floated toward her, as if on air. Men were so easily distracted.

When Ty stepped up onstage, she smiled, sucking her bottom lip. Cracking the whip, she slowly wound it around his chest, coming close enough to rest her breasts against him. "A little payback, Lieutenant," she whispered for his ears only. She wanted a *lot* of payback, but that would have to wait.

She tied him loosely to the pole. The crowd hooted and hollered, each man clamoring to be *the one*. Her eyes scanned the audience for the man who stood quiet, his anger apparent. Not wanting to appear obvious, she twirled back to Ty and ran her ass up and down his thighs and groin. She wasn't surprised to find him stiff. She twirled around him again and pretended to kiss him. "Watch the audience for the pissed-off patron," she murmured. "He'll be our man."

She twirled around the pole, dragging her fingers across his chest. The beat picked up and so did Siren's step. She swayed and swirled along the edges of the stage. Jase stood near the stage, and she acknowledged him with a sexy almost-lap dance. She didn't bother looking for Reese, knowing he was ensconced in the shadows, ever watchful. The zealots were the men she targeted with her fanny wagging and breasts thrusted, the obvious. It was the quiet, contemplative man she wanted to draw out.

Strutting back to Ty, Siren stripped off a long leather

glove. She wrapped it around his head, over his eyes. He pulled it off. She did it again, this time with the second glove. He pulled it off as well. Their eyes locked and she read heated lust there. She also read something else. Was it regret? Nonsense. This man at her mercy had no regrets because he didn't have a heart.

She twirled, dragging one glove along the stage floor as she did a split that nearly ripped her in half, then bent toward the crowd.

For a minute she thought she recognized . . . nah, couldn't be. She continued searching the crowd, her eyes watchful.

"Take it all off!" someone shouted. The music heated up and Siren rolled over and stood. In front of Ty, but facing the audience, she slowly slid the zipper down her leather pants. "More, more, more," they chanted.

She twirled around. Her butt facing the crowd, she wiggled out of the snug garment. The men whistled and screamed. The G-string she wore tonight was about as minute as she could legally get without fully exposing herself.

Phil didn't make it easy, torturing Ty with her sexy dance number. Without being obvious, he had to take advantage of his vantage point. How was he supposed to do that and not look like a fool? He couldn't not leer at the bodacious body swaying, twirling, and shimmying in front of him, especially after she flung her leather pants across the stage. The room had collectively gasped when her smooth honey-colored ass wagged in front of the jaw-gaping men.

Ty was not immune. The G-string did little to hide her charms. His dick rose, and so did his anger. He wanted her, dammit, despite her willingness to share herself with the world.

She dropped to her knees and pantomimed for the world a blow job. Ty felt his hips move back and forth with her head and he grit his teeth. The crowd erupted into a wild frenzy and he realized the stage was going to get rushed again if she didn't stop. He flung off the whip and gave the DJ the cut-off sign. She was down to a G-string, pasties, and her stiletto boots; he refused to allow her to take off more.

The music ebbed and the lights dimmed, the siren's wail quieted, and Siren exited the stage to the roaring crowd's displeasure.

"Shows over, gents," the DJ said. "File out calmly or end up in the po-po."

When Ty went backstage, he was met with Phil's fist, smack dab in the middle of his chest. "Don't ever do that again!" she snapped.

He grabbed her arm and hauled her along the short hallway and into one of the lap dance rooms. He slammed the door shut and glowered down at her.

"I swear to God, Phil, I'm going to give it right back to you one of these days. Keep your hands to yourself!"

She yanked free, her fury soaring. This was the man behind her father's death, and the same man was preventing her from doing her job. She wanted to do a lot more than sock him. "If our man was out there, I could have drawn him out. Why'd you shut me down?"

He growled, the sound furious, like a dog who'd had his bone yanked away. "Because you're a little too good at your job."

"What's that supposed to mean?"

He grabbed her hand and shoved it between his thighs. They both gasped. His erection was concrete hard.

Phil played it cool. She opened her hand and gently grabbed him. She pressed her palm against him and he reared in her hand. "Too bad, so sad, no more nookie for Lieutenant Jamerson."

She let go of him and backed away toward the door.

"That's the last time you get up on that stage. It's a safety issue. If you had stripped off another piece, I would have had a riot on my hands."

She stopped. "What's with you, Jamerson? You want me to play the part when it's convenient for *you*?"

"If I remember correctly, you were the one who suggested you strip for me at your house."

"A means to an end."

"So you used me?"

She laughed, genuinely amused. "How does it feel?"

"Like déjà vu. The age-old ploy. Delilah dances for Sampson to cut off his hair and take his power. You dance for me to take my power."

"You powerless? Give me a break. I'll dance until we get

our man, and you'll live with it because you know it's the only way."

"If you push it, you're off the case."

Phil resisted the urge to knock some sense into his thick head. She walked toward him and stopped a foot away. "You can talk the talk, sir, but when it comes time to walk the walk, trusting me to execute my part of the case, you can't. Hell, you can't trust me enough to give me information on my own father."

"I don't trust anyone."

"That's too bad. I think my father trusted you and you screwed him."

"You don't know what you're talking about."

"Don't I?"

Ty's features sharpened before they softened. "Maybe I just wanted to save you some heartache, Phil."

His statement startled her. "You give a rat's ass about someone else's feelings other than your own?"

"Yes, yours."

Her heart lurched. She almost believed him, but Mindy's words haunted her. "You're the biggest liar of all." She could kick herself for giving herself to him, for going with her desire and not controlling her animal urge to mate with him. She had wanted him so fiercely.

But that was before she knew what he did to her father.

She needed to get away from him. Now he was the last

person she wanted intimacy with. As she said the words in her brain she knew who was as big a liar as Ty. While her brain might say no to Ty, her hormones and part of her heart screamed yes. It made him all the more dangerous.

"I'm going to change and see if the boys spotted anyone." She grabbed the door handle, but then turned back to face him.

"I'm dancing again tomorrow night and every night after that until we get our man. If that doesn't work for you, then find another job."

She opened the door and slammed it shut behind her. She stomped past Candi, who stood open-mouthed in the hallway. Phil hoped she didn't hear anything. As much as she was at odds with the dancer right now, she didn't harbor any ill will. The last thing she wanted for the little blonde was for her to get tangled up in the quagmire of this case.

When she asked Jase and Reese if they'd seen anyone suspicious, they both said they hadn't detected anyone out of the ordinary. Even the several men who left just after she split from the stage, no doubt jerking off in the dark parking lot, were regulars who checked out.

"Go on home, Phil," Reese said, "and get a good night's sleep. We'll go through the tapes tonight."

Normally, the guys went over the tapes in the morning, but she guessed because of the note they wanted to jump on them right away. If she wasn't both emotionally and physically wrecked, she'd go through the tapes with them.

Her temper spiked when she pulled out of the parking lot only to find Ty tailing her. The urge to pull out her piece and shoot him toyed with her reality.

She tried to outrun him, but he stuck to her ass like a hooker to a john. Fine!

She pulled into her driveway and hopped out of the car, slamming the door behind her. "Okay, Lieutenant, I'm home safe and sound, no boogeyman hiding behind the bushes."

"Get inside," he commanded.

She dropped her bag and waited for him. She'd had enough. "*You* get inside. I'm not a little girl, and you're not my daddy!"

He yanked the keys out of her hand, shoved the right ones into the locks, turned the handle, then kicked open the door. He pushed her through, grabbing her bag and throwing it into the hallway after he stepped inside. Then he slammed the door shut, locking it behind him.

"Get out of my house!"

He stalked toward her, knowing he was being completely irrational, unprofessional, and downright egotistical. He knew it the way a junkie stole for a fix, knowing it was wrong but doing it anyway.

She backed up. "I mean it, Ty." She pointed to the locked door. "Out."

"No more stripping!"

"No more interfering with my judgment!"

"No more stripping!"

"Would you trust me to know my limits?"

"I don't trust anyone."

"Then what the hell do you want from me?"

The question slowed his steamrolling pursuit. What *did* he want? The answer surprised him. *More.* He wanted more of her. It scared the hell out of him.

"No more stripping."

Phil fisted her hand and raised it to his hard head. He flinched, expecting a blow. Instead, she pretended to be knocking on a door. "Hello? Anyone home?"

"I'm pulling you off the case."

She gasped. "You can't do that! We're so close."

"I lost one cop, I'm not loosing another."

Hot tears stung her eyes. "It's so easy for you, isn't it?"

She whirled away from him and strode toward the living room window. "You have no heart, Ty, no soul, no feelings except anger." She faced him again. "I won't allow you to pull me from this case. I'll go to Dettmer."

"You will not."

"I will. And unless you haven't learned something about me by now, there isn't a damn thing you can do to stop me."

Emotions skittered across his face, darkening his features. He looked like he was fighting a battle from within. For a moment, she thought he was going to concede. After all, there wasn't anything he could do to stop her, short of using force. He wouldn't do that.

When he spoke, his voice was calm, devoid of emotion. "Phil, I need you to trust me on this."

"Trust you? How can I trust you when I know you aren't trustworthy? Hell, you don't even trust *me*!"

He stood stock-still.

"I'm not your mother, dammit. I have integrity, and while I may like being up on that stage for my own reasons, I did it for the sake of the case, to catch a kidnapper. To find those girls. If that puts me in the same class as your mother in your eyes, then you need some serious therapy." She stepped closer. "Your mother was a troubled drug addict. I'm an inhibited woman trying to come to terms with her sexuality. There's a huge difference." As she spoke the words, the pieces fell into place. "There's nothing wrong with a woman wanting a physical release, sexual fulfillment. It doesn't make me wicked. It makes me human. The fact that you have your own demons to slay should have no bearing on this case, Ty. Right now, I'm the key to drawing out our man. Back off and let me do my job."

"No," he whispered.

The man was as stubborn as a stick. His eyes burned hot and the set of his jaw told her there was no compromising. She dug in deeper.

"So let me get this straight, Lieutenant Jamerson. You're taking me off this case because we're so close to the kidnapper, you're afraid he might kidnap me and in doing so make you look like an ass?"

"Wrong."

"Okay, then you want me off the case because you hate me so much you can't stand to see me on a daily basis."

"Wrong."

"Then spell it out for me, sir."

"I won't jeopardize losing another man."

"You won't lose me! You guys can shadow me twenty-four/seven. You can put a GPS chip in my scalp. Hell, you can sleep in my guest room! *I want to stay on this case.*"

Ty let out a long breath. She felt victory near and spoke again: "We've lost three women. We're close, the kidnapper is communicating with us, for crying out loud. What more do you want? For him to walk up to us, introduce himself, then hold out his hands to be cuffed?"

Ty shook his head. "I can't go into details. You'll have to trust me on this. I'm pulling you."

She moved in on him. "What do you mean, you can't go into details? I have a right to know everything you do about this case. Are you holding out on me?"

"As commanding officer, *if* I was holding out, I have that right."

He was holding out emotionally. Just like he was holding out info on her father.

She knew she shouldn't say it, but the words came out of her mouth. "Just like you held out information on my father's case?"

He didn't blink.

"I won't allow you to steamroll me like you did my father."

His eyes widened. She laughed harshly. "I know you forced Margery to testify against Mac. You forced her to lie, you threatened to take her daughter away if she didn't."

Her wrath mushroomed. "You stand there like Mr. Righteous. You're no better than a common criminal; hell, you're worse. You turned on one of your own. You pulled that trigger, ending my father's life."

"You don't know what you're talking about."

"The hell I don't! I met with Mindy Flint. She told me all about you and the guy you worked for. Sal, another crooked cop. Who is he, Ty? And why is he still alive and my father dead?"

Ty remained silent.

"You're StreetSmart, aren't you?"

Silence.

She launched herself at him, her years of anger, frustration, and sadness spewing forth. "You killed my father! You killed him!"

She pummeled his chest, she kicked his shins, she gut punched him. And he stood as still as a stoic oak.

"Murderer!" she screamed. How could he do it? How could he live with himself? Her life, her mother's life irrecoverably changed, her father's life gone forever.

Tears streamed down her face. "It wasn't time for him to die," she screamed. "He thought I was a bad daughter. I never had the chance to prove to him I was worthy of his love." She slammed into his chest with her fist. "Don't you see? He killed himself because he thought I saw him the way he saw me. He couldn't look me in the eye. He couldn't deal with the shame of it."

Her punches weakened. She hit him with her other fist. "He was a good man." Her voice wavered as tears choked in her throat, her vision blurred, her eyes stinging from the salt of her tears. Her body slumped against his, her energy gone. "He didn't deserve to die like that."

Ty scooped her up in his arms and she didn't resist. Her limbs were like Jell-O and her strength was sapped. She rested her head against Ty's shoulder and for a moment allowed herself to feel like a loved little girl, something she'd desperately wanted from her father, but had never received. Mindy, a stranger, had garnered more affection from Mac than had his own daughter.

Ty carried her back to her bedroom and gently laid her down on the bed. He smoothed her wet bangs from her face and sat down next to her. "I didn't kill your father, Phil."

With all the bitterness purged from her, Phil heard the truth in his simple words. She hiccoughed. "I never told him I loved him."

"He knew you did."

Ty stroked her damp cheek and ran his fingers through her long strands of hair. "You're a good daughter and a good cop." He bent down and whispered, "I'm proud of you."

She opened her eyes and gasped. His face was only inches

away. His warm breath caressed her cheeks. She wanted to slip her arms around his neck and bring his lips to hers. His eyes penetrated deep into her. As if he knew her thoughts, his lips lowered to hers. When they met, a shock wave went through her. His lips were soft yet firm, warm and inviting.

Gently, he tasted her, his tongue lingering on her lips before slipping between them and tasting more of her. Phil slid her arms around his neck and arched, pulling him closer. His scent engulfed her. His heat, his strength.

What began as tentative and exploring turned sure and demanding. Ty's chest thrummed and Phil's body responded.

For a man who had limited experience kissing, Ty took her breath away. He kissed her long, deeply, and wet and she wanted more of him.

It hit her that for him to kiss her as he did, so intimately, he must care for her. Had she penetrated his armor?

He lifted his lips.

"No, please, kiss me again," she begged.

"Phil," he whispered hoarsely, tracing her bottom lip with his finger.

"Don't talk, Ty. Make love to me."

His mouth swooped down on hers, taking what little breath she had away.

A moment later, he tore his lips from hers, his breath hot and fast against her own. His hands held her face and his eyes beseeched hers. "Baby, I can't make you any promises."

She kissed him hard. "No promises."

She'd live only for this moment and how she felt in his arms. Special, protected, and her inhibitions be damned.

Ty's fingers trailed up her arms. Disengaging them from around his neck, he pushed them up over her head, trailing his fingertips along the soft inner skin. Moving up on her, he couldn't stop kissing her. It was like a faucet had been turned on in a barren desert. He wanted the kiss to go on forever.

When she bucked against him, the friction of her jeans against his hard-on reminded him of other parts of her body that needed attention.

Releasing her hands, he trailed his fingers to her breasts, the full mounds greeting him like long-lost lovers. It had only been a day and he was starved for her again.

He wanted inside of her, he craved it.

Their lips broke only for the split second it took to pull her T-shirt over her head. Phil ran her hands up under his shirt, then scraped her nails down his back. She tore her lips from his. "Ty," she said, panting, "take my pants off, I can't wait."

Instantly, he had them off.

He smiled, brushing his fingers down the taut creaminess of her belly. "Naughty girl, where are your panties?"

She smiled seductively and scooted up on the bed, opening her knees just enough to give him a glimpse of her moist nether lips. "I like going commando."

In a slow slide, he pulled one bra strap down over her shoulder, his finger trailing across her skin, then he kissed the hollow at the base of her throat and shoulder. Her skin warmed to him, her vanilla scent wreaking havoc with his senses. "You're beautiful, Phil. Beautiful."

She laughed low and husky. "You're the first man to tell me that."

"Then all the men before me were blind."

His fingers trailed down her belly. Slowly, he circled her belly button. Her hips moved in a sensuous roll. His hand trailed lower, the heat of her pussy glancing his fingertips before he touched her there. When he slipped one long appendage into her hot depths, they moaned in unison. "I love the way you feel inside. So hot and wet for me." She clamped her muscles around his finger.

His lips found hers again and the long slow slide of his finger mimicked his tongue. Emotion welled up inside her.

Her lithe body drew taut in tension. A slick sheen of perspiration dampened her skin. She felt wanton, wild, and—surprisingly—loved. While they'd had a meeting of bodies, the action just blowing off steam, scratching an itch, the way his slow hand moved against her and his lips tortured her, this time the act went deeper.

Phil moaned, squeezing her eyes shut and arching against his sinful finger. The tension snapped, her hips jerked, her body unraveled. He caught her cry of ecstasy in his mouth as he pushed her through an orgasm.

Ty's chest tightened. He loved the way her body responded

to his touch, the way her skin glowed and her breasts drew taut and high when he touched them, the way she closed her eyes and bit her bottom lip.

He slipped his finger from her, trailing his fingers up her belly to circle one nipple then the other, spreading her juices. His lips trailed from her bruised lips to her nipple. Languidly, he lapped up her juices. Her breath hissed against his shoulder and she arched into him.

"Patience, baby," he murmured against the heated skin of her swelling nipple.

Phil moaned and Ty lost patience. He shucked his clothes in record time, then slid his body against hers, reveling in the hot smoothness of her. Grasping her hands, he entwined his fingers through hers and pushed their hands up over her head. He looked deep into her stormy eyes and in one slow sensuous dive, he entered her.

"Oh God," Phil moaned.

Pure ecstasy riveted her face. Instantaneously, he felt the rush of his seed and groaned, halting it. He wanted to make love to her slowly and completely.

"Don't move, sweetheart," he said, breathing against the hollow at the base of her neck.

Phil couldn't help her body's instinctive reaction to him. Her hips flinched, and the muscles deep within her constricted in sweet pain.

He thrust deeply, the action catching her off guard, and

she responded, meeting his next thrust with her hips. Ty's hands slid from hers and delved deep into her hair, holding her face immobile, his gaze burning hot. He kissed her hungrily, the tempo of his thrusts matching the beat of her heart.

Wrapping her arms around his neck, she hung onto him and her chest tightened. She wanted to cry, so much emotion clouded her senses.

Her body acted on its own, thrashing wildly in abandon beneath his thrusts. With the power of a tsunami, one raging orgasm after another swept through her body, giving her no break between each wave, her cries silenced by his lips.

Ty's hips battered into her, his thrusts deep and strong. When he began his climb to orgasm, Phil clutched his head hard to her and kissed him with every ounce of passion she possessed, silencing his cries of pleasure as he came deep inside of her.

Once their heart rates and breathing returned to normal, Phil snuggled into Ty's warm embrace. She felt safe, content, whole, and unashamed of her body's appetite and the measures she took to feed it.

"Thank you."

He laughed low, smoothing damp strands of hair from her cheek. "For what?"

"For being the tool to help me lose my hang-ups."

He hugged her close. "My pleasure."

They were quiet for a long moment. Silence wrapped securely around them. As the sexual haze cleared, reality slowly infiltrated Phil's brain. She'd just made love to the man who drove her father to suicide. She stiffened. He asked her to trust him, yet he crowed to the world he trusted no one.

She checked her emotions and her mood softened. Could she blame Ty for her father's decision to take his own life?

Just as quickly, her anger turned toward her father. How could he take his own life? It was a sin of the highest order. Did he care so little for his wife and daughter? Suicide was a permanent end to so many things, and the beginning of a hell for those left to deal with it.

Ty kissed the tip of her nose, then trailed his lips to hers. He knew how to kiss, this man. Not that she had anyone to compare to, she just knew he was good at it.

"I like kissing you," he murmured.

She didn't return the kiss; her mind had shifted gears. His hadn't, his resurging hard-on pressed against her thigh.

"What are you thinking, Phil?" His warm lips trailed a path between her breasts, her traitorous nipples hardening.

"I want you to tell me how it went down with my father."

It was Ty's turn to stiffen. "I told you, I can't discuss it." He took her face between his hands and gave her a pointed look. "There are things still in the works, Phil. I can't tell you more than that."

"You can't tell me how my own father was set up and killed?"

Ty rolled over on his back, clamping his hand across his

forehead. The muscles in his jaw twitched. "Sometimes, Phil, you have to trust people. Could you please, for once, trust me?"

She moved toward him, her hair hanging down around them like a dark veil. "Can you for once trust *me*? Tell me what happened."

He pulled on her hair, bringing her lips to his. "No."

The spell shattered. They were back to square one. The only thing Ty Jamerson and she had in common was great sex. If he couldn't trust her enough to fill her in on the facts regarding her father, then he was no longer welcome in her bed.

"Please leave."

Ty didn't waste a moment. He was up and dressed before she could roll over. "How lucky for you, I made it easy," she said. "This time you don't have to skulk out in the early morning hours."

He fastened his belt, his dark brows furrowed. "I owe you an apology for that. I thought it would be easier. I haven't changed my mind. After this case, I'm transferring out."

"Easy come, easy go, Jamerson. It's what you do."

He raked his fingers through his long hair. "Yeah, it's what I do."

Desperation washed over her; she didn't want him to leave, yet she didn't want to make a fool of herself. Holding onto an unwilling man was like chaining a tiger. "Take that fish with you. He doesn't like me."

Ty stopped at the door. "He'd like me less."

For a long moment, he stood silent and she felt the hard

rush of tears. Twice now she'd cried because of this man, and twice now he was walking out on her.

She wouldn't ask him to stay, especially when she was the one to tell him to leave. Be careful what you ask for, Phil, you just might get it.

"I'll see you at the club tonight," Phil said softly.

A single tear slid down her cheek.

He opened his mouth as if to argue, but he quickly shut it. "Maybe that's for the best."

He turned then, and walked out of her life.

Just like that, wham-bam-thank-you-ma'am.

Phil threw the pillow at the wall. "Bastard," she shrieked. "Bastard," she said more softly.

For the second time that night, tears fell. She cried for her father, for her mother, for herself, and most of all for Ty. He was a walking emotional wasteland, a man of honor in his own way. One capable of giving so much . . . yet holding back so much more. Because deep down inside, she knew while she'd been looking to blame someone, anyone, for pulling the trigger killing her father, Ty wasn't the guilty party. Her father had made the choice.

It was time to put her cop face on with her father and face the cold hard facts. She swallowed hard and realized her image of him would be forever tarnished with the acceptance of his deeds. Mac wasn't entirely blameless. He'd committed adultery; he'd destroyed her mother's faith in him and their marriage. No wonder she had receded so far into her mind.

Phil admitted the ugly truth, yet she didn't love her father any less. She knew her father was guilty of adultery, but assault and pandering? No, Mac hadn't sunk that low.

She sank back into the sheets, hugging the second pillow close, inhaling Ty's warm woodsy scent. As much as she wanted to stay on the case, she wasn't sure she could work with Ty any longer.

She startled at the knock on her door. Ty! She threw on her robe and dashed to the front door, flinging it open.

"Candi! What are you doing here?" And how the hell had she found her address?

Tears streamed down the little dancer's face. "I saw Ty leave."

Gently, Phil pulled Candi into the house. "I'm sorry, Candi." Phil led her into the kitchen and sat her down at the small table.

"Can I have a drink of water?" Candi asked between sobs.

As Phil turned to the fridge for a bottle of water, the unmistakable sound of a gun being cocked got her attention. Phil stopped in mid-stride.

"Turn around real slow, Officer Zorn."

Phil did just that. "My name is Kat—"

"Save it for the next idiot." Candi's blue eyes blazed, the sweet innocent dancer gone. In her place a harpy stood.

"Sit down. You're going to write a letter."

CHAPTER TWENTY-EIGHT

Ty drove like a fiend possessed, his flight instinct strong, his fight instinct gone. When the going got tough, Ty got going, as far away from emotional entanglements as he could get. He could still see Phil's tragic dark blue eyes blinking back tears.

Son of a bitch!

The feelings battling inside him were enough to make a sane person crazy. If this was love, the world could fucking have it! Love? Holy shit. He slammed on the brakes and pulled to the side of the road. Not love. He didn't know the meaning of the word, just that he was sure as hell he'd never felt it and no one had ever expressed it to him.

He thought of life without Phil. His gut twisted, the thought more than unpleasant. It was downright depressing. No one had ever mattered enough, only his mother, and after a while her memory faded and he stopped wishing for what could have been.

He gunned the truck back onto the road, continuing his flight path. He couldn't go back, he had a case to work, and while he was so close, he feared that if he told Phil about her father, all of her emotions would overrule her training and she'd screw up everything. No, he needed to keep focused, for everyone's sake.

Maybe, after the case was closed, they could try. He gritted his teeth. He was locked into the state department for the next two years on a state-sponsored UC sting. He'd made the call that morning.

You don't have to take the job, you can stay in house, he thought.

His knuckles whitened against the steering wheel. He pressed his foot harder on the pedal. He wasn't willing to put his heart on the line just to have it thrown back in his face. Besides, Phil hated him. The thought of her rejecting him was too much. He remembered the feelings from the years with his mother. The lasting hurt wasn't worth the momentary pleasure.

Their positions now reversed, Phil sat at the kitchen table as Candi trained the Sig in her hand on Phil's chest.

"You're going to write Ty a Dear John letter." Candi pulled a folded sheet of paper and a pen from her back pocket and tossed it onto the table. "I'll tell you what to write."

Phil looked up at the cagey blonde. "Why are you doing this?"

Candi smiled and waved the gun. "For the oldest reason in time. I want Ty, he wants you, I'm getting rid of you, me and Lola get Ty. Not to mention there's a market for your type."

Phil shivered as the fine hair on her arms rose. How could she have been so blind?

"*You* picked the girls?"

She smiled. "Yeah, I picked them and Mr. Sal picked them up."

Goose bumps scattered across Phil's flesh. "Who is Sal?"

Candi smirked and rolled her eyes. "Do I really come across as a moron?"

"You did it before Ty came into the picture. Why, Candi?"

She waved the gun at Phil. "Dear Ty."

Phil didn't move. "Write, bitch! 'Dear Ty, I feel confused about us.'"

Phil began to write, changing her handwriting from her usual style.

Candi continued, "I need time to figure it all out. I'm leaving. Please don't try to contact me."

As Phil slowly wrote the words, Candi talked, her voice high and sharp. "Lola's dad threatened to take Lola away. I couldn't let that happen, so when I was approached by Mr. Sal to pay me big bucks to make a few inquires regarding new dancers, I figured what the hell."

"You didn't know he was going to kidnap them?"

"Not at first, but after he gave me more money than I'd ever seen, I was okay with it. Besides, he told me they wanted to see the world and he was showing them."

Phil's hand stopped writing. "Do you know where they are?"

"Maybe." Candi stuck the gun between her eyes. "Keep writing." She smiled, genuinely amused.

"Cooperate and I promise you a deal."

Candi laughed. "No deals, just write."

When Phil began to write again, Candi stepped back.

"Tell me where they are," Phil said, glancing up from the paper.

Candi shrugged. "He has a contact in San Francisco. He sends them over to Saudi Arabia or somewhere. Those sheiks like American girls, and that being the case, they're sure gonna like you."

Phil's stomach roiled like a battery of fire ants marching through her gut. "C'mon, Candi, a deal. You and Lola can start over. Give me the contact in the city."

Candi's eyes glittered. "Does Ty come as part of the package?"

"No."

"Then no deal."

"You won't get away with this."

"I have and I will. Now sign it, then get up."

Phil signed the paper, her letters perfectly formed instead of her usual scribble.

She slowly stood and waited for Candi to come in a little

closer. Phil had size, experience, and strength on her side, not to mention she was in a fight for her life.

Candi wagged the gun, her hand tilted, the weight of the weapon taking its toll. "Why couldn't you leave Ty alone, Kat?"

Phil shrugged and watched the blonde's wrist sag under the weight of the gun.

"He's hard to resist."

Phil pounced the minute she said the last word, catching the blonde completely off guard. Grabbing Candi's wrist, she wrenched it and the stripper's fingers loosened. Candi screamed, twisting away from Phil. Gripping Candi's wrist with both hands, Phil violently shook her. The gun hit the floor with a thud and they both dove for it. Phil was closer and she grabbed it, pulling it to her belly, then rolled over and pointed it at Candi.

"I'll shoot you in a heartbeat, Candi."

"And leave Lola motherless?"

"Lola lost her mom the day she was paid for the first girl. She'll be better off with her father."

Candi shrieked. "Her father's a prick! You can't do this to me!"

"Turn over Mr. Sal and I'll make sure the DA goes easy on you."

Candi visibly paled. "He'll kill me."

"Who is he, Candi?"

Candi's eyes widened and she looked past Phil. Her face lost more color.

"I believe we've met, Philamina."

Phil's blood ran cold. Her nightmare worsened. She stood and backed away from Candi, then slowly she turned. "Captain Dettmer?"

He nodded. The nickel-plated semi in his hand reflected the ceiling light. "Candi, be a good girl and take the gun from Officer Zorn."

Candi snatched it out of her hand. Submissively, she cowered. "I wasn't going to tell her, I swear."

Dettmer smiled. His yellow teeth caught the ceiling light in an ugly glare. "I know you weren't, Candi. You know what would happen to Lola if you did."

"You were in the club tonight," Phil said.

"You read the note. Did you doubt it?"

Phil cursed. Despite his cover, she'd recognized him. She hadn't believed her own eyes. Once again, she'd ignored her instincts. She promised herself then and there she would never question them again—*if* she survived this nightmare.

"You were leaving the note on my door when I opened it."

His grin widened. "I made a quick recovery, wouldn't you say?"

"Why, Captain?"

He tsked and stepped closer. His dark eyes glowed malevolently. "Full of questions, just like Mac. It's what got him killed, you know."

Phil's chest ached. "What?"

Dettmer smiled. "There you go again." His eyes raked her from head to toe. "You look like a woman who's been recently well fucked."

Candi gasped.

"I have plans for you, Philamina. For the both of us." He had the look of a lunatic. Phil backed away. "I tried getting rid of that most interfering lieutenant of yours," Dettmer continued. "I was sure they'd nail him for Mason."

"*You* killed Scott?"

He smiled. "I didn't think you'd lie to IA, Phil. I know Jamerson left here well before eight A.M. But you lied to protect him. And he lied to protect you. How sweet. That man doesn't have a decent bone in his body and all of a sudden, he has integrity? You must be one hell of a treat in bed."

"How did my father die?"

"He put the barrel of a shotgun in his mouth and pulled the trigger." Dettmer laughed. "I watched."

"Why?" she whispered, pain tightening her chest.

"Because, Phil, Mac was on the verge of exposing him." Ty's deep voice startled them all.

He stood at the entryway to the kitchen, each hand filled with a Sig.

As cool as an ice cube, Dettmer laughed. "Ah, the prodigal stud returns."

"You've been found out, Captain," Ty said, the barrel of his gun aimed at Dettmer's chest.

Dettmer chuckled, unshaken. "So it would seem." The next instant Dettmer pulled the same trick Phil had earlier on Candi. He dove for Phil.

Confusion reined. In the blur of it, Phil ducked out of Dettmer's reach, heard Ty's yells to move away, and Candi's shrieks, followed by two gunshots.

Candi's body fell back on her, knocking her to the floor. In the fight for her life, knowing there was nothing she could do for Candi if she were hit, Phil grabbed the gun from her lax fingers.

She rolled away and popped up on her knees, training the gun on Dettmer, who leaned against the far wall of the kitchen, his free hand pressed to the spreading red stain on his shoulder, the gun in his other hand pointed right at Phil's head. Ty stepped deeper into the room, both barrels trained on their captain. Phil slowly stood up.

Fleetingly, she realized she hadn't been hit and then wondered why the hell the dancer had shot Dettmer. He was her ticket out of there.

They stood in her kitchen, Phil, Ty, and Dettmer in the classic Mexican standoff.

"Mac," Ty explained to Phil, "was set up from the get-go. Dettmer had us all believing your old man went rogue."

"What changed your mind?" Phil asked, not taking her eyes off the dirty cop.

"Mac had tapes. Margery kept them for him. But Dettmer knew something was up, and he kept Margery from her daughter. Dettmer got Margery hooked on heroin. He had her turned into a junkie in less than a week. She turned on Mac. Dettmer had complete control. He used Margery to get to Mac."

"Was my father unfaithful to my mother?"

Dettmer laughed. "He was as close to unfaithful as you could get. He took that addict under his wing and that scrawny daughter of hers and kept them. I caught them in bed one night. Not sex, just Mac acting like the knight in shining armor. I took a picture and threatened to tell your mother.

"That's when he threatened to expose me. I had Margery running whores for me, and I was selling them to my contact in San Fran."

"But the heroin won," Phil said, understanding so much now. "If my father was innocent, why did he kill himself?"

Dettmer grinned, the ceiling light bouncing eerily off his yellow canines. "I told him if he ate his shotgun, I'd make sure you and Vivian were taken care of."

"You forced him to commit suicide?" Phil asked, disbelieving the horror her father had endured.

"No one could force Saint Macdonald to do anything he didn't want to do. He refused. Said he'd never betray you or Vivian or the lousy department."

Phil's brows knit together in confusion. "But—"

"I did it for him." Dettmer's cold confession stunned her. Hate spiraled out of control from her gut. Grief hit Phil square in the chest. For a brief second, she saw black. She gulped for air. Her body warmed, cold perspiration coated her body, and for a minute she thought she might faint. Her father, a victim of the most heinous of crimes. Murder by cop.

"You son of a bitch. You shot him in cold blood!" Phil screamed, remembering how her mother pleaded with the chief and the city for money and continued benefits. Her efforts fell on deaf ears, the Zorn name blacklisted.

"He never had the hero's funeral he deserved and we never saw a penny from the association or the city."

Dettmer shrugged. "Shit happens."

Phil gasped. "You're evil, Captain. I hope you burn in hell."

He rewarded her statement with a slow acknowledging nod.

"We've got you, Dettmer," Ty said. "We knew you set Mac up, and we waited a long time to get you. Our patience paid off. We've got you on tape watching Phil, we have you on tape in the club, we have you on tape paying Candi. We have you."

Phil's anger erupted, this time at her lieu. A dawning settled over her. "You knew all along it was him and didn't inform me?"

Ty nodded. "I couldn't tell you. We needed him to lead us to his contact in the city. We needed him to hang himself. I was afraid your emotions would impede your work."

"Why did you force Margery to testify against my father?"

"Because I believed at the time he assaulted her. It wasn't until after his murder that I knew I'd made a mistake."

Phil dared not look at Ty as he spoke.

"I'm sorry, Phil. I'm sorry I didn't get to him in time."

The regret in his voice was deep and genuine. Emotions so deep, so painful, so utterly heartbreaking engulfed her. Phil pulled back the hammer of the hand gun and aimed at Dettmer's head.

"Don't do it, Phil," Ty said, moving closer to her. "He deserves prison."

She battled every moral she believed in—but an eye for an eye burned hotter than her ingrained moral fiber. Her finger pulled steadily on the trigger.

Dettmer's eyes glittered, malice emanating from his every pore. "Go ahead, Phil, do it. Make it easy for me." He laughed. "Make it easy for me, like your father made it easy for me."

"Shut up," she whispered.

"He cried like a woman, begging me to spare his life."

"Liar."

"Pull the trigger, Phil."

Ty stood six feet to her right. She felt his strength. She wanted it all to be over. "Phil, let's bring him in the right way."

Tears filled her eyes, their hot sting blurring her vision.

"Why should we?"

"Because," Ty said, "it's the right thing to do."

She wiped her eyes with the back of her hand. Dettmer made his move. He lunged straight at her and she pulled the trigger. The sickening sound of a bullet penetrating flesh, Dettmer's groan, and his gun hitting the floor, then skittering across it, all played out in slow motion before her eyes.

His expression incredulous, he pulled his hands away from his chest and stared in shock at the sticky blood covering them. Blood seeped onto his white shirt, spreading quickly. Slowly he backed up, stopping when his back hit the wall next to her desk. He slid down the wall, leaving a bloody smear in his wake.

Phil watched the spark of life flicker out of his eyes. She shuddered and with no regret hoped he'd be tortured in hell. Her hand dropped to her side, loosening its grip on the gun. She turned to Ty and took a step toward him.

Ty yelled something, her foggy state not deciphering his words. An instant later, the gun was ripped from her grasp.

In her foggy dream state, she turned to find Candi aiming the gun at her.

Phil shook her head. Slowly, the fog cleared. "Why did you shoot Dettmer?"

Candi's eyes darted to Ty, then back to Phil. "He's Lola's father. He told me if I screwed up, he'd take her." She sneered and jabbed the gun at Ty. "Give me your keys," she said.

"Don't do this, Candi," Phil pleaded.

Candi turned hate-filled eyes on her. "You've ruined everything. He was supposed to love me, not you!"

Ty dangled the keys to his truck in front of Candi. She grabbed them, keeping the barrel of the gun pointed at Phil. The second she turned, Phil rushed her, shoving her against the wall. Air rushed with a *whoof* from Candi's chest. The gun went off and time stood still.

Phil expected to feel pain, but she felt nothing. Candi's body went limp, then mimicked Dettmer's slow slide to the floor.

Phil stood in stunned silence. Candi's blue eyes dulled as her life ended. A bitter wave of sadness swept over Phil. Little Lola would never grow up knowing the love of her parents.

Ty grabbed Phil and pulled her out to the front porch, away from the carnage, and hugged her close. He stroked her hair and whispered against her forehead, "I'm sorry about your father, Phil, but I didn't kill him." She nodded against his chest, grateful beyond words that Ty had no hand in her father's death. She drew in a deep breath.

"He can finally have an honorable burial," Ty offered.

Phil's heart swelled. It's what her father had wanted, it was what he deserved. Maybe then they could all move forward.

Phil pulled back from Ty just enough to see his face but still stay wrapped in his comforting embrace. "Why did you come back here?"

His jaw twitched and his face went rigid. She drew back. Her heart steeled for another blow. She didn't know if she could take more. She took a deep breath and when she exhaled, her breath wavered. "Tell me."

He inhaled a deep breath and let it out slowly. "Because, I want you."

Relief flooded her system. "Oh, really? What about me do you want?"

"Everything."

"Not just sex?"

"Not just sex."

Joy lit up her world, despite the bodies in her house and having learned of her father's betrayal by one of their own. Accepting that her father was not perfect, she smiled, hopeful there might be a future with Ty.

"Promise to tell the truth, the whole truth, and nothing but the truth, so help you God," she said.

"I promise."

She smiled brighter and wrapped her arms around his neck. "You have to kiss me whenever I ask."

His lips lowered to her and he kissed her, long, deeply, and wet.

"You don't have to ask," he whispered against her mouth before kissing her the way she wanted to be kissed for the rest of her life.

EPILOGUE

3 months later

"You look beat, baby," Ty said.

Philamina nodded. She reached over and squeezed Ty's hand resting on the steering wheel. She closed her eyes and let out a long, tired breath. Her eyes were sore, scratchy from her tears. She knew when she opened them she would wince. Her heart, while so full in one area, was depleted in another.

She missed her father.

"C'mon," Ty urged, turning off the ignition. "We're home."

Phil nodded, not wanting to open her raw eyes and feel the sharp sting of sunshine on them.

Instead she let Ty come around and open the truck door for her. He literally dragged her out, her body useless.

Ty gathered her up into his arms and finally she opened her eyes. His eyes met her gaze, and fresh tears welled. Ty's deep green eyes expressed his heart. He kissed the tip of her nose and hugged her close. She melted into him.

He turned with her in his arms and kicked the car door shut with his right foot.

As he walked from the driveway of his house to the front door, he said, "It was good to see Mac finally laid to rest with the honor he deserved."

Phil nodded and hiccupped against his chest.

Keys in hand, Ty slid one into the lock and pushed the front door open, then kicked it closed.

Instead of taking Phil down the hall to their bedroom, he walked into the sunroom off the kitchen, her favorite room.

If any room could spark life into her it was this one. After the work she'd put into transforming the space from a storage area into a living, breathing entity, he wasn't sure which one of them had been more amazed by her talent. Ficus, rhododendron, ivy, and orchids colored the walls and floor, bringing the room alive, the scents almost as intoxicating to him as her own. In the corner, away from the sunlight, in a large bowl, Bubba happily swam around. The bowl next to him teamed with colorful fish.

He set her down on the cushioned rattan chair nearest Bubba.

"Your fish is floating," Ty said.

Phil gasped and came to life. Her eyes popped open and she jackknifed out of the chair. When her eyes landed on Bubba swimming at the surface, blowing bubbles for food, she turned around and punched Ty in the chest.

His loud whoosh of breath made her smile.

"Don't ever do that again."

Ty took his punishment, and would have done it again to get her to react. This depressed state she'd assumed the last few weeks more than concerned him. The PD shrink said it was delayed Post-Traumatic Stress Disorder. Ty thought that was bullshit. The woman was still grieving for her dead father. His heart tightened with compassion. He'd move heaven and earth to ease her pain.

He sat facing her, their knees touching. He smoothed the fabric of her skirt across her knees and looked her directly in the eyes.

"Phil, you need to stop this."

Her eyes filled with tears. "I can't."

"Yes, you can. Today, believe it or not, was a good day."

"How can you say that? I buried my father for a second time." Slow tears tracked down her cheeks.

"Did you ever think you would see Mac get the honor guard he received today? Hell, cops from five states showed up to pay their respects. Over five hundred strong. He got his due. A Medal of Valor, a full police funeral, and his rank and pension reinstated."

"He never should have died in the first place."

"You're right, but we can't change the past, only our future choices." He moved closer. "Look, even your mom has started to come out of her twilight zone. She smiled at me!"

Phil attempted a smile through her tears, but it looked more like a grimace.

"She needs you, Phil, and while you may not think so, you need her too." He looked intently at her, and squeezed her knees. "I need you."

She nodded and wiped her cheek with the back of her hand. "I know."

"You did good, baby. Your first time out. We got the bad guys, found the kidnapped girls, and learned the truth about your dad. Now it's time to move on—or all of the what-ifs will eat you up."

"Martens is in serious therapy."

"She should be. All three of them have been through hell."

"I'm going back into IA."

Ty wasn't surprised. "You're a damn good investigator."

Her tears slowed, she hiccuped and sniffed. "You taught me there are two sides to every cop's story. I think I'm better qualified now to see that and not rush to judge. I don't want what happened to my father to happen to another cop." She looked at him and more tears welled in her eyes. "If I was left to my own devices three years ago, I would have hung you out to dry." She slid her hands over his on her knees. "I'm sorry."

Ty smiled, and his heart filled. It was a strange and wonderful thing what this woman did to him. He still wasn't sure how to deal with her. He learned something new every day. But so long as she was willing to put up with him, he'd decided he wasn't going to let her go.

Ty traced his knuckles across her cheek. "I've learned from you too, Phil. I've learned to look deeper and not take a veteran officer's word over my gut."

"So, Captain Jamerson, does that mean you won't be breaking my balls every time one of your men comes through my office?"

Ty grinned. "I'll make reasons to break your balls, Inspector Zorn."

He gathered her up into his arms and hugged her close. "There are a few other things I've learned from you."

He felt her smile against his shoulder. "Oh yeah, what?"

"I'd rather show you."

Several minutes later Phil sat in Ty's big recliner in the living room. The afternoon sun began its daily journey to the hills in the west, casting long pink shadows through the curtains.

"What are you doing?" she called craning her neck toward the hallway.

"Be patient," Ty called back.

Phil smiled and settled back into the inviting leather of the chair. She closed her eyes and ignored the sting from her gravelly eyes. Taking several deep cleansing breaths, Phil tried to clear her mind of sad thoughts.

She started when the touch of smooth fabric covered her eyes.

"Easy, baby," Ty whispered against her ear. His warm breath instantly stirred her. She smiled when the soft scent of a vanilla spice candle flirted with her nose.

The familiar sound of a low saxophone infiltrated the room.

Her blood quickened and she smiled lazily. "What are you up to, Captain?"

"I want to show you what else I learned from you."

"Can I take off the blindfold?"

"Yes."

Phil yanked it off and almost drowned in giggles. Ty stood three feet away from her, his body swaying as he tried to undo his shirt buttons in a slow sexy movement. He was all thumbs.

"Are you going to strip for me?"

His eyes flashed and she could swear he blushed. He yanked at the third button, his frustration mounting. "If I could get this damn shirt unbuttoned!"

He grabbed each side of the shirt and yanked, buttons flying across the room. She gasped, and his glare dared her to laugh. She settled back into the chair and put her hands over her mouth. Her heart swelled and she felt the well of tears again.

She loved this man. She loved him heart, body, and soul.

For him to attempt a striptease for her was beyond anything she ever thought he would do for her.

His jerking body movements told her he was not comfortable with his act, yet for her he continued. He grinned like the devil himself when he caught her eyes and freed the top button of his trousers. His jerky undulations stopped and he stood ramrod stiff when he pulled the zipper down.

"You're very good, Captain."

He attempted to do a sexy little dip, at the same time he tried to kick off his shoes. He stumbled and landed face first in her lap.

Phil couldn't help it—her laughter rang out, mingling with Ty's deep chuckles.

He looked up, her laughter faded, and she took his face into her hands and pulled him toward her lips.

He rose to the occasion.

"I see, Captain, you still have some learning to do."

His lips pressed against hers. "Teach me," he whispered.

"It could take years."

"I predict decades."

She melted against him. "I've been told I'm pushy and overbearing."

"I've heard."

"I can't cook."

"I know."

"And I have commitment issues."

"We'll work through them."

"You may be sorry."

Ty smiled and backed up just enough to pick her up. Her arms slipped around his neck and she gave him a coy glance.

"Are you sure you're up to the challenge, sir?"

He pressed her hips against his erection. "I'm up for it in more ways than one. Now shut up and kiss me."

Happily, Phil obliged.

Turn the page for an excerpt from
Karin Tabke's next steamy novel,

SKIN

Coming soon from POCKET BOOKS

CHAPTER ONE

"Strip."

"I beg your pardon?"

"Drop your drawers, take off your clothes, *get naked.*"

Reese hesitated. The woman sitting behind her desk stood, the movement slow and fluid. Her features, though, screamed impatience.

"Look . . ." she glanced at the file he'd handed her when he was ushered into her office. "Reese, *Skin* is an upscale chick rag. How the hell can I tell if you have the goods if I don't see them first?"

He'd never been shy about shucking his clothes for a woman, but he'd never been commanded to do it in the middle of the day in the downtown office of a very attractive and very irritated female. He stood.

Miss Donatello had legs long enough to wrap around him

twice and a waist he bet he could span with his hands. Her full breasts bobbed in rhythmic sensuality with her every move under the fitted white shirt that topped the black leather skirt that hugged her lush ass like a second skin. His taste usually ran to tall, lithe women, but this voluptuous drink of water would quench his thirst any day. He warmed to his assignment.

"Reese, I'm a very busy lady. I need to see your package, *now*." Her eyes narrowed. "If you can't drop your drawers for me now, how the hell are you going to drop them for my camera?"

Too much was riding on him being picked as *Skin*'s first centerfold.

He grinned, the gesture rare given his generally antisocial demeanor. He'd gladly produce more skin than she could handle. Slowly, he unbuttoned his 501's, his eyes catching her hazel ones.

Reese held her gaze as he slid the denim down his thighs, his muscles slowing the process. Like a stunned rabbit her nostrils flared. He knew she was more than curious. His eyes continued to hold hers, daring her to look before he was ready to extend an invitation. He'd lay odds she didn't normally allow a model to control the show-and-tell stage of this type of interview. His black boxer briefs followed his jeans to his knees. Reese grinned big.

Warily, Frankie's eyes dipped. She gasped, for a moment unable to control her female response to his male. Her reaction was one of basic attraction, and she was having a hell of a time breathing normally. She'd seen a lot of the male anatomy in her business and more cocks in the last twenty-four hours than she could count, but she'd never seen a package this beautiful, this complete, and never so eager to salute her. The models she'd interviewed the previous day and this morning shriveled up in shyness. Not this guy. She wracked her brain for his name. She was lousy with names. Oh yeah, Reese.

She cleared her throat. "Nice salute you have there, sailor." Leaning a hip against the edge of her desk she crossed her arms over her chest. She wanted to touch him, to see if his tan skin was as warm as she suspected. His erection bobbed and she wondered what he was thinking.

Collecting herself, she pursed her lips. Resisting the urge to smile, Frankie silently thanked God for this blessing. "I'm so glad you're not gay."

"What makes you so sure?"

Frankie laughed and cocked a brow inclining her head toward his impressive erection. "The fact that you haven't shriveled up or failed to rise to the occasion." Her eyes locked with his. "And the fact that your boy there keeps growing."

"He likes what he sees."

Her skin warmed, and while she didn't want to admit it, she was glad on a personal level he was very obviously heterosexual. She allowed her eyes to ravage the smooth hard planes of his belly and lower to the smooth thickness sprouting between his thighs.

He would do very nicely for what she had in mind.

"Well, tell your little man the only job he's being interviewed for is to perform for my camera. Nothing more."

Reese stood perfectly still, his sailor coming to full attention. A prominent vein sprouted from the thick patch of dark hair at the root of his cock jutting its way toward the wide, silky breadth of his head. She knew if she touched him he would be warm, and she'd feel the thick surge of blood course through him. She squirmed in her heels, and quelled the urge to brush her fingertips down his shaft. This was business, and with the one exception she'd paid dearly for, she made it a hard and fast rule not to touch the models, except to position them on a shoot."

"Is there a hands-on segment to this audition?"

His deep husky voice sent chills cascading along her neck. The guy had "trouble" stamped all over his arrogant face.

She nodded. "Maybe. Let's see what you have upstairs."

He cocked a dark brow. She smiled when he pulled his form-fitting black T-shirt over his head. "You learn quick, sailor."

His chest was almost as irresistible as his astute cock. Hard, defined, tan. Several pale slashmark scars tattooed one side of his ribcage. Her imagination ran wild with scenarios of how they got there. Instead of detracting from his maleness, they intensified it.

Thick arms rippled with the slightest movement, his biceps bouncing softly as he smoothed his dark brown hair back into place with both hands. She swallowed hard, the image of his arms up over his shoulders, his chest flexed and his cock growing inches by the second burned in her memory banks. Warmth infiltrated the moist spot between her thighs. Dormant desire roused deep inside her. She might run a skin rag for chicks but she wasn't one to sleep around, especially with her models. Goosebumps coursed down her arms. Even if she was attracted to this guy, she wouldn't go down that road with him. One time had been more than enough. Since the Sean incident two years ago, her knees were welded together when it came to mixing business with the obvious pleasure Reese was capable of giving.

"Do I muster up?"

She gave into a rare smile. Crossing her arms over her chest, Francesca slowly walked around him. "Very nice glutes." He did have a fine ass. Smooth, muscular cheeks screamed for her hands to test their hardness.

"How'd you get the scars on your chest?"

"Old girlfriend. Really sharp nails."

"Are you Italian?"

"I am if you want some Italian in you."

Frankie gasped. "For someone who's looking for work you sure are cocky." She snorted. "Pun intended."

She grabbed a digital camera off her desk, focused, and began clicking away. As she worked her way back to the most excellent front view of this man, she knew that even though she had more men to interview this was *the man* to launch her magazine into the ranks of *Playgirl*. He was perfect. He had an edge to his features that inspired women to want to tame him. His tanned skin and deep-set crystal blue eyes contrasted, giving him the predatory look of a lone wolf. A faint thin scar ran behind his right ear down his throat stopping just above his collar bone, giving him an air of danger. She needed to capture that danger on film and sell it to delirious women across the country. Her smile widened behind the camera.

His body spoke for itself. She could see the handwriting on the wall. The entire staff would want to be in on his photo sessions. An idea sparked. They'd go with location shots. A day in the life of Mr. *Skin*. She quickly warmed to the idea then scowled. Could they afford location shots? Unk had hinted there were some accounting issues, so had her father the day before he died.

Her lips drew into a firm line. Since her father's death two weeks prior she'd been off-balance, unsure—afraid. The turmoil in her personal life and here at *Skin* sent her control-freak nature into a tailspin. Yesterday, her first day back at the office, she'd forced herself to produce and not lament what she could not change. And the winds of change blew hot and heavy through her family. If she had ever thought her family was dysfunctional, now they were downright scary.

A shiver skittered across her skin, and her belly flip-flopped. Papa was dead now and playing the rebellious daughter was a moot point. But God how she wanted to best him, to prove to him she had what it took to be involved in the family business, to change his perception of her after the

Sean debacle. Now she couldn't, dammit, and even worse, their last words to each other were harsh.

Frankie shook off the malaise. She had a job to do. Happily she gave Reese her undivided attention. She focused and shot, getting every conceivable angle she could of the man who would launch *Skin* into the stratosphere.

Despite her sexy chore, emotion welled. She'd not only lost what little respect her father gave her as a business woman but she had become the laughing stock of the family. Proving once again women were not worthy of the same respect as the male members. The hot sting of tears caught her off guard. The trauma of the last two weeks caught up with her. She took a deep breath and exhaled slowly. A deep chuckle jerked her out of her musings.

"I have to admit you're the first, Miss Donatello."

Lowering the camera, her eyes focused on Reese and his glorious erection. "First what?"

"The first woman I've brought to tears without laying a finger on her."

Her eyes narrowed and warning bells sounded. The man was too intense, too bold, too distracting, and right now even though she wanted to loosen up, to get back into her groove, she resisted.

"I—" The door to the office flew open with a bang and Reese and Frankie started.

"Son of a bitch, Anthony, don't you know how to knock?" Frankie demanded.

Tony stopped in his tracks, and gave Reese and his erection a cause for pause. "Back to your old tricks, sis?"

Francesca set her camera down on her desk and stepped around toward the door.

"Excuse us—?"

"Reese."

"Sorry—Reese."

Frankie pushed her brother out the office door and into the crowded anteroom of her offices, where Tawny, her assistant, sat surrounded by hunky male models. A dozen sets of eyes looked expectantly at her. Frankie smiled and continued down the hall with her brother in tow until she came across the office recently vacated by one of her father's accountants. She hustled Tony in and shut the door behind them.

"What the hell, Tony?" she demanded.

His dark brows shot up. Good looks ran in the family— lean, olive-skinned features accentuated Tony's Italian heritage. He was a miniversion of her handsome father. Santini wasn't known as Don Juan for nothing. He was a lady's man until the day he died, much to the chagrin of Tony's mother, Lola.

"You're asking me what the hell? What the hell was that naked guy doing in your office?"

"I'm interviewing for my centerfold."

"The hell you are!"

"The hell I'm not!" He might be the heir apparent for all things nefarious but *Skin* was legit and it was hers.

"You are not going through with that."

"I sure as hell am. *Skin* needs a shot in the arm and the anniversary edition is launching our first centerfold."

"Father forbade it!" Tony shrieked. He sounded like a teenage girl on a roller coaster ride.

"Father is dead."

"And you have no more respect for him dead than you did when he was alive. No wonder he disowned you."

"He did no such thing." He only threatened it. How did Tony know?

"That's not what he told me the morning he was killed."

Shit! Frankie chewed her bottom lip. They had quarreled, she and her father. She wanted complete creative control over *Skin,* and that meant giving her permission to go with the full nude centerfold. Santini was violently opposed to his only daughter, a daughter who had in his mind proven to be naïve, emotional, and impetuous, to take pictures of naked men and then publish them for the world to see. He had his honor, he told his daughter.

"But, Papa, you own strip joints and peep shows!"

"That's different, Francesca. It's what men do. I will not have my daughter, my flesh and blood, take pictures of naked men. I'll lose respect in the family. My answer is no!"

When she refused, and threatened to enlist the aid of her uncle, his older brother, his last words to her were, "Then you are dead to me."

The next morning he was dead to her.